ON BORROWED TIME

BY THE SAME AUTHOR

The Goddess of Macau

ON
BORROWED
TIME

THE CHOICES WE MAKE.

LOVE OR REVENGE.

GRAEME HALL

FOR ANNE WITH LOVE

PROLOGUE

EVEN WITHOUT OPENING IT SAM knew at once who the letter was from. It stood out among the junk mail and bills, and there was no mistaking the hand that had written the address. The vertical strokes in the H and the K, the tails of the 'g's. It was handwriting he had seen in messages on his desk telling him to return a call he had missed. He recognised it from notes left on the fridge reminding him to buy milk. It was handwriting that had been on the first Valentine's card he had received in years. The letter was from Emma.

The envelope was postmarked Winchester, so that meant she was back with her parents. He shouldn't really have been surprised. After all, that was where she'd said she would be going, but he hadn't been sure if she was telling the truth. Her sudden unexpected departure, leaving with barely a warning, had left him doubting everything. He held the envelope in his hands. He should open it, of course, and he would when he was ready, but it had been a long day. He threw his jacket over the back of a chair and slumped on the sofa, leaving the letter on the coffee table in front of him.

The office had become his anaesthetic of choice: losing himself in his new role as a partner; working late so that he had an excuse when colleagues tried to drag him out to a bar, cutting himself off from even his closest friends; trying to overwrite his memories and thoughts with contract terms and warranties, agreements and memoranda. He had to keep going because the dark times came when he stopped. That was when his mind went back to those final days, only a few short weeks ago. The day Emma told him that it wasn't going to work, the day she said that they couldn't be together, that she was going back to the UK. When he stopped moving, when he stopped running away from his thoughts, that was when the memories came rushing back. He re-lived their final conversations on a permanent loop, looking for an explanation that he never found. Looking for something he might have missed.

'But why?' he would ask.

This was then followed by a ritual exchange, a catechism:

'Is there somebody else?'

'No.'

'Don't you still love me?'

'Yes.'

'Is it something I've done?'

'No.'

Every time they had this argument Emma would fall back on her story, which had the great advantage of being true. At least in part anyway.

'You know how it is, Sam, I need a visa and I don't have a chance of getting one. I'm going to have to leave in the end, so it's better we don't get too involved.'

This never satisfied him. It couldn't be the reason, it didn't make any sense. It never even sounded as if she believed it herself. You didn't end a relationship because of a visa problem. And what was with this *'better we don't get too involved'*? Weren't they already deeply involved? He knew he was, anyway. He'd never been so much in love. Yes, her visa would be an issue, but he also knew that it wasn't insurmountable, and besides, they had months before it expired. In the end he had reluctantly accepted that explanation rather than know the real reason, for fear that somehow it was his fault. Certainly, Emma hadn't been herself in the weeks beforehand. The sleepless nights she'd spent staring out at the harbour. The times she'd been anxious and twitchy and he knew that something was wrong, but when he'd tried to broach the subject she would always back off. He wished now that he'd pressed her more. Things could hardly have turned out worse if he had.

On the day she finally left he'd helped Emma with her bags. They took a taxi into town so she could get the airport bus, and while the driver sang along to the radio Sam had been reduced to looking out of the window, the loud Cantopop ruling out conversation.

At first he'd been grateful for that, until he recognised that the song was the latest Andy Lau hit: *You are my woman.* The irony of the title had not been lost on him. Perhaps it had been a mistake asking her to stay in his flat until the end. A clean break might have been less painful, but he hadn't been able to stop himself from wanting to hang on to her for as long as possible. He suspected that she may have felt something similar, given the way she'd held him in her sleep on their last night together. He felt a sharp pain as he remembered how it was to feel her body pressed against his, her head on his shoulder.

When they reached town Sam paid the driver, who continued to sing tunelessly, leaving the two of them to unload Emma's luggage. The bus station was busy and they struggled with the bags as they worked their way through the crowds to the queue for the airport bus. Sam had offered to go with her, but she had declined. He held her as they stood in the queue, but there was no kiss and after wishing her a safe journey Sam turned and walked away. He heard her call out something but didn't look back. He'd known how much it would hurt if he did.

And now here was a letter. How much would it hurt to read it? The pain hadn't even started to ease, even if his time with Emma was beginning to seem like a different life. Something that belonged to a different Sam. Would there be an explanation? An apology? What could she possibly say that would explain, let alone justify, what happened? For a moment he was tempted to tear the thing up, leaving it unread; rip it into a thousand pieces and scatter them out of the window. Let them rain on the street below like confetti from the wedding that might one day have been. But the moment passed, the temptation to give in to anger and resentment eased. He opened the envelope.

Halfway through, Sam was disbelieving. She'd written the letter while still in Hong Kong.

'Why the fuck couldn't you just have told me this? Didn't you know what I'd do? Didn't you trust me?' he berated the absent Emma as he absorbed her words. By the time he came to the final paragraph though, he was crying.

My love, I hope you understand that I couldn't stay in Hong Kong any longer. I made my choice and the file will be in California by now. I don't really know what will be done with it, but she promised that nobody will connect it to you. That's one of the reasons why I left – if you do stay then I didn't want it to look like we were in it together. But you have to make your choice, and you need to make it on your own, without me around, without me influencing you. If you decide that your future is in Hong Kong, then I wish you a happy life. If you decide to leave, then please forgive me and write to me or call me at my parents'.

Whatever you decide, I love you.
Emma

CHAPTER 1

HONG KONG, SEPTEMBER 1996

THE FLOWERS EMMA HAD BOUGHT were a mixture of white lilies and small yellow orchids; she thought that the colours were appropriate for the occasion.

So much had changed since she had been at this Wan Chai junction on the same day last year. An attempt at gentrification was beginning, and on one corner a five-storey walk-up was in the process of being demolished to make way for upmarket apartments; the pavement made impassable by protective hoardings that displayed posters of happy, smiling families with perfect teeth and hair, enjoying a perfect life in their perfect homes.

Opposite, the road was being excavated by an electricity company, and although it was a Sunday the sound of a pneumatic drill breaking up tarmac was starting to get to Emma as she looked around for somewhere suitable for her flowers. Nowhere seemed quite right until she noticed a spot between a bank and a 7-Eleven. Emma placed the lilies and orchids next to a drainpipe and then used a piece of ribbon to secure the flowers in place.

A couple of passers-by looked curiously at this young blonde woman and what she was doing, but for the most part nobody paid any attention to her. In this part of town few were ever surprised by anything a Westerner did.

***

'I heard there was mainland money involved?' Rob looked at Sam inquiringly, his estuarine accent rivalling Cantonese in tonal complexity.

'Where did you get that from?'

'Just some gossip from a trader I play football with. He was surprised that the government would allow it.'

'Well it's nonsense. It's a Bahamas-registered company for a start,' said Sam.

'Which – as you well know – means fuck all.'

Sam did know only too well, and for a moment a number of bad memories briefly surfaced.

'It's just an investment company Leung Hing-wah has set up. You know he's looking to get into telecoms. That's all.'

Sam and Rob were on the top deck of the junk belonging to McShane Adams, the law firm they both worked for. It was half-eleven on a Sunday morning and they were on their first beer of the day. Kate joined them, making her way unsteadily as the boat pitched and rolled in the wake of a passing tug.

'God, can't this thing keep still? Are you two talking

work?' she said. 'It's a glorious Sunday morning, we've got the whole day ahead of us and I don't want to be trapped on a junk with a pair of corporate lawyers who can't talk about anything else. If you're going to talk shop I'm going back down to the others.' The rest of the party were sensibly in the shade on the main deck.

'I love the way she talks about lawyers,' Rob said to Sam. 'To hear her speak you'd never guess that she was one as well.'

'Not on a Sunday I'm not. Now, which one of you two is going to be a gentleman and rub sun-cream on my back? Sam?' Sam took the proffered bottle. 'Thanks … don't miss under the straps … You'll make someone a great husband one day, Sam. Who knows, the way things are going it may yet be me.'

Kate and Sam had started at McShane Adams on the same day three years ago and had worked together ever since. They were good friends who offered each other a shoulder to cry on when romantic liaisons were not working out. Only once had the mutual comfort gone further and they'd kissed, before they both pulled back not wanting to spoil a friendship. But one night, after a party and at least one margarita too many, and when they were both more maudlin than normal, they'd vowed to get married if they were still single when they hit forty.

'Oh that's nice … Has anybody ever told you you've got great hands?'

'Sam,' said Rob, 'you should come to Manila with us next weekend. Play some golf.'

'No thank you.'

'Why not?'

'Well, for one thing I don't like golf.'

'What's that got to do with anything?'

'And that's the other reason. I know you're not going for the golf.'

'Now, boys,' interrupted Kate, 'no fighting on my birthday.'

'That's not until tomorrow,' Rob protested.

'Close enough.'

Another roll of the junk in the swell caused them all to hold on to a handrail until the boat steadied itself again.

'So why haven't we been invited to your birthday bash tomorrow?' asked Sam.

'Girls only, I'm afraid. It's *Ladies Night* at Carnegies and a bunch of us are going. No men allowed, or at least no men that we might have to meet again the next day. It's a bummer it's a Monday though.'

'I wish I hadn't asked now.'

'Don't be a prude, Sam,' said Kate, 'you should try it sometime. Just not tomorrow.' Kate lay back on the deck, sunhat covering her face.

***

On a Sunday morning Wan Chai looked even seedier than normal; at least at night the neon gave an illusion of fun and glamour, a suggestion of parties and good times. The detritus of Saturday still hadn't been completely cleared away, but even at this early hour some of the bars were starting to open, or perhaps they had never closed. Sometimes Emma wished that she could enjoy Wan Chai the way others did, and occasionally she tried and let herself be dragged there, but it had too many associations and normally she made a point of avoiding it if she could.

Checking the time, Emma spent a quiet moment with the flowers and then flagged down a taxi.

***

When the second bottle of champagne was opened Sam wished they'd given more thought to the food they'd brought with them. He was starting to feel light-headed. Rob seemed unaffected, while Kate was in party mode.

'Come on, Sam, answer the question: myself excepted, of course, who is the best-looking woman in the firm?'

'There's no way I'm going to answer that. You're just trying to trick me into embarrassing myself. You should have been a litigator.'

'Ah, you're on to me. There's no pulling the wool over your eyes.'

'There's no pulling at all where Sam's involved,' said Rob.

'Oooh! Cruel,' said Kate. 'Are you going to stand for that?'

'If we don't have something to eat soon I'm not going to be able to stand full stop.'

***

Alice was already at the restaurant when Emma arrived. Tall but with a slight build, Alice was a local the same age as Emma; they had met when Emma was working in one of her first temping jobs. Emma didn't make a habit of being late, but running a few minutes behind she wasn't sorry that Alice had arrived first. The restaurant was a very traditional *dim sum* place where *gweilos* were unusual, and while Emma wouldn't have been turned away, they both knew that she would have felt uncomfortable on her own. Brightly lit and almost full just after noon, it was a world of shouted conversations and the staff barking orders.

Emma squeezed her way between the crowded diners to where Alice was already seated at a small table in a corner.

'Emma!' Alice got to her feet and they embraced, Emma's English reserve overcome by Alice's natural ebullience.

'Heavens, this place is heaving. Sorry I'm late. It's just as well you've grabbed a table.'

'*Mo man tai.* No problem.' Alice poured two small cups of jasmine tea. 'How are you?'

'Good thanks,' said Emma, picking up one of the cups and then putting it down hastily until it had cooled a little.

A waitress was hovering nearby with a trolley of *dim sum* to choose from.

'We'd better order. Food first then gossip,' said Alice. With the queue for tables already growing, polite chit-chat before ordering food was not the restaurant's business model. 'Is there anything special you want?'

'No, you choose, you know what I like.'

Emma let Alice order and wondered if she would ever be able to master Cantonese. Like many of her friends she had started lessons, but soon gave them up and made do with a few basic phrases and just enough to get her home in a taxi. The food order sorted, they returned to their conversation.

'So what have you been up to this weekend?' asked Alice.

'Something I had to do this morning – that's why I was late, the traffic was bad getting back – and then yesterday I had lunch with a crowd down at Shek O.'

'Anybody interesting there?'

'Just some people I worked with the other week. Oh … you mean were there any single men? Only boring business types. You know what they're like. Full of talk of money and deals … unsavoury tales of Wan Chai bars.' Emma sipped her tea cautiously and found that it had cooled a little. 'What about you?'

'You forget I'm a Hong Kong girl. I went to that new mall in Mongkok yesterday. It was a break from studying.'

'How's the course going?'

Alice worked as a secretary but was doing a part-time law degree.

'It's okay, I guess, but a lot more boring than I thought it would be. You think it's going to be all about defending the innocent, human rights and so on, but the reality is so dull. Land law, contract, remembering the names of all these stupid cases from years ago. Just dull and boring. But I can't stay a secretary forever and either I get myself a qualification or a husband. At the moment the law degree seems easier.'

Emma smiled. 'No luck on that front then?'

'Alas no,' Alice sighed, after an almost imperceptible pause.

The food started to arrive. Bamboo steamers of *har gau* and *siu mai*, plates of bok choi, turnip cake, noodles and – to Emma's alarm – chicken's feet. To her they were one of the mysteries of Cantonese food that she was happy to leave to the locals. Seeing the expression on Emma's face, Alice was quick to reassure her.

'Don't worry, they're for me' she said, taking one with her chopsticks. A waitress stopped at their table with another trolley and Alice took a plate of pork buns. 'I saw my cousin Kwok-wah on Friday,' Alice continued, picking small chicken bones from her mouth. 'He's finished his degree, and would you believe he's going to Shanghai to do his PhD?'

'Shanghai?' The noise in the restaurant was starting to bother Emma and she wasn't sure if she'd heard correctly.

'I know. My aunt and uncle are furious. They wanted him to go to the States or Canada – Australia at least – but he says China's the future, where it's all happening. Who knows? Maybe he's right but it seems scary to me. It was Ah-yeh – you know, our grandfather – who came to Hong Kong from China in the fifties, so he's particularly unhappy.'

'What's his subject? Kwok-wah.'

'Something to do with electronics or computers. Something like that anyway. He did try and explain it to me once but I can't say I understood much. Yesterday was my last chance to see him before he left. He leaves this week.'

Another waitress approached with desserts and Alice took a plate of pastries and then refilled the teacups before biting into an egg tart.

'So, are you going to get another job?' asked Alice.

'Well, nothing permanent. I've got more temping work starting tomorrow. Nothing special but I need some money and I'd like to save for some travelling. A holiday at least.'

'Again?' Emma had only recently been in Thailand. 'I'm so jealous. Where do you want to go this time?'

'My parents want me to spend Christmas and the New Year with them, but I'm not thrilled with the idea of England in the cold and wet. I'd really like to go down to Sydney but I don't have the money.'

'But Emma, they're your parents!'

'I know, I know, don't you make me feel bad as well. It's hard enough the way they make me feel guilty about it. Anyway, we'll see. Christmas is a long way off still.'

Emma knew that her parents would have liked her to be at home now, but this was a day above all when she felt she had to be in Hong Kong. In fact Emma's whole approach to life was a matter of some concern to her parents, who hadn't wanted her to go travelling in the first place, least of all in this part of the world and especially now she was an only child. Emma had landed in Hong Kong two years previously at the end of a trip through Southeast Asia with her then fiancé Mike. A trip that started with Emma engaged and ended with her being single again. Her parents had been looking forward to a wedding, followed in a year or two by grandchildren, and to them Emma's apparent contentment with life in Hong Kong, without a boyfriend and without a career, was not part of the plan.

Emma never told them what had happened with Mike, but a succession of arguments had escalated until they ended in a heated row in Thailand when he'd been flirting with a good-looking Chinese-American girl. This hadn't been the first time she'd caught him either; as far as Emma could tell Mike seemed to be more interested in the young Asian women they met on their travels than he was in her. She had had the last laugh though; after dumping Mike in Chiang Mai, she spent the next few weeks travelling with the object of his attentions.

Later, when she looked back on that trip, Emma rationalised that it was probably better to discover an incompatibility quickly rather than ten years on with children. Perhaps all soon-to-be-married couples should be forced to spend two weeks in a cockroach-infested guesthouse with no air-conditioning.

***

The junk moored for lunch in the sheltered waters off Tai Tam. Sam and Kate took refuge from the heat and sun and watched the others as they took turns trying and failing to waterski.

'Not your cup of tea?' he asked.

'I gave it a go once when I was looking to catch the

eye of a guy I was interested in. I caught his eye alright, but repeatedly falling off wasn't giving him quite the impression I was hoping for. How about you?'

'Too much of a coward. Too unfit and uncoordinated.'

'A triple whammy, eh? Here …' Kate filled his wine glass. 'This stuff is better than any macho posturing.'

'I shouldn't have any more … You're a bad influence, you know? I blame the convent education.'

Kate laughed. 'It's true – there's nothing quite like a convent girl who's gone off the rails. Look – hah! That will teach him to show off!' They both laughed as Rob fell in a cloud of water and spray.

***

'Do you want that last pastry?' Alice was inspecting what was left on the plates.

'How can you eat so much and stay slim? It's not fair. Go on, you have it. How are your mum and dad?'

'They're well,' said Alice, through a mouthful of pastry. 'But still arguing over whether to stay in Hong Kong.'

'Pardon?' Emma was struggling to follow the conversation.

'Sorry. I said they're still arguing over whether to stay or leave.'

'I thought they'd decided on Vancouver?'

'They did – sort of. They've got their residency rights sorted, and we have other family there, two of my mother's cousins, but now they can't decide whether to go or not. My mother wants to but my father wants to stay. He thinks there might be good business after the handover.'

'And what do you want?'

'I want them to make up their minds and stop arguing. Seriously? I don't know. I don't know what I want. Changing the subject, are you going to come to our meeting on Friday?'

Alice was active politically and for some time she'd been trying to persuade Emma to join a human rights group she was involved with. Emma didn't think this was very likely to happen and kept gently declining all invitations. She'd had a fairly conventional Home Counties upbringing – father a retired civil servant, mother a teacher – and had never been involved in politics before leaving the UK other than going on the odd student demo. Even then she had once chickened out of a poll tax march by claiming to be ill, when in truth she had simply been worried about what her parents would think if they found out.

'I don't know, Alice, you know I'm not really into that sort of thing, and with my hearing I do sometimes struggle in groups.'

For once there was a hesitancy in Emma's answer that Alice picked up on, as if for the first time her resolve seemed to be eroding under the constant action of Alice's repeated invitations.

'Just come and give it a try. Just for once. If nothing else we're quite a fun bunch and afterwards we often end up in a bar or getting something to eat. You might be surprised.'

Recognising that Alice was going to keep asking

until she said yes, Emma decided that it would be simpler to give in. After all, she only had to go once.

'You win, I'll come.'

'Good.' Alice smiled at her victory. 'I promise you won't regret it. I'll call you later in the week to tell you when and where. You won't be the only newcomer – there are a couple of other new people coming along.'

'I'll give it a try – beyond that … who knows, we'll see.'

***

At the end of a long afternoon the junk deposited its passengers in Aberdeen. No amount of cajoling and begging could persuade the crew to take them back to Central. The junk lived in Aberdeen and they weren't going to make an extra trip halfway round the island just for the convenience of a bunch of drunken *gweilos*. Tired from a mixture of sun, alcohol and activity, they fell into waiting taxis. Rob and a gang heading to Lan Kwai Fong for a beer or two; Sam and Kate shared a ride home.

'Sorry about Rob,' said Kate. 'He was particularly obnoxious today. Such a wideboy sometimes. Perhaps I shouldn't have asked him along.'

'Oh, he doesn't bother me, and you had to invite him. He'd have moaned like hell if you hadn't. I've just never fitted in with that crowd. You know that as well as anyone.'

'And you're all the better for that. But … ah, here we are … *Ni douh, mh'goi*,' Kate said, leaning forward to ask the taxi driver to stop. 'Do you want to come in for a drink?'

'No thanks, it's been a long day. I'll see you tomorrow.'

**

That night Emma had a familiar dream, a variant of a dream that often came to her over the years. The dream always involved water. Water and fear. In this particular version, which was one of the most common, she is walking in a forest by the edge of a river as it runs towards a waterfall. There is enough growth on the trees that she knows it must be spring, but in the shade of the forest canopy it is cool and damp. She knows that it is dangerous to walk so close to the fast-moving water, and the rocks are wet and slippery, but the temptation is too great. She picks her route from stone to stone and tries to keep her balance, but the rucksack she is wearing is heavy and makes it difficult, so she tries to take it off. In the attempt she loses her balance and, as her feet slip on the moss-covered rock she is standing on, she knows that she cannot stop herself from falling into the river.

She wakes with her alarm just before hitting the turbulent water but almost at once recognises the familiarity of the dream.

A dream that has become a friend.

A companion, at least.

CHAPTER 2

SHANGHAI, SEPTEMBER 1996

YEUNG KWOK-WAH MOVED TO HIS right to close down the opposition. Shoulder to shoulder, he leant into the mathematician from Nanjing, and when the mathematician briefly lost control of the ball he was quick to steal it. Kwok-wah was shorter than the others, but in compensation he was fast and agile. He turned and spun away, leaving his opponent flailing behind him. Sighting the basket, he took a shot. The ball rattled the hoop and hesitated briefly before dropping through the net.

'Yes!' shouted Kwok-wah, raising an arm in triumph. His three-pointer from near the halfway line was the cue for everyone to decide that the game was over. They had been playing on an outdoor court and storm clouds were building up in the west. There was a distant rumble of thunder and everyone knew the weather was changing. By the time they had gathered their belongings and started to head to the dorm, the first heavy drops of rain were beginning to fall.

Granny Sun watched from her room as the basketball players came back, pushing and shoving each other out of the way in their rush to get out of the rain.

'No running!' she shouted.

***

'I need your papers.'

Kwok-wah's arrival in Shanghai several weeks previously had not been encouraging. The guard had been abrupt and aggressive, his uniform ill-fitting and his tie loose. His breath smelt of raw onions. A second guard sat in the gatehouse with his feet on the desk and a cigarette in his mouth.

'Sorry?' Kwok-wah had had a long journey and only wanted to find his room.

'You new here?' the guard grunted, approximating speech.

'Yes.'

'From down south I guess by your accent?'

'Hong Kong.'

'Xiang Gang you mean … Remember where you are, sonny. I need to see your papers. Some kind of ID as well.'

Kwok-wah handed over his letter of acceptance from the university, counter-stamped by the Shanghai Ministry of Education, along with the letter he had received telling him when to arrive and where to go, his temporary residence permit issued by the Shanghai Municipal Government, his China Home Return Permit, his Hong Kong identity card, and finally his

British National (Overseas) passport. The guard threw the last one back at him and took the rest back to the gatehouse, leaving Kwok-wah standing alone and hoping for the best. It didn't seem the most promising beginning to his time in Shanghai. Shortly the guard returned bearing a clipboard that he clutched protectively to his chest as if he thought Kwok-wah might make a lunge for it. The guard struck Kwok-wah's name off a list before returning his papers and directing him to the main administration block.

Kwok-wah made a mental note to never be without his student ID. He wasn't particularly interested in politics but even he was acutely aware that Tiananmen Square was only seven years ago and most of the dead had been students. His older cousin Alice had been on the protest march in Hong Kong when a million people filled the streets. She had wanted him to come along with them but he'd only been fifteen and his parents said no. Kwok-wah hadn't been that bothered. All that interested him at that age was building a basic home computer from scratch. His mother was constantly frustrated to find his bedroom full of circuit boards, power supplies and the smell of burning solder. Kwok-wah had been taking things apart – and putting them back together again, most of the time anyway – for as long as he could remember. He had started with simple things like toasters and kettles, and then moved on to radios and televisions. There was a time when his parents thought he had a psychiatric problem and they took him to see Dr Chan, but the doctor had been relaxed about Kwok-wah's obsessive interest in household appliances.

'Mrs Yeung, some children can play the piano very well. Others the violin. Some can learn foreign languages quickly, others are good at sports. Your son just has a natural aptitude for technical things. Trust me, he'll do well in life.'

After getting the seal of approval from the medical profession, Kwok-wah's parents encouraged him, and it was soon after that he moved on to computers. When it was realised that he also had a talent for maths, his future seemed predestined.

In spite of everything Alice had said about him coming to China, Kwok-wah didn't regret choosing the Shanghai University of Science and Technology. Already one of the best in the country, it had been marked for expansion and growth. More importantly, at least as far as Kwok-wah was concerned, the university was home to his supervisor, Professor Ye Zhang; his number one reason for coming to Shanghai. For those in the know, Professor Ye was fast becoming a world leader in the areas where computational mathematics overlapped with computer science and telecommunications, and he was a regular speaker on the international conference scene. That was how Kwok-wah had first come across him. Professor Ye had given a talk in Hong Kong on mobile data transmission and its future potential, a talk that inspired Kwok-wah and was probably the main reason that he had wanted to go into the field. On one occasion Kwok-wah tried to explain to Alice his interest in fast Fourier transforms and their potential use, but he had quickly realised that her polite nods were only a way of pretending to listen when in reality she had no idea what he was talking about. In truth not many of his friends understood or cared either. Quite a lot of them had a mobile phone, but few seemed to see the potential for them in the future, and even if they did they weren't interested in the technology that would be needed.

After several false starts, Kwok-wah found the administration building and was directed to an accommodation block where he was to share a small dormitory with three others. Bunk beds occupied the walls, and there was a small cupboard each and a single large table. A communal bathroom at the end of the corridor smelt of cheap disinfectant.

But Kwok-wah soon discovered that the most important aspect of his new home was Granny Sun who lived on the ground floor by the main door, ideally placed so that she could keep an eye on comings and goings. She was of an age that could only be described as ancient; missing most of her teeth save for a single gold tooth that would glint on the rare occasions when she smiled, and with a tuft of hair growing from a mole above her upper lip. Nobody knew her real name, she was simply Granny Sun, and nobody knew how long she had been there, only that she had seen off several generations of students and would probably see off several more. Her exact role was also unclear; at times a combined caretaker and mother, but more often a gatekeeper. Bringing girls back to the dorm was a particular crime, and if anyone attempted it she would be out of her room at a speed remarkable for her age, scolding whoever was foolish enough to try, while the guilty party would stand there staring at his feet and apologising profusely.

To begin with, his new room-mates – a physicist from Hunan, a Beijing engineer, and a Shanghainese chemist – regarded him with a confused mixture of disdain, suspicion, curiosity and jealousy. They were fascinated by him and were always asking about life in Hong Kong (*'Can you always get the latest American movies?', 'What's the stock market doing?', 'Who is Michelle Yeoh dating?'*), but at the same time they took every chance they could to tell him how much better everything was in China (*'Look at the way Shanghai is growing, it will overtake Hong Kong soon', 'China – the next superpower'*). His poor Putonghua hadn't helped either. Kwok-wah had taken some classes but evidently not enough.

***

The first few weeks in Shanghai proved frustrating. Eager to get on with what he thought of as his real work, instead Kwok-wah found himself spending most of his time in compulsory courses in advanced mathematics. He was relieved to be excused the political classes his room-mates had to sit through, but it was still a month of boredom before he was finally able to meet his supervisor.

Professor Ye's office was in one of the older buildings on the campus. A creeper had spread up the front, giving it an air of Ivy League or Cambridge. The building itself had once been a school dated from the 1920s and had more than a little flavour of old Shanghai; the Shanghai of the French concession, the days when everybody wanted a piece of China, and the Bund was the most important concentration of wealth and power in Asia. It was an unlikely building for a computer science department and less than ideal. A new home was planned but for the time being the computer science department occupied three floors in one wing of the building.

While he waited for his supervisor, Kwok-wah made small talk with the departmental secretary about how he was settling in to Shanghai. He'd quickly worked out that being friendly with her would pay dividends.

'Good morning, Mr Yang,' said Professor Ye when he finally arrived. Kwok-wah was becoming used to people using the Putonghua form of his family name. 'Please, come in.' Professor Ye unlocked his office and Kwok-wah followed him in. 'Let me go and get my secretary to bring us some tea.'

Kwok-wah stood, unsure whether to take a seat. He absorbed the room while he waited for the professor to return. He had been there before, when he was interviewed for his PhD, but he'd been so nervous at the time he hadn't taken much in. There were wooden beams in the ceiling and a window that looked out over a well-tended rose garden. Kwok-wah watched as a team of gardeners worked on the flower beds. A notice in both Chinese and English prohibited walking on the lawn. In the office itself, tidy well-organised bookshelves contrasted with the piles of papers stacked on the large wooden desk that dominated the room. To Kwok-wah's mind it all seemed rather old-fashioned and in contrast to the nature of Professor Ye's research, and yet at the same time it seemed appropriate and gave a sense of gravitas; a feeling of academic weight and authority. Kwok-wah was nervous and found himself fiddling with his hands.

'Please, sit down. It's good to see you again. Welcome to Shanghai.' They had met only twice before: that one time in Hong Kong after Professor Ye's talk, and then once in Shanghai after Kwok-wah had first applied to do his PhD. When he first saw Professor Ye in Hong Kong, Kwok-wah had been surprised that he was only in his early thirties. Smartly dressed in a good suit and wearing modern-looking metal-rimmed glasses, Professor Ye looked as much the successful businessman as a university professor.

'How are you settling in?'

'Well, thank you, Professor.'

'Good. And how did you find the lectures?'

'Useful, thank you.'

'I'm sure they weren't.' Professor Ye smiled. 'I'm sure you knew all that stuff anyway, but we're a bit rigid in our procedures here, and if the rules say you have to take a course then you have to. We like to make sure everyone is starting at the same place. Even our star foreign students.'

'I understand.'

'Now, on to more interesting things. Your research ...'

They discussed Kwok-wah's planned PhD. The subject had been agreed before: Kwok-wah was to carry out a comparative study of different algorithms to be used in mobile data transmission. There would be a mixture of theoretical studies, some computer modelling and a little experimental work.

'I know you've been round the department before,' said Professor Ye, 'but I'll get my secretary to show you everything.'

And that was it. After a few more pleasantries Kwok-wah was dismissed. In time, he settled into a routine. Mornings were spent in the library researching the literature, afternoons at his desk in the department. Kwok-wah was far too junior to warrant an office of his own, and instead shared a space with one of the post-docs, who grumbled and made it clear this was completely against his will, but in spite of that gave Kwok-wah the desk by the window.

***

Importantly his Putonghua improved and his room-mates realised he wasn't an alien after all. When they discovered a common interest in basketball, barriers quickly came down and he began to be accepted as one of them.

'That shot was as lucky as fuck,' said Zhao Zhanyuan – the physicist from Hunan. 'But I'm not complaining.

It showed those tossers from Block D a thing or two.' In Hong Kong Kwok-wah would have been shocked by the language, but he was becoming used to his room-mate's turn of phrase.

'Pity about the rain,' said Li Lao, the engineer from Beijing. 'Did you see those girls watching us? That tall, slim one, she was something, didn't you think?'

'I certainly did, though if you'd paid more attention to the game and less to the skirt we might have won more easily.'

Kwok-wah was quiet as he changed out of his wet kit and thought about taking a shower. He had also seen the young women who had been watching them play, and while he knew he was probably imagining it, he would have sworn that the tall, slim one Li Lao had mentioned had been paying particular attention to him.

CHAPTER 3

SAM STOOD AT THE BUS stop contemplating the day ahead. The first without his secretary. Sam had been incredulous when she'd told him her holiday plans. Two weeks was her entire allowance for the year. He'd have to suffer a temp. It was always a nightmare having to work with someone who didn't know their way around the files and how he liked to do things. He was busy enough as it was without that hassle.

Apart from one or two small clouds, the sky was clear and the sun was already unrelenting. Although the extreme temperatures of summer had passed, it was still undeniably warm and humid, with the fresher autumn weather yet to come. To make things worse the bus stop seemed to have been located in something of a suntrap and heat radiated from the pavement.

'God, it's hot again.'

The words came with a Texan accent. Sam recognised the speaker as someone from his building. He thought it odd that a Texan would find this weather hot, but not particularly wanting to engage anyone in conversation Sam muttered a reply, while a well-dressed older Chinese woman delicately mopped her brow with a handkerchief. A passing cloud briefly hid the sun, giving a moment of respite.

Sam hated having to wear a suit and tie, and while he wouldn't admit it in public in private he had to acknowledge that he was putting on weight. He reckoned he'd added an inch to his waistline for each year he'd been in Hong Kong. He didn't care for the heat either. He'd been standing for no more than five minutes, but already he was feeling like a damp rag. There was always a magical day in autumn when suddenly the humidity would drop and everyone knew the worst was finally over, but until then it seemed at times as if summer was never going to end and the city became increasingly fractious in the heat. Sam could only envy friends who worked in more relaxed fields, but the law was stubbornly traditional and McShane Adams more so than most. But then it had been like that ever since Sir James McShane met Hector Adams Esq. at the Hong Kong Club in 1853 and decided to go into practice together. Sam took off his jacket and carried it over his arm. He stood as still as possible so as not to make the heat any worse. A bead of perspiration meandered down his neck and under his collar.

***

The traffic was heavier than usual and Sam arrived at work feeling prematurely stressed. Never a good start to the day. Kate and Rob were already at their desks but otherwise the corporate law department was quiet. He made himself coffee and enjoyed the calm.

Kate appeared at his door.

'Morning, Sam, how you doing? Recovered from yesterday?'

'Just about, I think, though I could have done without the journey in this morning.'

'Well, you're the one who wanted to live in the sticks.'

Sam's first apartment had been closer into town and, on the rare occasions when the weather was neither too hot nor too wet, he could even walk to work, but when the lease was up he had moved further out in search of more space and a little greenery. On his first morning there he had enjoyed being woken by the cicadas on the hill behind his building, rather than the city sounds he had been used to, but sometimes there was a price to pay with the commute.

'A bit quiet here this morning?' said Sam.

'I think the merger team were in over the weekend,' said Kate. 'When I got in there were still a couple of pizza boxes the cleaners had missed.'

'That would explain it. More importantly, happy birthday.'

'Thank you. You busy today?'

'Working on my telecoms deal, Paul wants a draft contract ready for when he gets back.'

'Well, if you're free for lunch do you want to grab a bite?'

'Of course.'

'Good. Half-twelve by the lifts.'

Conscious of his late start, Sam started to immerse himself in the papers: reports from the auditors and accountants, schedules of assets and liabilities, draft contract terms, memoranda of understanding. He enjoyed the minutiae of the work and the need to pay attention to detail. It appealed to something in his nature, a desire for order perhaps. Soon he was lost to the world to the extent that he didn't notice the arrival of Clara Chang, the firm's HR manager, until she announced her presence with a discreet cough. Sam looked up and saw Clara, and standing next to her a thirtyish slim fair-haired woman in a light summer dress, wearing a beaded necklace and silver earrings that spoke of a market somewhere in Southeast Asia.

'Morning, Clara, what can I do for you?' asked Sam.

'Good morning, Sam. Sam, this is Emma Janssen, she'll be working for you while Annie's away. Emma, this is Sam Hebden.'

For a moment Sam was slightly taken aback. The last thing he'd expected was a *gweilo* as a temp, and an attractive one at that.

'Hello, Emma. Welcome to McShane Adams,' he said.

'Thanks.'

'Sam's one of our bright young things,' continued Clara.

'Hardly.' Sam blushed.

'You see, Emma, he's also very modest. Paul thinks very highly of you anyway.'

'Paul?' asked Emma.

'Paul Ridgeway, senior partner in the department.

He's away at the moment but you'll meet him while you're with us. That's right isn't it, Sam?'

'Yes. He's back next week.'

'I've already given Emma a tour of the department,' said Clara, before turning to Emma and adding: 'But just give me a call if you need anything.'

'I will.'

'So I'll leave you two to get acquainted.' Clara smiled as she left Sam and Emma.

'Grab a seat,' said Sam, gesturing to a chair in the corner of the room. Emma pulled the chair over so she could sit facing Sam across his desk.

'Emma … Jenson?'

'Janssen.' Emma spelt it out. 'It's Dutch. My grandfather moved to the UK at the start of the war and stayed on.'

'So how long have you been in Hong Kong?'

'Just on two years. The usual story of ending up here by accident and enjoying it. And you?'

'A little longer, three years now.'

There was an awkward pause in the conversation. Sam didn't want to go down the route of the usual conversational clichés about life in Hong Kong, but he was somewhat wrong-footed by Emma and didn't know what to say.

'Well … perhaps I should show you some of the things that need doing,' was the best that Sam finally managed. He went over to a table covered in papers neatly arranged in piles.

'Of course,' said Emma, getting up from her chair

and smoothing down her dress. 'There is one thing I should mention though. Clara already knows this but I do have a slight hearing problem. Tinnitus and a little hearing loss. It's not usually an issue, especially if I'm facing someone, but if occasionally I seem to be ignoring you I promise I'm not really. Just tap me on the shoulder or whatever to get my attention.'

'Oh … okay.' Sam was again nonplussed. Not only had he never had a Westerner as a secretary before, but he had never had one with a hearing problem either. He wasn't quite sure how that was supposed to work.

***

Kate and Rob were waiting for Sam by the lifts when he arrived. They were looking at him expectantly.

'Well,' said Rob, 'who's the blonde?'

'Emma.'

'And?'

'And what? She's my temp for the next couple of weeks.'

'Clara must like you is all I can say, I've never had a temp who looks like that. If you feel like introducing me some time …'

'Stop it, Rob,' said Kate. 'It's my birthday so I'm supposed to be the centre of attention. Is she any good?'

'She is, thank God,' said Sam, before Rob could make the inevitable crude remark. 'She's picked things up very quickly. Is it just the three of us?'

'I'm afraid so. Everyone else pleaded pressure of work. I'll try not to take it personally.'

'Their loss.'

Later, after a longer than intended lunch, Sam returned to find Emma sitting at her computer, a cup of green tea in her hand.

'How are you doing?' Getting no answer, Sam realised that Emma hadn't heard him, so he moved to the other side of her desk and repeated his question.

'Oh, hi, I was lost in the work,' said Emma.

'Sorry I was gone so long. It's Kate's birthday today and we got a bit carried away.'

'While you were gone you got a call from Paul Ridgeway … Where's my note? Ah, here it is. Can you call him back?'

'Did he leave a number?'

'Yes – it's on here.'

Sam took the proffered note and reflected that it was Sod's Law the call would have been when they were out for lunch. He gathered the papers he imagined Paul probably wanted to talk about and then rang back. To Sam's relief his efforts in the morning meant he was able to answer all of the questions and avoid any embarrassment over the late return from lunch.

'Everything okay?' asked Emma, standing at the door to Sam's office.

'Yes, fine thanks. He's not a bad person to work for but he can be quite strict at times.'

'And you need to impress him, right?'

'If I want to progress in the firm then yes, and I think I do.'

Even as he said this Sam wondered why he was telling so much to someone he had only met that morning. He wouldn't normally admit his ambitions to friends and colleagues – in fact, certainly not his colleagues, not even Kate, perhaps especially not Kate. Perhaps it was easier to talk to a stranger about these things, someone who couldn't use it as a weapon against him later. He'd learnt that lesson before and it wasn't a mistake he was going to make twice.

Sam had the sense that Emma was about to say something in reply but instead she simply returned to the green tea and her work. He watched her for a while then forced himself to get back to his papers.

***

Emma came into Sam's office at the end of the day.

'Is there anything else you need from me today?' she asked.

'No, I don't think so, thanks – we've made good progress.'

'I'm glad to hear that. I know it must be a pain when you have a temp. Do you have to stay late?'

'I'll probably do a bit more to make up for the long lunch.'

'Well, I'll be off now, if that's okay.'

Sam worked on quietly after Emma had gone until he was interrupted by Kate. She was wearing a plastic tiara and a sash saying 'Birthday Girl'. In her right hand she was carrying a balloon. Sam raised his eyebrows.

'Gifts from the secretaries,' she explained. 'I'll lose

them when I get out of sight. Has Emma gone?'

'Of course,' said Sam, 'it's only idiots like us who are still working at this hour.'

'Emma's a good-looking girl.'

'Not you as well. I've only just met the woman and know nothing about her.'

'Well, we'll just have to do something about that. I'll see what I can find out from her tomorrow. Until then I shall love you and leave you.' Kate headed for the lifts, singing a rather approximate rendition of 'I Feel Pretty'. Sam winced at how out of tune she was.

***

Back home Sam switched on the air-con, which stuttered half-heartedly into life. There was much noise, clanking and whirring but not a lot of cooling. He'd have to get it looked at. He changed into shorts and a T-shirt, and then went to the fridge to see what there was for supper. Not much was the answer, but he found a supermarket ready meal and a can of beer. They'd have to do. He tried to watch television while eating, but noisy renovations in the flat above had been going on late into the evening for weeks now with little sign of finishing soon. Giving up on television, and hoping to drown out the hammering, he put on a Coleman Hawkins CD, turned up the volume, and went back into the kitchen to find something else to eat. While he looked at the bag of potato chips that had the potential to be dessert, the telephone rang.

'Sam, glad I caught you. Sorry for ringing you at

home.' It was Paul Ridgeway. Sam turned off the music.

'No problem, Paul. What can I do for you?'

'Nothing urgent, but Mr Leung wants a meeting as soon as I get back. Can you organise something and confirm the details with his PA?'

'Sure. No problem.'

'Thanks.' Paul abruptly cut short the conversation. Sam wondered why if it wasn't urgent Paul had bothered to call him at home. Restless for the remainder of the evening, Sam was troubled by thoughts of mainland money and Bahamas companies, and the last time that he allowed his ambition to overcome his judgement.

**

It was Friday, and with Hong Kong looking forward to the weekend the heavens had opened.

The weather had broken from the heat of the beginning of the week, but not in a good way. Instead it was a type of day that was depressingly common in a Hong Kong summer. A day when it rained so heavily that at times it was dark enough for the street lights to come on. There was an intensity to the rain as it drove through the heavy air; a constant background to accompany the cadenzas of thunder. The rain formed torrents flowing down the roads, bringing an uncontrolled wild element into this most urban of environments. When the weather wasn't ridiculously hot and humid, it would rain instead. It was moot which was worse.

Nor was this a short, sharp summer shower where

you simply took shelter until it passed. This was rain that Noah would have recognised. This was rain that could continue for days, flooding streets and floating away taxis with the rising waters. Rain that could work its way through permeable walls in badly built apartments. Rain that closed schools and airports. Rain that could bring the city to a halt. This was rain that could cause landslips. Rain more than capable of bringing down a hillside and homes with it. Rain that could take lives.

Emma collected her umbrella and bag and stuck her head round the door of Sam's office.

'Is it okay if I leave now?' It was only 5 pm. She knew it was a bit early but she had worked through lunch and needed to get to the meeting. 'Is it still raining?' Emma looked past Sam and through his window.

He looked himself. 'Yes, I'm afraid you'll get soaked.' Sam turned back towards Emma before adding: 'But sure, I don't think there's anything that can't wait until Monday. Oh … and don't forget you're welcome to join us for drinks later, if you like. We'll be at Hennigan's from seven-ish.' He had invited her to the department's usual Friday post-work drinks.

'I'm not sure I can, but if I'm finished in time I'll try and see what I can do. If not, I'll see you Monday.'

As Emma stepped out into the street, rainclouds still filled the sky and the downpour showed no signs of relenting. Sheets of water covered the pavements, and small lakes were starting to form where the drains were blocked with litter and rubbish. Emma had hoped to get a taxi, but as soon as she saw how bad the rain was she knew it would be next to impossible, and anyway the traffic was already almost stationary. Confident she could get there faster on foot, Emma put up her umbrella, although it would scarcely be enough to keep her head dry, and headed out into the early evening crowds.

Alice had given her the address of a flat in Mid-Levels that was close to the series of covered escalators and footbridges that snaked their way uphill, taking people home from the shops and offices of Central. By the time Emma had reached the escalator, she was relieved to be under shelter again; water dripped off her while she was carried between buildings and above narrow streets. She found it next to impossible not to be drawn into looking through the various windows she passed and always felt uncomfortable at seeing so many private lives on display. Couldn't they use curtains? She would in their place, blinds at least. Short of closing her eyes it was difficult not to watch the overweight man in a grubby singlet and shorts; the housewife cooking in a tiny kitchen; the older woman hanging laundry.

Leaving the escalator at Caine Road, just as she was finally starting to dry a little, she once more had to rely on her umbrella to try and fend off the rainstorm that wasn't showing any sign of easing. If anything, it had somehow managed to get worse. When she found the building she was looking for, an unremarkable high-rise barely distinguishable from its neighbours,

Emma hesitated. She really wasn't sure about this and was regretting that she had allowed Alice to twist her arm. Especially when she was now soaked to the skin. Would it hurt if she just went home? She couldn't think what difference she could possibly make to anything. She could always blame work. Tell Alice that her boss had needed her to do something. Her finger hovered over the intercom with indecision before she remembered it was a friend she had promised. She pressed for flat number 14E; she was committed now. A man answered in English and the door catch was released to let her into the dry. She shook her umbrella to get some of the worst of the water off and took the lift to the fourteenth floor.

The door was opened by Alice.

'Oh dear ...' Alice looked at a bedraggled Emma and tried not to laugh. 'Come in.'

'Thanks. Is there anywhere I can tidy myself up a bit?'

'End of the corridor on the right.'

A few minutes later, and looking a bit more presentable, Emma joined Alice in the living room. A black leather sofa took up one wall and there was a small dining table with a number of chairs. In spite of the rain it was still warm and a ceiling fan gently stirred the air. In addition to Alice, there were five others seated or perched on various spots around the small room.

'Emma, this is Kelvin.' Alice introduced a Chinese man who Emma guessed to be about forty. 'This is Kelvin's flat.'

'Welcome, Emma, please have a seat.' Kelvin rose and offered Emma the chair he had been sitting on.

'Thanks. Sorry though, I'm going to get everything wet.'

'Don't worry about it. Hong Kong in the rain, what can you do?'

Kelvin left to fetch another chair and Alice introduced Emma to the others. One was a Westerner, Charles, probably in his sixties; Lily and Yannie were local women, both around Emma's age. 'And this is Liang-bao.' Alice placed a hand on the arm of a tall – at least six foot – young Chinese man with high cheekbones who was sitting at one end of the sofa. 'Like you, he's a new member. Everyone – this is my good friend Emma.'

'Hello,' said Emma to the room, adjusting slightly the position of her chair so that she could more or less see everyone's faces, which always helped her hearing.

Kelvin returned with the extra chair. 'Can I offer you a glass of wine?' He picked up a bottle and offered it to Emma.

'Please, thanks.'

Kelvin poured Emma a glass and then took his seat before beginning the meeting.

'So, now we are all here, let's get started,' he said, looking around at his guests as he spoke. 'Firstly, welcome to Emma and Liang-bao. It's always good to have new members. As the rest of you know, we need to discuss Yan Xiao-ling, but for the benefit of our new friends I should perhaps explain a bit.' Kelvin turned his attention towards Emma and Liang-bao in particular. 'He's a medical researcher in Beijing, a lecturer at Tsinghua University. He's been doing work on recent sharp increases in infectious diseases in China but his figures don't match those of the government. He's been suspended from his university position and put under house arrest. The Chinese Communist Party never likes bad news. They always shoot the messenger.'

'Sometimes literally,' added Yannie.

'How did you come to hear about him?' asked Emma.

'I'm in the medical faculty at Hong Kong University,' said Kelvin. 'I haven't worked with Yan Xiao-ling myself but some of my colleagues have. They put me on to him when they realised he was suddenly, how do you say ... *persona non grata.*'

'So what do you propose to do?'

'Well, that's mainly what we need to decide but there are some fairly standard things we can do. To start with we need to get the media involved, and that's where Yannie comes in. Her husband's a journalist.'

'Kelvin exaggerates,' said Yannie. 'He's a sports reporter for the *Sing Tao Daily* but he does have friends on the news desk.'

'Which is what we need. What we don't have though is a contact in the English language press.' Kelvin turned to Emma. 'I don't suppose you have any journalist friends by any chance?'

'Sadly no. But temping, I do tend to come across

quite a range of people so I can keep my eyes open.'

'I can use my professional contacts to keep Yan Xiao-ling's name remembered in the academic community,' Kelvin continued, 'and meanwhile we can all write to the Chinese government to protest.'

'Do you think that will do any good?' asked Liang-bao. It was the first time he had spoken and Emma was surprised by how good his English was. Not only was it fluent and natural, but his accent sounded very proper. He was one of those Chinese people she came across from time to time who somehow managed to seem more British than the British themselves.

'Who knows, but we have to try, don't we?' said Alice.

Kelvin started handing out papers that had been on the dining table.

'What I've done is to prepare a basic information sheet so you have all the right facts to hand, and just in case you don't know it – or you've lost it – I've added the address of the Xinhua News Agency.' Although technically a news agency, everyone knew Xinhua was the *de facto* Chinese embassy in Hong Kong. The unofficial representative of Beijing and the Chinese Communist Party in colonial Hong Kong.

After a little while the business of the meeting came to an end and conversation drifted to more general matters. Kelvin brought out another bottle of wine and some food, while Emma got to know the others. Charles was a retired civil servant who had spent his whole working life in Hong Kong, Yannie worked in the same trading company as Alice, and Lily was Yannie's sister.

'So how did you find the meeting?' Kelvin asked Emma.

'Interesting, thanks. Have you been involved in this sort of thing for long?'

'I guess it was after Tiananmen Square I started thinking about politics. There was a guy I knew when I was a student who was killed that night.'

'Sorry, I didn't know.'

'It's okay, we weren't close or anything, but still … it was a wake-up call.'

'I bet it was.'

'So I joined Amnesty and then a couple of years ago I started this group.'

'What made you want to do that? After all, Amnesty is so well known.'

'It is and it does great things. But sometimes it gets dismissed by China as being too Western. It's too easy for Beijing to paint Amnesty as a bunch of interfering foreigners. I wanted to try and build something more local. Something grown here in Hong Kong. We're only small at the moment though. There are a few others not here tonight but it's just so hard to get local people involved in politics. Hong Kong people often just want a quiet life, you know? As long as they have good jobs and *dim sum* they don't like to cause trouble.'

'Even with the handover next year?'

'Even with that, yes. Tiananmen did make some people stop and think, at the time anyway, but that was seven years ago so any panic that caused has largely died away. You probably know how many people tried to make sure they could go to Canada and so on if they needed to, but even that was just insurance. They don't really want to leave unless they have no choice. So, trying to get people interested in human rights, well … it's not easy, but you've got to start somewhere, haven't you?'

'Indeed.'

Charles was waiting for a chance to cut in.

'I think Charles wants a word with you.'

Leaving Kelvin and Charles to talk, Emma couldn't help but notice that Alice was spending a lot of time with Liang-bao, and when Liang-bao excused himself Emma took the opportunity to get Alice to one side.

'Okay, are you going to tell me what's going on?' Emma asked.

'What do you think of him?'

'I don't know, I've only just met him. He's good looking though. Tell me more, and anyway, why didn't you tell me on Sunday?'

'I nearly did. We met in the cafeteria at Hong Kong U about a month ago. He's a student there as well. We got talking, found we had some common interests.'

'Is he a mainlander?' Emma was a little shocked. She'd always thought of Alice as being a very traditional young Hong Kong woman. That she might be dating someone from the mainland was unexpected.

'I know. It feels exciting somehow. Almost illicit. It's like I'm having an affair with a married man.'

'I take it your parents don't know?'

'Of course not. Shhh … here he comes.'

Liang-bao came back into the room and Emma was curious to find out more.

'Alice tells me you're a student at Hong Kong U?'

'That's right. I'm doing a Masters there.'

'You have very good English.'

'For a mainlander?'

'Sorry.' Emma blushed, embarrassed. 'I didn't mean to sound rude.'

'It's okay,' Liang-bao laughed. 'It's a fair question. I did my first degree in London. I lived in a flat in Stepney for three years.' Emma knew Stepney and knew that Liang-bao didn't have a Stepney accent.

'Well if I'm going to make a fool of myself I might as well go the whole way. You're very tall for a Chinese person.'

'Emma!' Alice looked shocked at Emma's blunt questioning.

'Again, a fair comment.' Liang-bao was unconcerned. 'I'm from Harbin in the north. We do tend to be taller than average for China.'

'Enough,' said Alice. 'Enough of this interrogation.'

'Sorry.' Looking at her watch, Emma saw that it was half past eight. 'Anyway, I need to be going. I hadn't realised what the time was.'

'So what's the rush?' asked Alice.

'Just some work drinks I said I'd try and make. I'll give you a call tomorrow.'

***

'Now that the others have gone, I can tell you what I found out about Emma.'

Kate and Sam were sharing a table in Hennigan's. The rest of their gang had moved on to get something to eat before hitting Wan Chai later. Kate had declined going with them, pleading, with some truth, that she was still feeling the effects of her birthday, but also guessing that Sam wanted to stay on in the hope that Emma might yet make it.

'Currently single and unattached. Not sure whether or not there was a boyfriend when she came to Hong Kong. She was a bit coy about that.'

'How did you find this out?' asked Sam.

'I happened – by pure chance, of course – to be in the ladies at the same time as her and we got talking. As you do.'

With the rain still falling, the bar was predictably full and they had been lucky to get a table. Friday night partygoers taking shelter where they could. Hennigan's was not the smartest bar in town – nobody could remember when it had last been decorated, and the chairs were worn and threadbare – but the 70s music made it popular with expats and locals alike, and above all, tonight, it had the very great advantage of being indoors.

'And what makes you think I'm interested in her anyway?'

'God Sam, I love you and all that, but you can be so dim at times. For one thing I've seen the way you've been looking at her all week. I bet she's noticed as well. And to be fair, why wouldn't you? She's very good looking. And you're sitting here hoping she's going to turn up when you could be with the others. Oh, and by the way, sometimes I think I know you better than you know yourself.'

'That's all very interesting,' said Sam, 'but it doesn't look like she's coming.'

'Perhaps not, but to be fair she did say that she might not make it. Let's have one more drink and then go and get some food ourselves.' Kate waved to get the attention of a waitress.

'I haven't asked how your birthday drinks went,' said Sam, 'though given how late you were the next day I take it they were fun?'

'They were, though somewhere along the way I managed to lose a shoe. I didn't even realise until I got out of the taxi going home. It was an expensive pair, as well.'

'Poor Cinderella.'

'Sorry?'

'Waiting for Prince Charming to turn up with your missing slipper.'

'Oh, I get it now, yes, I suppose so, though at four in the morning Wan Chai is short on charm.' Two beers arrived together with a bowl of popcorn. 'Still,' continued Kate, 'the night must have been quite good because the next morning I found a slip of paper in my handbag with a man's name and telephone number on it.'

'Somebody you met?'

'I guess so.'

'You don't know?'

'I *think* I know who it was. Tall guy, bit of a jock.'

'So are you going to call him?'

'I already have.'

Sam always had confused feelings when Kate started going out with a new man. It wasn't that he was jealous of anyone dating her, they had never been an item, and although they joked about it they both knew they never would be, but he feared that one day Kate would find someone and he would lose a close friend. When they'd finished their beers, Sam and Kate left the bar and found that the rain had finally stopped. With the downpour over, the crowds were starting to fill the street again, and as they got into a taxi they didn't see the young blonde waving at them as she came down the road.

CHAPTER 4

'You must be excited about Hong Kong returning to China.'

Once a week the basketball players would go out for beers, and Kwok-wah found that after a few drinks his new friends started to open up to him a bit more. But he was already getting tired of this question; the question everybody seemed to want to ask him.

'Glad to be rid of the British, I expect.' This was from Zhao Zhanyuan. Kwok-wah didn't pay much attention to politics but even he had recognised early on that Zhanyuan was the most hard-line. Li Lao had warned him that Zhao Zhanyuan's father was a major in the People's Liberation Army and Kwok-wah learnt to be careful and non-committal in anything he said. In truth Kwok-wah never knew how to answer these questions, if they were questions at all. They seemed more like slogans that had been learnt by rote. He had never thought of himself being under any colonial yoke; he had grown up under British rule and had simply accepted it as a fact of life. Just one of those things, as inevitable as June rain and cockroaches. His answers were always quietly neutral, and if he could he'd try and change the subject.

Mostly though they talked about girls. A couple of his room-mates had girlfriends back in their home towns, but that didn't seem to stop them eyeing up their options.

'Have you seen that girl in the calculus class?' asked Li Lao in a typical conversation one evening. 'The one that sits in the front row wearing a short skirt. She keeps crossing and uncrossing her legs until Professor Wang mixes up his second order derivatives from his partial integrals.'

But Kwok-wah soon came to the conclusion that they were all talk. He never saw his room-mates actually go up and speak to any of the female students. Kwok-wah himself was unattached. There had once been a girlfriend in Hong Kong but she had dumped him when she concluded – completely correctly – that he was more interested in his research than in her, and he wasn't particularly looking for anyone.

The bar they were in one Friday was one of their favourites. A little away from the university, there was less chance of bumping into any of their teachers and it was also popular because it had an American theme with a jukebox and pictures of NBA stars on the walls. The fact that his friends could switch so quickly from praising China as the next great superpower to a fascination with all things American never ceased to surprise Kwok-wah, but he was learning discretion. He knew better than to say anything.

'It's your round, Hongkonger,' Zhanyuan said. He'd taken to calling Kwok-wah that as if to emphasise the difference between him and the rest of them. Kwok-wah was far from sure it was his turn to get the drinks, his round seemed to come more often than the others, but he didn't feel inclined to argue. Anyway, the drinks were much cheaper in Shanghai than back home. The waitresses seemed busy so Kwok-wah went to the bar himself. Once he'd ordered, his eye wandered over the room. It was busy, as always on a Friday. Mainly young, probably mostly students since the bar was close to Fudan University. Some slightly older customers, dressed more smartly as if they had jobs in media or law but were not yet ready to move on to the expensive downtown places.

Four women sat at a table beneath a large action photograph of Michael Jordan. Kwok-wah looked at the picture, trying to work out when it was taken. He couldn't tell who the Bulls were playing; was it the Phoenix Suns? If so it might have been from the 1993 Finals. Or was it Portland from 1992? While he tried to decide, Kwok-wah realised one of the women at the table was looking straight at him. Slim, long hair in a ponytail, she smiled at Kwok-wah, who immediately looked away, embarrassed that she might have thought he was staring at her.

'Here, let me help.' Li Lao appeared on Kwok-wah's shoulder as the barman set down the last of the glasses. 'I'll take these.'

***

Fourier Transforms in Frequency Division Multiplexing Systems read the title of the book Kwok-wah had out from the university library on a semi-permanent loan. Scraps of paper were placed between pages to help him find his way back to interesting sections and he had to resist the temptation to scribble notes in the margin. It was his bible. He told himself that when he was next back in Hong Kong he would try and get hold of his own copy. Here in China buying new textbooks printed overseas was less straightforward. Not always possible and expensive when it was.

He was reading a chapter on Laplace transforms while sitting at his desk in the department. The December weather had come as a surprise to Kwok-wah; the one or two slightly chilly days in a Hong Kong winter were no preparation for the genuinely cold weather here. There was frost on the inside of the window and the heating was struggling to cope with the cold snap. Kwok-wah pulled his collar up and breathed on his cupped hands to try and get some warmth in them. Granny Sun had given him a flask of herbal tea she assured him would keep his blood hot during the winter months. Kwok-wah wasn't convinced it was working, and it tasted foul. Immersed in his reading, he didn't hear Professor Ye enter.

'Mr Yang?'

Kwok-wah, surprised, jumped slightly. 'Professor …
sorry … I …'

'Sorry. I didn't mean to alarm you. I just wanted to
tell you I need to cancel our meeting this afternoon.'

'Oh.' Kwok-wah didn't want to show it, but he was
disappointed. He was supposed to have regular meetings
with Professor Ye, his supervisor, but the previous two had
been cancelled as well. It seemed to be becoming a habit.

'I have a visitor that I must see. Speak with my
secretary and we'll try and reschedule for next week.'
Professor Ye left before Kwok-wah could even think
of commenting that he had said the same thing last
time but nothing had come of it. Not that he would
have dared say any such thing.

***

As he became more confident in the months since his
arrival, more comfortable in his new home, Kwok-
wah started to explore Shanghai. He knew some of
the city's history from his school days and from the
reading he'd done before coming, but he learnt even
more when he walked the streets. He learnt how the
trade with the outside world that had brought Shanghai
its riches had been a double-edged sword and had also
brought different people with different ways. They'd
built churches and houses, tennis clubs and dance halls.
They raced horses and played croquet on the lawn; no
locals or dogs allowed.

Kwok-wah walked the broad avenues of the old
concession districts, roads lined with *faguo wutong*

– French plane trees that had seen so much change in Shanghai. Rulers and revolutions came and went while the trees continued unconcerned. He investigated the older Chinese areas around Xiaodongmen; telephone lines crossing the streets in a giant cat's cradle, hawkers selling street food from carts, and prematurely aged men on bicycles pulling large loads on trailers. It was obvious many of these districts would soon disappear under various redevelopment schemes. Some had gone already, others were clearly not going to be still standing in a year's time. Perhaps even the plane trees were not safe.

He walked along the Bund with what were once banks and trading houses, mostly now repurposed, along the curved bank of the river. Neoclassical vying with Beaux Arts, Gothic revival with Art Deco. The other side of the Huangpu River, the Flash Gordon skyscrapers of the rapidly growing Pudong district faced down the grey-stone monoliths of the past. Two different eras, almost two different worlds, staring at each other across the water. In the mornings he took to jogging in a park near the university, passing young and old enjoying *tai chi* or ballroom dancing, music playing from speakers hanging in the trees like some futuristic fruit.

It was on one of these explorations of the city, when he was near the Yuyuan Garden, that he saw the woman from the bar. She was standing on a zigzag bridge that led across a lake to the Huxinting Teahouse, leaning forward, arms resting on the wall, while she peered down into the water. Even with his limited interest in fashion he couldn't fail to notice she was better dressed than most other women he'd seen in Shanghai. Tight jeans that showed off her long legs, and a blue woollen jacket with a fine scarf wrapped round her neck. A pair of black leather gloves complemented her ankle boots.

Kwok-wah was still a little embarrassed by what had happened in the bar, the way it must have looked as if he'd been staring at her – his mother would have scolded him for bad manners – but in spite of that memory he took the opportunity to observe her from a distance. He was considering how he might find a reason to talk to her, perhaps explain what had happened that night in the bar, when she left the bridge and started towards the entrance to the gardens themselves. He had already been in there once that day, but his interest was piqued. He bought another ticket and followed her in. His curiosity in who she was overcame any concerns that he was stalking her.

But soon, in trying too hard to keep his distance, he found he had lost sight of her completely. Even in December the gardens were full of couples and families; the noise and crowds creating an atmosphere that was a far cry from the peace and calm intended by the sixteenth-century designers. He wandered through the gardens, not paying any attention to the pavilions and ponds he had admired only a couple of hours ago. Instead he concentrated on looking for the woman. He saw her. Her profile framed like a portrait within a circular opening in one of the dragon walls. Had she glanced at him? For a moment it was as though she had seen him, but then she was gone. Kwok-wah spent another fruitless hour in the gardens with no success.

Only later, back in his dorm, did Kwok-wah realise he'd seen her before that night in the bar. She'd been one of a bunch of students watching them play basketball: slim, taller than the rest, long hair in a ponytail.

***

The Friday morning departmental seminar on the Cooley-Tukey algorithm would normally have absorbed Kwok-wah's full attention. But not today. When the lecturer came to the end of his presentation Kwok-wah realised that he had scarcely taken in one word. He hadn't seen the woman since the Yuyuan Garden, but now that he had started to think about her he found her very absence was distracting him. He didn't have the faintest idea why. He'd seen her twice, no, three times, and only from a distance. He hadn't spoken a single word to her and he had no idea who she was.

So he was more than a little surprised when he saw her in the cafeteria at lunchtime.

'Here, Hongkonger, I got you a banana,' said Zhao Zhanyuan as he sat down at their table, tossing the fruit in Kwok-wah's direction.

'Very funny,' said Kwok-wah in a flat tone that made it clear he didn't think it was funny at all. It was an old joke – yellow on the outside, white on the inside – that Kwok-wah was tiring of. He didn't even think it applied to him at all. Back in Hong Kong he knew many people who fitted the description far more than he did. But he guessed it was all relative, and to Zhao Zhanyuan perhaps he did seem less Chinese. It was still tiresome though.

'What on earth does that mean?' asked Kwok-wah, looking to change the conversation.

'What?'

'Your T-shirt." Zhanyuan was wearing a T-shirt with the words *'SCENE: IT'S AMERICAN ANSWER'* emblazoned on it. Zhanyuan looked down at his chest for a moment.

'Dunno.' He shrugged.

Kwok-wah picked at the remains of his lunch. He wondered if there was any meat at all on his chicken or if it was all bone and gristle. He gave up on what was left and was starting to tidy his tray with a view to leaving when he saw the woman at the food counter. There was no mistaking her; she was at least eight inches taller than the friend she was with.

'You see that woman in the queue?' he said to Zhanyuan. 'Tall. Jeans, long hair, talking to the girl in the red tracksuit top … just being served. Do you know who she is?'

Zhao Zhanyuan turned to have a look.

'No, I don't think so. Why? Somebody you fancy?' Zhanyuan raised an eyebrow. 'I can understand why. Wait a minute … didn't she watch us play basketball once? I remember – she was the looker … Yeah, now I know why you're interested. But you're wasting your time, she's way out of your league.'

Kwok-wah felt his face blush and kicked himself for mentioning her to Zhanyuan. There were times when he wondered if Zhanyuan wasn't taking too much of an interest in what he was up to. Almost as if he had been given the job of keeping an eye on him. 'I've just seen her around a couple of places since then. No matter. I have to be getting back to the lab.' Kwok-wah carried his tray back to the counter. As he did so he passed the woman, and this time there was no doubt that she smiled at him.

***

Kwok-wah was pleased to have some relatively mindless work ahead of him that afternoon. Using a program he had written himself, he had been allocated time on one of the department's mainframes to run multiple simulations of different algorithms. Kwok-wah sat at a terminal and watched the flickering ever-changing display on the monitor that showed the progress of the software. He found it restful and strangely beautiful to watch as the ephemeral letters and digits passed in and out of existence. It was soothing and allowed his mind the freedom to wander. Who was she? Was she really interested in him or was it just wishful thinking on his part? He'd had girlfriends before, but not many, and he would be the first to admit he was useless at trying to read people's body language; useless at telling the difference between a friendly smile and something more significant.

He told himself he was being ridiculous. He was

cross with himself for being so stupid. How could he imagine she was interested in him? He hadn't even spoken to her. Surely she must have a boyfriend? If not here then back at home, wherever it was she came from. He had no illusions about his appearance and didn't think he was particularly good looking. His teenage acne had only recently become less of an issue and there was no doubt that Zhanyuan was right; she was out of his league, unless she had some special interest in Fourier transforms. Which he doubted. The printer clattered into action. The results of the first simulation were in and Kwok-wah stood over the machine guiding the paper as it spooled out so that it didn't get tangled or jam, as often happened.

While he was occupied with the printer, he saw Professor Ye enter the lab. These days it was unusual enough to see him in the lab at all – Kwok-wah had been surprised and a little disappointed at how little time Professor Ye spent there, he seemed to prefer meetings with the great and the good – but what caught Kwok-wah's attention most of all was that the professor was accompanied by a military uniform, a man not much older than Professor Ye himself, early forties perhaps, with thinning hair. Kwok-wah knew nothing about military uniforms – he couldn't even have said whether it was army, navy or air force – and had no idea of the man's rank, except that judging from the smartness of the uniform and the high density of badges and insignia, it was apparent he must be reasonably senior.

Kwok-wah kept a low profile and concentrated on

folding the printer output. Professor Ye was showing his guest the equipment they had.

'We've got three mainframes. This is the most powerful. But they're all several years old now. We've tried to update them as best we can, to upgrade their processing speed, but there's no getting away from the fact that they are not up to the job any more. Things move so fast in our field.' Kwok-wah wasn't eavesdropping as such but he couldn't avoid hearing what was being said. His Putonghua still wasn't perfect but he got the gist of things.

'When the new building is ready we'll be in a position to increase our capability, but we'll need a substantial amount of money if we are to maximise our potential and give you what you want. The mainframes will all need replacing with the latest models, and I want to replace the PCs as well. It's going to be expensive.' The uniform didn't reply; he was looking around at the machines. 'Our normal departmental budget won't even come close to covering the costs. We need to look at the special projects money but even that is going to need a boost.'

'Can you prepare a proposal?' They had moved to the other side of a large computer cabinet. Kwok-wah couldn't believe they didn't know he was there, unless they simply weren't bothered about being overheard.

'Of course. I'll put together a report with the things we need. The other thing to remember is the lead time. We can't waste time if you want to get this project moving. We'll need to start planning exactly what we want at least two years before we move to the new building. For the large mainframes, I'd like to get things underway as soon as possible. Especially for anything the US won't sell us directly.'

'There are ways and means round that. Let me have something in writing and I'll pass it on to my brother. And your staff? Are they onside with this?'

'They don't know. They don't need to know. I simply point them towards certain research areas that are useful to us. They don't need to know anything about the final product.'

With that, Professor Ye and his guest left the lab, and Kwok-wah suddenly realised that he'd stopped breathing.

***

'Hi,' said the woman.

Kwok-wah was clearing his thoughts while shooting a few baskets when he heard the voice of a woman, speaking in English with an American accent. The surprise of hearing English, the first time he'd heard it spoken since arriving in Shanghai, along with the gender of the speaker, caught him off-guard and he missed his shot badly. He turned to see her standing at the edge of the basketball court; slim, tall, long hair in a ponytail. The woman who had been occupying his thoughts.

'Sorry,' she said. 'I didn't mean to put you off your shot.'

'It was just a bad shot.'

'I've been watching you for a while. You're good.' Kwok-wah felt himself blush. He went to retrieve the basketball to hide the fact. 'My dad's a big Warriors fan,' she continued. 'He takes us to see them sometimes. I'm Susan, by the way, Susan Khoo. I think I've seen you around? I thought I'd come and say hello.'

'Yeung Kwok-wah. Or Yang, as I'm known around here. Your English is very good. Better than mine, if I'm honest.'

Susan laughed. 'I'm American. From California. Oakland, to be precise.'

Kwok-wah blushed again. 'Now I feel stupid.'

'No need. You're from Hong Kong, right? Didn't you want to go back home for Christmas?'

'I didn't think I did but I'm not so sure now.' His mother was a churchgoer and when he'd called to say he wasn't coming home for the holidays, Kwok-wah could tell she was upset. 'But it's too late now. How about you?'

'Too expensive to go back to the States again. I was back for Thanksgiving not that long ago.' Susan sat down on a bench by the side of the basketball court. She was wearing a tracksuit and trainers as if she had been out for a run. 'So what are you doing here? In Shanghai, that is. What are you studying, I mean?'

Kwok-wah hesitated before deciding to sit down next to her on the bench. Having been intrigued by this woman, now that he was in her company he was unsure of himself.

'I'm doing a PhD in computer science,' he said.

'Would I regret it if I asked what it was about?'

'Do you know what Fourier transforms are? Sorry, if it turns out you're studying maths that's going to sound like a stupid question. You're not, are you? Studying maths?'

'No,' she laughed, a light laugh that made Kwok-wah smile without knowing why. 'I'm doing building sciences. There's some maths, of course, but nothing particularly advanced.'

'Building sciences? What does that involve?'

'It's a kinda multidisciplinary thing. A bit of architecture, some civil engineering, materials and so on. Y'know, anything that might go in to the construction of new buildings.'

She was sitting turned towards Kwok-wah and he noticed the gold stud earrings she was wearing.

'So what brought you to Shanghai when there are so many good schools in the US? It's pretty unusual, isn't it? For an American to come and study in China?'

'Look around the place,' Susan said. 'Shanghai, I mean. You must have seen just how much building is going on. This is where it's all at. There are so many new developments using new techniques and new technologies. People here are more interested in trying new ideas and new ways of building. They have to be just to try and keep up with the demand. There's such a pressure to build quickly. Back home everything is more traditional. But what about you? You were going to tell me about your ... what are they called again? Something transformers?'

'Fourier transforms. It's hard to explain in detail if

you don't have a maths background, but basically I'm doing research into a number of mathematical techniques that can be used in data transmission. Mobile phones, computers and so on.'

'Phones?' Susan frowned.

'Well not yet, but soon enough.'

'So the same question you asked me: why here?'

'My supervisor – Professor Ye – is a leader in the field. It wasn't so much that I wanted to come to Shanghai, but I really wanted to work with him. I heard him give a lecture in Hong Kong outlining some of the things we'll be doing with our phones in the future. It was inspiring.'

'That's a cool reason. Is this your block?' Susan gestured to the nearby accommodation building.

'Yeah, I share a dorm room.'

Susan rubbed her arms.

'It's starting to get cold,' she said. The sun had started to disappear behind a building and the day had not been warm to start with.

'True. Probably time to get going,' Kwok-wah said reluctantly. He wanted to continue the conversation but in his shyness couldn't think of a way of doing so.

'You know,' Susan said, 'being here over Christmas is a bit sad. Do you want to get together sometime? Maybe grab a bite to eat? Not tonight, I'm out with my room-mates, but tomorrow? I know one place I'd like to try.'

'Sure. Why not?' Kwok-wah tried to sound relaxed.

'Cool. Let's meet here again tomorrow at … what

shall we say? Seven? No, I've a better idea. Let's meet at the countdown clock.' The countdown clock was a large digital display, some twenty feet high, counting down in days, hours, minutes and seconds to the return of Hong Kong to China. The clock occupied a prime spot in front of the main administration building.

Kwok-wah continued to sit on the bench as he watched Susan head back towards her dorm. Only then did it occur to ask himself what she was doing so far from her own building in the first place.

CHAPTER 5

'SAM HAS EVERYTHING READY FOR you to sign, Mr Leung,' said Paul Ridgeway as he ushered Mr Leung and his companion into the boardroom where Sam was waiting with the papers to be signed. Paul Ridgeway had come to Hong Kong in the seventies and unknown to him the joke in the department was that he'd brought with him a seventies hairstyle that he had never relinquished. Over the years his wife and colleagues had managed to dissuade him from wide lapels and kipper ties, but he wouldn't budge on his hair, which today was particularly bouffant and rested gently on his shoulders.

'Yes, Mr Leung, it's all here,' Sam said, gesturing to the bundles of papers laid out on the mahogany table that took pride of place in the boardroom. The room had a look common to a traditional Hong Kong law firm; prints of colonial Hong Kong designed to give clients a sense of history and continuity decorated the walls, while a Chinese vase that rested on a well-stocked drinks cabinet acted as a reminder of where the office was. For visitors from overseas, the windows from the nineteenth floor offered the perfect tourist view of Victoria Harbour and Kowloon, the Star Ferry weaving its way across the water, the afternoon sun glinting off the windows of the Peninsula Hotel. Before Paul and the client had arrived, Sam had been watching a plane as it banked making its final approach into Kai Tak. All the clichéd images of Hong Kong in one single convenient vista.

'The pages needing your signature are all marked with a red tab.' Sam opened the papers to the first page. Mr Leung took a fountain pen and began to sign while his companion looked on. Mr Leung had been a client of the firm for many years. Now in his seventies, but still with a good head of hair, dyed black and parted in the centre, he remained very much the patriarch of his family company. He had a number of children who were responsible for parts of the business, but there was no sign of Mr Leung stepping down from the top any time soon. Mr Leung's companion was not family and was a couple of decades younger, though in contrast to Mr Leung, his hair was carefully combed to hide its relative absence.

Sam had done little else recently other than to prepare the contracts. Good though Emma had been, Sam had been grateful that Annie was back while they worked long into the evenings, and the time difference didn't help with Sam often on the phone to lawyers in the Bahamas. But still, when he had time to reflect,

Sam missed Emma. On her final day they'd made one of those 'must get together sometime' arrangements, but Mr Leung had had to come first, and apart from one after-work drink – which hadn't gone well – little had happened.

While Mr Leung signed, Sam considered his companion. Sam had seen him in a couple of meetings now, but he never gave anything away and had rarely spoken at all unless in reply to a question. At first Sam thought it might be a language issue – perhaps his English wasn't that good, and he seemed to be a Mandarin speaker – but when he did speak he had good, albeit American-accented, English. Mr Leung seemed respectful of him though, treated him as an equal, which was in itself a little surprising. Sam had met Mr Leung a number of times before and he had always been very clearly the man in charge. Even his children always knew their place.

'Thank you, Paul. I've been impressed with your work, as always,' said Mr Leung as he turned the papers to find the next signature page.

'We try our best, don't we, Sam?'

'Especially for such long-standing clients,' Sam echoed.

'We've known each other for quite a while now, haven't we, Paul?' said Mr Leung.

'It must be the best part of twenty years, I think. You were one of my first clients when I came here.'

'And I hope it will continue that way,' said Mr Leung as he continued to sign. 'Even after next year.'

'Why wouldn't it?'

'I know some expatriates are thinking of leaving, but not yourself?'

'No, not me. It will be business as usual, as far as I can see.'

'Quite right, Paul. But still, things will be different will they not? Are you not at least a little bit … how shall I say … concerned about our … our friends in the north?' Mr Leung's companion looked up and smiled at this point.

'Some things may be different perhaps, but also the same,' said Paul. 'We all still want the same things don't we? Stability, prosperity – no rocking the boat.' This had been the Hong Kong business mantra for some time now.

'And young Sam here? Is he the future?' Mr Leung turned to Sam. 'Will you be staying on, Sam? After the handover?'

'I certainly hope so, Mr Leung.' Sam didn't think any other answer was politic in the situation, and anyway, it was true. Sam saw his future in Hong Kong and like most expats he didn't see any reason why the handover would make any difference to him.

Mr Leung had signed the last page and he passed the papers back to Sam.

'Congratulations, Mr Leung,' said Paul, acknowledging also the companion who had been silent while he watched Mr Leung sign. 'You now own 55% of Bright Talk Telecommunications.'

'Most satisfying.' Mr Leung rose from the table and the others followed suit. His companion whispered something in Mr Leung's ear. 'We have to be going, Paul, but perhaps you and your charming wife would care to join me in my box at Sha Tin on Sunday?'

'We would be delighted. Is your horse running?'

'She is, yes, in the fourth race. But please – and I only say this because you are a good friend – I would not put too much money on her. She is too young at the moment, but she has promise.'

After Sam had accompanied the clients to the lifts he went to Paul Ridgeway's office.

'That seemed to go well,' said Sam.

Paul looked up from his desk where he was signing letters his secretary had left for him.

'Yes. Thanks Sam, you've done good work on this deal.'

'I don't know Mr Leung's partner well. Is he a mainlander?'

'Why do you ask?'

'I was just curious. He seems out of keeping with Mr Leung's usual style of doing business.'

'And what do you think is Mr Leung's usual style?'

'A bit old-fashioned perhaps, very traditional. Quite proper. This guy seems … I don't know … a sharp suit compared to Mr Leung's three-piece?'

'Perhaps, old school though he may be, even Mr Leung has to move with the times.'

'It's just that …' Sam hesitated before continuing, uncertain whether to broach the subject but knowing from experience what could happen if he didn't. 'It's just that there are rumours going around.'

'Rumours?'

'About mainland money being involved in this deal.'

Paul Ridgeway sat back in his chair and studied Sam for a moment.

'Three pieces of advice for you, Sam, if you want to get anywhere.' There was a severity in the voice that made Sam wish he'd kept his mouth shut. 'Firstly, you shouldn't listen to gossip. Secondly, we are professional advisers. Our clients expect discretion. Thirdly, sometimes the best questions are those that are left unasked. Understood?'

'Of course.'

'Good. Now, I've things to get on with. Please close the door on the way out.'

Sam went back to his office, inwardly cursing himself for raising the subject. After all, it was only rumour and gossip, which had come from Rob. Not the most reliable of sources. But he'd been stung once before by being an unwitting accomplice, and that was how he had come to be in Hong Kong rather than London. Sam wasn't sure if Paul Ridgeway knew how he had come to be looking for a new job; it had never been mentioned, but there were occasions when Sam was in a more cynical mood and wondered if it might even have been viewed as a positive. Just the sort of skill and experience he was looking for.

Still angry with himself, Sam slammed his office door shut with such venom the flimsy partition wall shook. After a short pause the door opened again.

'Is it safe to come in?' asked Kate.

'Of course. Sorry.'

'No need to apologise to me, but you may have woken up the conveyancing department downstairs.'

A faint smile briefly toyed with the idea of crossing Sam's lips before thinking better of it. Kate took the chair facing Sam across his desk.

'Do you want to talk to Dr Kate about it?'

This time the smile decided to give it a try and rested briefly on Sam's mouth before concluding the time still wasn't right.

'Sorry. I've just made a fool of myself in front of Paul.'

'That's it? Some of us do that all the time. What did you say?'

'I just … I mentioned there were rumours and gossip that the deal was being done using mainland money. He basically told me to shut up and stop asking questions. It wasn't so much what he said as the tone of voice he used. A bit like a headmaster scolding a troublesome child.'

'What? You came out with all that on the basis of what Rob said?' Kate laughed. 'Are you an idiot or something? You know what he's like. Anyway, so what if there's mainland money involved? Pretty much every deal I've dealt with these last three years has included some China aspect to it. It's normal these days. You know that.'

'I know, you're right, of course. But telecoms is a bit different, it might be viewed as a sensitive industry, sensitive in political terms that is, but still it probably wouldn't be an issue if it was all out in the open. But if there is mainland money and it's being hidden from view using a Bahamas company, then you start wondering why.'

'You think there might be some ulterior motive?'

'Perhaps,' said Sam. 'Perhaps it's just being laundered. But whatever the reason, somebody would be hiding something.'

'If it's true, of course,' said Kate.

'Indeed. But Paul certainly didn't deny the rumours.'

'Maybe he doesn't know?'

'Unlikely. But anyway, that's what happened. Nothing more. I'm going with him and a client to Shanghai next week so we'll see how that goes. See if I can get back in his good books again.'

'Fair enough,' said Kate. 'Let's talk about something more interesting. How are things with Emma since she was here?'

Sam was sufficiently embarrassed by this question that he almost wanted to go back to the subject of mainland money and Bahamas shell companies.

'We had a drink after work one day.'

'And?'

'And what?'

'Is that it?' Kate sounded horrified. 'Please tell me you've seen her since then.'

'I'm afraid not. I've been busy with this deal, she's been busy …' Sam knew how pathetic all that sounded.

'Oh Sam, please, enough with the excuses already. Stop being so feeble. I hope you're not just sitting around waiting until you and I are the last ones left on the shelf, because I'm not. I have a date this weekend.'

'Anyway, I don't think anything is going to happen. The one time we did meet up was all a bit strange.'

'Strange? What do you mean?' asked Kate.

'Well, we went for a drink in Causeway Bay because she'd been working in an office there. That was all fine; we had a couple of glasses of wine and then I suggested we go get something to eat.'

'Sounds like a standard first date to me.'

'Exactly. So far so good, but it was what happened on the way to the restaurant that was odd.'

'Will you just get on with it?' interrupted Kate. 'Cut to the chase. What was so strange about the evening?'

'I'm getting there, I'm getting there. Causeway Bay was really busy, well, it always is of course, but it was particularly busy. I think there might have been something on in Victoria Park. We were walking against the flow of people who were all going the other way towards the park, and there was this family, a couple with two small kids who were messing around. One of them – a small boy – wasn't watching where he was going and ran straight into me, knocking me off-balance.'

'Did you fall?'

'No, not really, but I stumbled off the pavement into the road and a taxi had to brake sharply to avoid hitting me.'

'Shit. We're you alright?'

'Sure. The taxi driver gave me a gesture or two and I could see him mouth something I probably don't want to know, but I was fine. It was afterwards everything was weird. Emma just totally freaked out. When I'd recovered from the initial shock, she was standing there shaking and her eyes … they were just staring blankly. It took me a while to get her back to something like normal. After that she wasn't interested in dinner and we just went our separate ways. But you should have seen her, Kate. You'd think she'd been the one who was nearly run over, not me. It was weird, so I don't know—'

'Oh. But—'

'—but, if you'd let me finish, as it happens we're going to a movie tonight.'

'A movie!' Kate clapped her hands in delight like a child at Christmas. 'That makes it a date. A proper date – just make sure you're not still in a bad mood. Believe me, there's nothing attractive about a man in a sulk. What are you going to see?'

'The new Maggie Cheung film, what's it called …? *Almost a Love Story*.'

'Good choice, I saw it at the weekend. A perfect date movie. Mind you, I didn't have you down as an aficionado of Hong Kong cinema.'

'I'm not,' Sam acknowledged. 'It was Emma's choice. I think she likes having the subtitles. They help with her hearing.'

CHAPTER 6

'How are you finding it here? In China?' Susan asked a few days after Christmas. They were sitting on a bench by the athletics track, taking a break after a morning run; a common interest, they'd discovered. Kwok-wah and Susan were spending an increasing amount of time together. Kwok-wah wasn't sure what the definition of a date was, and whether they had been on a date or not, but they had explored some of the bars and cheaper restaurants they could afford on their monthly allowances.

The day was cool, if not as cold as it recently had been; overcast and the air damp and heavy. Susan took a swig from the water bottle she was carrying and offered it to Kwok-wah.

'Is it what you expected?' she continued. 'Compared with Hong Kong.'

'I don't know. I don't know that I'd given it any thought. I don't know what I expected. What do you make of the place? I mean it must be even stranger for you than it is for me. You know … coming from the States.'

Susan laughed. 'Oh my God, you've no idea how weird China is to an American – even when you're Chinese. It freaks me out sometimes. I mean, I've done a bit of travelling around Southeast Asia but China is still something else.'

'What do you miss most about home?'

'Pretty much everything! The food for a start. I'd kill for a plate of pancakes with maple syrup. Or just hanging round the mall with my friends. Driving along the Pacific Highway in a convertible with the top down. The weather. Especially the weather … or, to be more precise, the air. I mean' – Susan was getting into her stride – 'when did we last see the sun? It's just day after day of this horrible grey smog. Except when it's raining, of course. Then it's just wet.'

'And yet you're here?'

'And yet I'm here.' Susan smiled. 'Well it's not all bad, of course, and like I said it's got to be good experience for my career. But we weren't talking about me. What about you? What would you be doing now if you were in Hong Kong?'

'Much the same as here mostly. I'd play basketball. Chat with friends. Go see movies. Mostly though I'd be doing something on the computer. Playing games, writing programs. That sort of thing. Go to the Golden Shopping Arcade.'

'I didn't have you down as a shopping addict.'

'It's not a regular mall. It's a place devoted to computers and so on, there are loads of little shops selling all the latest stuff.'

'Ah … I see. You're passionate about your subject, aren't you? I like that. I don't think I am. For me it's just a way to a job, but I really like the way you're so into it. I really do. It's cool.'

'Cool? People normally call me a geek, but I just want to do my research.'

'And is it going well?'

'It's okay, I guess.' Kwok-wah hesitated before going further. If he was honest with himself, he had been feeling a little dissatisfied with things for a while, but he wasn't sure he could identify exactly what was wrong. He was making progress with the research, considering it was early days, but he was largely ignored by the rest of the department and felt rather isolated.

'You sound unsure?'

'Perhaps I expected too much.'

'In what way?'

'I don't know … I think I expected to spend more time with Professor Ye. After all, he was the reason I came here in the first place.'

'Isn't he very helpful?'

'Oh, he's great,' said Kwok-wah, backtracking, anxious not to bad-mouth his professor. 'I just wish he was around more often. He's often away or in meetings. He has a lot of visitors, which means his door is often shut all afternoon. It can be hard to pin him down and get him to spend some time with me. But then, like

I say, perhaps that's just me expecting too much from him. After all, I'm just a lowly PhD student, not some general or whatever.'

'General?' Susan looked at Kwok-wah. Her eyes were alert and suggested that he had piqued her interest.

'Major, colonel … I don't know. He may not even be army, for all I know.'

'What on earth are you talking about?'

'There's this one guy who is always visiting the labs. I've no idea who he is but he has a military uniform of some sort and Professor Ye always gives him a lot of time.'

'They do like their uniforms here, don't they? Even the traffic cops look like five-star generals. But you don't know who he is?'

'No idea at all.'

'Why don't you just ask?'

'You're joking, I hope?' Kwok-wah was horrified by the thought of asking something like that. 'I'm pretty sure I'd be told it was none of my business. But whoever he is, Professor Ye shows him a lot of respect. He can be quite sharp to other members of the department, but when it comes to this guy he always seems to be very … I don't know … what's the word in English?'

'Obliging?'

'Yes … well, no … it's more than that. It's as if Professor Ye owes this guy something.'

'What do you mean?'

'Well, perhaps that's going too far, but certainly it's as if he'll do anything to help him. As you say, obliging.'

Susan looked at her watch. 'I have class in half an hour. You still okay for this evening?' They were planning to explore more of the city together. There was a rumour of a new pizza place off Nanjing Road their stipends would cover.

'Yes, no problem. I'm looking forward to it.'

'Me too.' Susan laid a hand on his shoulder as she stood up and headed back to the main campus.

***

The damp air of the morning turned into afternoon rain. A persistent heavy downpour that worked its way through the old window frames of the computer science department. The window near Kwok-wah's desk was particularly leaky. The first time it had rained he'd finally worked out why the post-doc had been so willing to let him have the spot with the view. Kwok-wah had taken to keeping an old towel nearby so that he could dry the window sill when the water started to come through.

He was stuck in a dilemma. The research paper he was reading didn't make any sense to him. He had found what seemed to be a glaring inconsistency, which as far as he could tell undermined the whole argument. Kwok-wah had decided that either the authors were just plain wrong or he didn't understand the topic as well as he thought he did. Logically he knew it was far more likely the problem was his, the paper came from a good university in the States and the researchers were well known in the field, but he had enough confidence in his own abilities to consider that perhaps he was right and they were wrong. He looked at his watch: ten past three. Professor Ye should be in his office. Perhaps he might have time to help resolve the question.

Kwok-wah sighed inwardly when he saw that the professor's door was closed. When he was available, the door was normally slightly open; a closed door usually meant either he was not there or he didn't want to be disturbed. Kwok-wah took a chance and knocked anyway but there was no answer. The departmental secretary wasn't around either so there was nobody to ask where the professor was or whether he might be back any time soon. Frustrated as usual Kwok-wah turned to head back to his desk when he was stopped by a voice behind him.

'Oi! You there!' It was a rough Shanghainese dialect Kwok-wah had difficulty understanding at first.

Kwok-wah turned and saw a small delivery man carrying a large box. The man was wiry but struggling under the weight.

'Can I help?' asked Kwok-wah.

'Damn, this fucking thing is heavy.' The man just managed to put the box down on an empty desk before he dropped it. He shook his arms, which had been straining under the load. 'I'm looking for a Professor Ye Zhang. This is computer science, isn't it?'

'Yes, but he's not here at the moment.'

'This is for him. Is there anybody I can leave it with?'

'Well his secretary should be here but I don't know

where she is either. That's her desk behind you, perhaps you could just leave it there?'

'It needs signing for.'

'Oh.'

'You couldn't sign for it, could you, mate?'

'Well, I …'

'I've got five more fucking deliveries to make and I can't hang around here, and it's too bloody heavy to take back.'

'What is it?'

'How the fuck should I know? Come on, mate. It just needs a signature.'

Kwok-wah was reluctant to take responsibility but realised he didn't have a choice.

'Where do you want me to sign?'

'Just here.'

Kwok-wah signed the crumpled piece of paper the delivery man thrust into his hands.

'Can you just help me get it over there?' asked Kwok-wah, gesturing to the secretary's desk. When they moved the box, Kwok-wah discovered just how wet it was from the rain. The cardboard was sodden and before they could get the box down onto the desk the base tore under the weight of the contents, which came falling out, narrowly missing his feet. Books. Loads of them. No wonder the box was so heavy.

'Shit. Sorry about that.' The delivery man turned to leave. 'Still, they're only books. I'll leave you to sort them out.'

Cursing, Kwok-wah gathered the books from where

they had fallen. They hadn't suffered from being dropped, though some of them were a little wet. Curious, he looked at the titles as he arranged them on the desk. They were all in English, apparently from the United States and England: *Advanced Cryptography, New Techniques in Digital Cryptography, Mathematical Techniques and Prime Number Theory in Data Security, Applications and Techniques for Cybersecurity, Data Encryption Using Public and Private Keys.* Kwok-wah wondered how any of this related to Professor Ye's research.

**

The library was a new building four-storeys high and impressively stocked with journals and textbooks in both Chinese and English. Kwok-wah found it a congenial place to work. Quieter than the dorm, and warmer – and drier – than his desk in the department. He favoured an area on the second floor by a window that looked over a small ornamental lake, with the buildings of central Shanghai in the background. He had only been there for thirty minutes and was settling in to the textbook he was reading when Susan turned up unexpectedly.

'Thank God I've found you,' she said, in too loud a voice. A chorus hissed at her to be quiet. 'I was counting on you being here,' she continued in a whisper.

'What is it? What's wrong?' Susan sounded anxious and Kwok-wah wondered what on earth the problem was.

'It's my laptop.' She pulled out a black computer from the shoulder bag she was carrying. 'I don't know what's wrong with it.'

'Let me see,' said Kwok-wah, placing the IBM ThinkPad on the desk in front of him and powering it up. Susan pulled up a chair so she could sit close to him. In the confined space of the library desk, Kwok-wah felt her leg pressing against his. It was a good feeling. 'What does it run?' he asked.

'Windows 95. Nobody here knows anything about Windows.'

'It's a nice machine,' said Kwok-wah admiringly.

'It was a gift from Daddy when I got the place here. It's been great up to now, but all of a sudden it's like so slow and freezes all the time.'

'So I see.' The computer was taking its time to boot up and the hard drive was making an unhealthy amount of noise. 'Do you use it for your work?'

'Sometimes. It's got an unfinished project on it at the moment. That's why I'm panicking.'

'How do you print from it?' The machine had finished booting up and Kwok-wah started to explore the operating system. 'Do you mind if I look around?' he asked.

'No, not at all. I save my work on a floppy disc and there's a little shop I know that must have some form of bootleg Windows because they are able to print for me.'

'If you ever need help I should be able to print from it in the department for you … Ah … I think …' Kwok-wah had found what he was looking for.

'What is it?' Susan asked, trying to keep her voice down. 'Can it be fixed?'

'When did you last run a defrag of the hard drive?'

'A what? Kwok-wah, I've no idea of what you're talking about.' She punched him gently on the arm.

'Your hard drive just needs cleaning up. Do you want me to do that for you?'

'Can you? Please just do what you have to.'

'It's straightforward.' Kwok-wah set the computer running a defragmentation routine. 'It might take a while though.' Kwok-wah was finding their hushed voices gave an unsettling sense of intimacy to what was otherwise a routine conversation. 'Shall we go get some coffee?'

'You're a hero. I'm paying.'

CHAPTER 7

GOING BY THE NOISE IT might have been a flock of starlings. In reality it was a myriad simultaneous conversations echoing in the open space beneath the Hong Kong and Shanghai Bank building. Sunday morning and the sharp suits and briefcases of the week had gone, replaced by thousands of Filipina maids as Central became Little Manila. For the women who worked to make the lives of Hong Kong professionals more comfortable – women who brought up other people's children while being apart from their own – Sunday was a day of release after a week of hard labour. The sound of laughter and friendship was everywhere, every space a picnic spot with flattened cardboard boxes in place of blankets, and tastes of home passed between friends while they watched impromptu dance troupes practising routines to boom boxes. In one corner a game of cards, in another young women waited their turn while a hairstylist recreated the latest fashions at a bargain price.

Sam headed for the MTR station, picking his way through the mass of people. The movie on Friday had been a success, he thought, or at least it hadn't gone as badly as their first date. Afterwards they'd gone for a drink in a bar where middle-aged Western men danced to Abba covers with young Asian women. Sam had wanted to ask what had happened with that taxi business, why Emma had acted so strangely, but he thought it better to let sleeping dogs lie and all that, and instead they'd discussed what Sam had mistakenly hoped would be the safer topic of their first experiences in Hong Kong.

'So you were met at the airport by a driver and then put up in a serviced apartment?' Emma had said, in mock horror, when Sam told her how he'd arrived in Hong Kong that first day.

'You do realise what a cushy start you got? I took the bus from Kai Tak, stayed in a youth hostel for the first three weeks, crashed on sofas when I started to make friends, and then moved up the ladder to renting a spare room. It was six months before I had the money together to get my own place.'

'I suppose that's true – I did have it pretty good.'

'Sorry, I didn't mean to come over all self-righteous. I didn't mean it like that. It's not like it was your fault or anything – why shouldn't you take those things if they're offered? I would. It's just that sometimes the expat world seems to be a bit of a bubble. A very comfortable bubble with housing allowances, maids … everything on a plate, but still a bubble oblivious to the world outside.'

'I don't have a maid,' said Sam in his defence.

'That's very commendable of you. God, what must I sound like? Getting on my soap box. Sorry.'

'No offence taken.'

'So, you were in a serviced apartment for a while?'

'In Wan Chai. Then I shared a flat in Mid-Levels for a time but in the end I wanted my own place. I also wanted to get out of Mid-Levels, move to somewhere quieter, so now I'm in Pokfulam. What about you?'

'Western. A small flat on Des Voeux Road but it suits me.'

'Isn't it a bit noisy?'

'I guess so, but with my hearing it doesn't bother me. If anything it's a plus because the traffic masks my tinnitus when it's bad. The worst thing is that there's a McDonalds on the ground floor. Sometimes the smell of cooking fat can be a bit much. That's probably why it's so cheap.'

At the end of the evening they'd walked the streets for a while. Even at the late hour many of the shops were still open. The crowds weren't quite as busy as earlier in the evening, but even so it was urban Hong Kong at its most frenetic, glamorous and exhilarating; the light from the advertising signs and the shop windows illuminating the streets as if it were daylight.

'Do you ever go hiking?' Emma had asked out of the blue. 'I was thinking of doing the Pat Sin Leng trail on Sunday. Why don't you join me?'

The night before, as he rummaged in a cupboard for his hiking boots and rucksack, he'd wondered what he was doing. What he had failed to mention was just how infrequent his forays into the hills actually were. It had been at least a year since he'd last been hiking in the New Territories, but when Emma had suggested it he hadn't wanted to say no and didn't hesitate. Nor had Sam wanted to admit that he wasn't exactly sure where Pat Sin Leng was. When he'd looked on the map he discovered that it was a ridge of high hills to the north of the Tolo Harbour – quite deep into the New Territories, close to the Chinese border. He had also noted, with some alarm, that judging by the closely packed contour lines they were obviously quite steep.

Emma was waiting for him at the entrance to the subway station. He was embarrassed by the contrast between her smart running shorts and singlet with his own rather more aged kit, but there wasn't much he could do about it now. Two trains and a taxi later they arrived at the village that Emma had identified as a good starting point.

'Is this the right place?' asked Sam.

'I think so,' said Emma, slightly doubtfully. 'It looks familiar anyway.'

Sam's reservations were understandable. The handful of houses arranged around a small square looked an unlikely starting point and scarcely justified the status of a village. In the middle of the square stood a banyan tree with roots that wrapped themselves around the trunk like a predatory snake, while a straggly beard of aerial vines hung from the lower branches. None of the houses were in good condition and no more than a handful of them showed signs of being lived in; it seemed only the elderly remained in the village now, the young having long ago moved to the city – or to Toronto or Sydney. The distinctive click-clack of mahjong tiles sounded from one of the houses and a radio somewhere was playing Cantonese opera, but other than a pair of village dogs no one paid any attention to Sam and Emma.

The walk began with an easy concrete path leading through bamboo groves on the edge of the village. Emma led the way – occasionally checking her map – and when the path became too narrow for them to walk side-by-side Sam would drop behind. He tried to concentrate on the walk and not be too distracted by Emma's legs. A dragonfly flew into his face and he brushed it away, putting aside the thought that they often seemed to foreshadow a storm. The trail was simple to follow, which allowed them to talk as they went along, Emma turning to face Sam from time to time to better catch what he said.

'So you enjoyed the movie the other night?' Emma asked.

'I did, yes.' Sam had surprised himself with how much he had liked the bittersweet love story. 'Promise you won't tell anyone?'

'I promise. I wasn't sure because you seemed a bit tense that day. I hope it wasn't me.'

'No certainly not, not you at all. The day was a bit mixed if I'm honest and didn't end that well.'

'In what way?'

Sam gave Emma the same summary he'd given Kate of his dressing down from Paul Ridgeway.

'I see,' Emma continued. 'Good, well, not good perhaps, but you seemed nervous. I thought perhaps I was making you anxious. You're a little shy, I think. Not like the average Hong Kong alpha-male expat.'

'I think I'm getting a compliment ... At least I think it's a compliment?' said Sam. It was true that Emma did make him anxious; nervous, wanting to say the right things, not wanting to look like an idiot.

'It's certainly not a criticism that's for sure. Too many men in Hong Kong are so full of themselves. I don't get the impression that you'd walk over somebody to get what you wanted the way so many guys here do. Kind, I think.'

Sam flinched when he remembered those months in London before he came to Hong Kong; there were plenty of people there who might take issue with Emma's assessment of him. He was glad that they weren't around to say anything.

'I didn't ask you what brought you to Hong Kong in the first place,' said Emma. 'Did you always want to come here?'

'Not especially. I was recently qualified and happy enough in London, but I knew that I would have to move to get on ... Also, I suppose I was a bit restless anyway.' Sam comforted himself with the thought that none of that was exactly a lie even if it only skirted along the fringes of truth. 'Then I saw an ad for a job in Hong Kong. I'd done a bit of travelling and been to Hong Kong before and the idea of coming back appealed to me. To be honest, had the ad appeared three months earlier or three months later I probably wouldn't have noticed it, but the time seemed right and I thought *"Why not?"*

'I guess there was no girlfriend in London then?'

'Not really.' Sam didn't want to tell Emma that his girlfriend of three years dumped him when he was sacked. He had hoped that a new start in a new place would be a chance to reinvent himself where nobody knew him; he thought he would be able to become someone else, but of course that hadn't worked and he was just the same person with the same emotional baggage and hang-ups he'd been in London.

The path continued to snake its way through what might once have been a wetland before starting to slowly climb into the hills and the easy level walk that Sam had been enjoying came to an end. They passed through a grove of acacia trees and then the path opened out into a rough track that rose steeply past ancestral graves dug into the hillside. The remains of incense sticks and offerings of fruit lay scattered in front of each grave.

'This is the worst bit,' said Emma as they took a rest and a drink of water. 'Once we get to the top the path follows the ridge, and apart from one or two ups and downs it's quite easy.'

'One or two ups and downs?'

'Come on, we can stop for lunch when we get to the top.'

Sam would have preferred a longer rest but male pride wasn't going to let him say so. Conversation dwindled as they climbed. It wasn't long before it became clear that Sam was holding Emma back.

'You go on,' he said, 'just wait for me at the top.'

Sam continued to struggle up the hill while Emma went on ahead. He kept stopping to catch his breath and those rests became more frequent as the climb went on and on. Trapped beneath his rucksack, his shirt stuck to his back with perspiration and he wished he was wearing lighter clothes. When he finally reached the summit, Sam found Emma sitting on a rock. She was staring northwards, looking over the border at Shenzhen, the new city that had grown in under two decades from almost nothing to being larger than Hong Kong. From their hilltop vantage point it looked like an army of tower blocks had been marching towards Hong Kong until they'd suddenly come to a halt at the border, as if there was an invisible barrier that they couldn't pass. Perhaps they were waiting for permission to continue their journey south. Sam took a drink from his water bottle and tried to get his breath back while Emma continued to gaze at the view.

'It's quite a sight,' said Sam, when he had finally recovered.

'A friend of mine was telling me the other day that there are tens of thousands of illegal migrants living in Shenzhen,' said Emma. 'Most of them from remote parts of China. All of them looking for a job, all of them willing to work long hours for a pittance and with no rights at all. Those without the right papers are arrested, beaten up and returned to their home towns. They may be the lucky ones. Have you been there?'

'A couple of times on business.' Sam had taken a client to Shenzhen the month before. They stayed in a smart five-star hotel where they had a fine dinner. Afterwards their Chinese business partners bought them drinks in a bar where they were served by young women in cheongsams. It was made pretty clear to Sam that the women would offer more than drinks if he was interested, but Sam had played dumb and pretended not to pick up on the hints. Sam thought that it was probably better not to mention this to Emma. 'It's an interesting place, that's for sure,' he said, settling for something neutral.

'In what way?'

'Well, for a start, simply the way it has grown so fast, and like you say it's full of people from all over China – whether legally or not – which gives it a very different feel from Hong Kong. For one thing you don't hear much Cantonese and people have quite a different look about them. Different facial features compared to Hong Kong. It's a sort of microcosm of the mainland in one place – for better or worse. You can't help but admire the progress, but it's also a bit Wild West, as if anything goes. Every time I've been there I've always been very relieved to get back to Hong Kong. I've heard about people who get into trouble, get beaten up or something, stabbed in some cases even, who insist on getting back to Hong Kong before going to hospital.'

Sam and Emma ate the lunch they had brought with them while they admired the view. A charcoal grey hillside was clearly visible where earlier in the year five people had died in a hill-fire. A group of hikers – the first people they had seen since setting off – arrived at the summit by the same route, and after saying hello the group continued along the ridge. Sam and Emma let them get ahead before continuing in the same direction.

'Did you know that Pat Sin Leng means the "Ridge of the Eight Immortals"?' asked Emma. 'I've been out here a few times. It's one of the advantages of not having a proper job.'

Sam was relieved to find that Emma had been right and the going was much easier now that they were following the contour of the ridge. To the south the sun still glistened off Tolo Harbour where a flotilla of sailing boats spread over the water, but dark clouds were starting to build to the north.

'We'd better press on,' said Emma, looking at the approaching weather. She picked up her pace and after a while Sam again started to struggle to keep up and found himself falling behind. Compounding his general unfitness he had a nagging pain in his left knee that was starting to bother him on the downhill sections, and his left heel hurt with each step. Reaching another summit, Sam found Emma waiting for him.

'You okay?' she asked.

'Just a twinge.'

The temperature was starting to drop as the pressure fell and a wind began to pick up. Looking north, lightning could be seen in the distance and Sam ignored the pains in his knee and heel knowing that an exposed high ridge was not the best place to be in a thunderstorm. It wasn't long before the rain started, a few drops at first but soon getting heavier. They could both see and hear that the storm was getting closer and they hurried to get to the final summit and then start the descent into the village of Tai Mei Tuk. By the time they made it down from the hills they had long given up worrying pointlessly about the rain; a restaurant with a large open area where they could sit outside, but still be under cover, gave them the chance to start to dry off. They ordered a little food and some beer and Sam noticed a small puddle developing under his chair as the water dripped off his clothes. Soon they were both laughing at how ludicrously wet they were.

'Sorry,' said Emma, 'you must be wishing you hadn't come.'

'It's okay,' Sam lied. 'I'm sure I'll dry off soon enough.'

The thunder and lightning had stopped but the rain had settled into a groove so they ordered another beer.

'How do you know so much about Shenzhen?' asked Sam.

'Sorry?'

'That business you were telling me about illegal migrants.'

'Oh, that came from a friend of mine. She's quite involved with that sort of thing. She's a member of a small human rights group that she's been trying to get me involved with. In fact that's where I was that Friday when you invited me for work drinks. I just missed you and Kate, I was coming from one of their meetings.'

'You're a member too?' Sam had never imagined that Emma might be involved in politics.

'Not really, Alice – my friend – had been nagging me to go along and I sort of gave in to stop her going on about it. But it was quite interesting so I'll probably give it another go. With the handover and everything, it makes you think, even if as expats we're not that affected.'

They were interrupted briefly by a man from another table who asked Sam to take a photograph of a large family gathering.

'To be honest you don't look like a human rights activist.' Sam realised as soon as the words had left his mouth how stupid they must have sounded.

'What should I look like then?'

'I don't know but probably not soaking wet in running kit.'

'Actually it's not so bad now; my clothes are more or less dry. But my hair …' Emma ran her hands through her hair, pushing it back as she did so, revealing a small scar on her forehead just below the hairline that Sam hadn't noticed before. He wondered how that had happened. Emma caught his eye and he looked away embarrassed and felt himself blush. 'Anyway,' continued Emma, 'you're probably right. Certainly my parents would be surprised.'

'Where do they live?'

'Hampshire, near Winchester.'

'Any brothers or sisters?'

This time it was Emma's turn to look away briefly. 'No, just me.'

'And what are your plans next year, after the handover?'

'Nothing at the moment. Part of me would like to go on to Australia, but then I get a lot of pressure from my parents to go back to the UK.'

'Would you stay here?'

'Perhaps. If I could, anyway. It may all depend on what the visa situation is going to be. Who knows whether I'll be able to stay even if I want to?'

By the time they had finished their second beer the heavy rain had become a slight drizzle and they decided to make a move when they had the chance. An hour later they were back in Central. The maids had mostly left, leaving behind the evidence of a day well-spent.

'We're going the same way, aren't we?' said Sam. 'We might as well share a cab.'

They sat in silence in the back of the taxi. Sam knew that he only had until they reached Emma's apartment to pluck up the courage to say something, but before he knew it they were on Des Voeux Road and pulling over to let Emma out.

'Sorry about the rain,' she said. 'I hope today wasn't too awful for you.'

'Of course not, I enjoyed it. Perhaps ...' Sam hesitated momentarily as Emma started to climb out. They'd had drinks once, been to a movie and now gone hiking, but he was still unsure of himself with Emma. Were they dating? Only one way to find out. 'Would you like to have dinner or something … sometime?' Sam knew how corny that sounded and was relieved that Emma smiled.

'I thought you weren't going to ask. I've got your number,' she said. 'I'll call you.'

Sam watched Emma cross the road before the taxi pulled away. His knee was still hurting, his legs ached and he suspected that he had a cold coming on from the rain, but he thought that it was worth it.

CHAPTER 8

LUNAR NEW YEAR – THE Year of the Ox – and everywhere was dead. The university had closed down and even the city itself, sprawling megapolis that it was, appeared as if asleep. A slumbering giant. There was little traffic on the roads and for once all work had stopped on the countless building sites. Cranes were stationary, pile drivers silenced. The background sounds of the city, which the rest of the time Kwok-wah hardly noticed, were now conspicuous by their absence. At the university only a handful of a people were still around; Kwok-wah and Granny Sun the only ones in his building. He was glad he had Susan for company, and she seemed to appreciate having him around as well.

'Like you I'm the only one there at the moment,' she had said. 'Everyone else has disappeared to all four corners of China. It must be a nightmare though. I mean, did you see the TV news the other night? It was completely crazy. The queues outside the main railway stations were just horrific.'

His room-mates had left over the previous couple of days to catch overcrowded trains to all parts of the country. It was the largest peacetime movement of people in the world, and the numbers increased every year.

On the first day of the holiday Kwok-wah saw that Granny Sun was in her room.

'Gong Xi Fa Cai!' he said brightly.

Granny Sun muttered something in reply that Kwok-wah didn't quite catch, but he got the sense she was not completely enamoured of the holidays.

'Don't you have family to visit? Or will they come to you?' he asked.

'No, not me, Xiaoyang.' Kwok-wah was the only student in the dorm to be honoured by Granny Sun with an affectionate pet name. He received this singular distinction after fixing her rice cooker. 'It's just me these days. Come, sit with me for a while and have some tea.'

Kwok-wah was coming back after a morning run. He wanted to get on with some work, the quiet of the campus gave him a perfect opportunity, but he didn't really have an excuse for not taking some time out, and anyway, he liked Granny Sun. He also had enough sensitivity to realise that his question had touched a nerve and perhaps she would like some company. Granny Sun had only a small single room. In one corner was a two-ring hob; the repaired rice cooker was next to it on an old card table. The only decoration was last year's calendar, which still hung from a nail on a wall, along with faded photographs of two men, one older than the other. A camp bed occupied another corner, while a single chair and a small table made up the remaining furniture. A door leading to a small bathroom was the only concession to the fact that this spartan room was in fact a home.

'Come, Xiaoyang, sit down.' Granny Sun gestured to Kwok-wah to take the chair while she filled a kettle and put it on one of the rings to boil. Kwok-wah quickly discovered that the chair was perfectly placed to watch the entrance to the building.

'Are they family?' asked Kwok-wah. 'The pictures on the wall?'

'My husband and son.'

Kwok-wah wondered what had become of them but didn't know whether he should ask. She would tell him if she wanted to.

'I expect you're wondering what became of them.' Kwok-wah tried not to look embarrassed. 'The one on the left is my husband, Honggui, the other one is my son, Shu-ming. Such a lovely boy.'

Granny Sun took a small metal caddy down from a shelf and spooned tea into an old silver-plated teapot. 'We were farmers. Our parents were farmers and their parents before them. Back in Liaoning province. We were never rich – just peasant farmers – but as the saying goes there was always food in our stomachs and clothes to wear.'

Kwok-wah turned his chair so that he could face her. He made a mental note to himself to put the chair back in its original orientation before he left.

'You've heard of the Great Famine?' she asked.

'A little. Well, not much to be honest.'

'That's still probably more than most of your room-mates have. They're not interested in hearing about the past. All they care about is making money, getting a girl and a good job. You try and tell them about the hard times and you can see they don't care. Their eyes glaze over and all they want to do is get away from you as quickly as possible. Sometimes they yawn right in front of me. I think they do it deliberately to make fun of me.'

Granny Sun took the kettle off the heat and left it for a moment before filling the teapot and pouring two cups. She passed one to Kwok-wah and then sat on the edge of the bed with the other.

'What happened to your family?' Kwok-wah didn't tell Granny Sun that her assumptions about his fellow students were spot on.

'First they took our land off us. Not that we had much – just enough to grow some vegetables and keep a few chickens. We could feed ourselves with a little left over to sell. But apparently that was bourgeois. Whatever that meant, to be honest I never really understood. All the land in the village was seized and we had to send most of what we grew to a nearby town. We were happy to do that. It wasn't a large amount we had to give and we were told it was for the good of the country. It was for the people, they said, and we still had enough to eat. But then they started reducing the amount we could keep for ourselves. Bit by bit.

We used to have rice and vegetables every day, then the vegetables were only every other day. Then it was down to once a week. I used to take Shu-ming and go searching in the hills for edible flowers. Honggui set traps for animals but all he caught were rats. We ate those sometimes. If you cook them for long enough and use enough chillies you can't taste what you're eating.'

Granny Sun paused and took a sip from her tea. Kwok-wah wondered how hungry he would have to be before he could contemplate eating a rat.

'Didn't anybody say anything?' he asked. 'What about the village authorities?'

'Pah!' Granny Sun almost choked on her tea. 'Don't talk to me about those scumbags. They always seemed to have plenty to eat. Bunch of thieves, they were. No, things just got worse ... Do you know some people were reduced to boiling leather belts to eat? Hours they had to be boiled for and they were still inedible and as tough as ... well, as tough as old leather.' Granny Sun chuckled at her joke and then was silent for a minute. Kwok-wah was beginning to change his image of Granny Sun. He'd thought she was just a harmless little old woman who stopped the students from doing whatever they wanted. Clearly she was more than that.

'If it had just been Honggui and me I think we'd have been alright. We could have managed.' Granny Sun appeared thoughtful, looking into the distance, almost as if she had forgotten Kwok-wah was there; as if she was looking into the past and in her mind's eye

Honggui and Shu-ming were there in front of her. 'But we had Shu-ming to think of. He was only five at the time. He used to cry all night. He was always hungry and his skin was covered in sores. Honggui couldn't bear it so he started to give some of his own food to Shu-ming. I should have done the same ... even today I feel bad about that but I was just too hungry.'

'What happened to your husband?' asked Kwok-wah, even though he could guess.

'He started to get thin. Well, thinner, I should say. Also, he lost his hair. That was strange because before he had such a full head of hair. But even worse was the way the spirit seemed to go out of him. It was as if he'd just given up, and one day he did just that. Gave up. He lay down on the bed, closed his eyes and that was it. He was gone.'

'I'm sorry.'

'He gave his life for Shu-ming. I think he knew what he was doing.'

Kwok-wah had no idea of what to say, or indeed whether he should say anything at all. He thought about his own grandparents who had escaped from China after the war. What would have happened if they hadn't? Should he ask what happened to Shu-ming? Granny Sun raised herself from the bed and refilled his tea. She opened a tin and offered Kwok-wah an almond biscuit.

'Shu-ming was such a lovely boy. He was really bright, good at school, we had such hopes for him. We thought he would go far, make something of himself.'

Kwok-wah wiped biscuit crumbs from his mouth and plucked up the courage to ask the difficult question.

'Did he die in the famine as well?'

Granny Sun paused for a moment and Kwok-wah wondered if he had gone too far.

'Not in the famine, no. But I don't know if he's alive or dead.' This was not the answer Kwok-wah expected. Granny Sun was silent again before she was ready to go on. 'You see it was so hard after Honggui died, so hard to keep going. I couldn't feed Shu-ming, I barely had anything at all, so there really wasn't anything else I could do. But I think if he was still alive he would have tried to find me, but then again he may not know where I am. Or perhaps he has simply never forgiven me.'

Kwok-wah was confused, uncertain what had happened to Shu-ming.

'So, what did happen?'

'I sold him. I sold my only son to a family from the city. They were childless and I thought he would have a better chance with them than me, and the money saw me through the winter. But there hasn't been a single day since then that I haven't thought of him, wondered if I did the right thing, what became of him. So much has happened in China since then that I don't even know if he's still alive. Later I had to come to Shanghai to try and find some work. I left details of where I was going with my neighbours in case Shu-ming ever went back to the village, but I've moved so often since then I shouldn't think anybody knows where I am now. I don't suppose they even remember me at all. It's been thirty-five years since I left.'

'Have you ever returned to the village since?'

'No, it has too many bad memories. Anyway, you'll forgive me if I don't get carried away with the New Year hoopla. That's for people with something to live for. People like you, Xiaoyang, who should be at home with your family, not spending all day with your books.' Granny Sun wagged an aged wrinkled finger at him. 'They must be missing you.'

***

Kwok-wah could hear voices coming from his dorm before he had even started to climb the stairs. Three days later and his room-mates were obviously back from the New Year holidays. There was no mistaking Zhanyuan's voice:

'Yeah the whole family was there including my cousin. Damn, she's hot. She wears these tight sweaters that show off her breasts and I'd swear she wasn't wearing a bra. You could make out her tits. I think she was doing it just to tease me. Tell me, is it okay to want to fuck your cousin?'

'It depends. Is she in the Party as well?' asked Li Lao. 'I mean if she's just a commoner like the rest of us then I guess anything goes. But you Party members are supposed to have higher moral standards, aren't you? Setting an example for the rest of us?' Li Lao enjoyed winding up Zhanyuan about his family status.

'How many times do I have to tell you that I am

not a Party member?'

'Yeah, so you keep saying, but your father is and you will be soon enough. But if she's that good looking, why don't you invite her here so we can meet her? I'd be more than happy to give her a personal tour of Shanghai and a one-on-one tutorial ...'

'Shut your filthy mouth, smart-arse, that's my cousin you're talking about.'

'What are you complaining about? You started it. You're the one going on about how hot she is ... Well, look who we have here.'

Kwok-wah had come into the room.

'How's our very own capitalist running dog doing? How was it here – all on your own? Just you and Granny Sun.'

'Not bad. Got plenty of work done.'

For a moment he thought about telling them what Granny Sun had told him about her life, but he knew instinctively that she was right. They wouldn't be interested. In truth it was a disappointment to Kwok-wah that everybody was back. He had enjoyed the quiet of the campus and the chance to get on with things. He had also enjoyed the time he spent with Susan. They'd had dinner together and they met up to go see the New Year fireworks. Once he began to get over his initial nerves, he found her easy to talk to. She had a way of listening to him that put him at ease. She was attentive and never seemed bored even when he started going on about his research. It was a refreshing change to find someone who was so interested in what he was doing.

He found himself positively wanting to talk to her, to tell her about his family and his work. And then there was her Californian accent. Together with her looks, there was something almost Hollywood about Susan. He could imagine her in a movie or a TV show. He certainly felt he had more in common with Susan than with his basketball friends.

A small voice in his head told him not to mention her to them.

CHAPTER 9

'DID YOU SEE THAT CHAN Wah Man has been released early?'

Emma suddenly felt a chill at Yannie's words. Her hand stopped in the act of picking up a glass, before she gathered herself and took a sip of her wine. She glanced around, hoping nobody had noticed anything unusual. Liang-bao was pouring Alice a glass of sparkling water, Kelvin was taking an olive from a bowl, and Charles was trying to catch the attention of a waiter. They were in a bar one evening after a meeting, and with most of Hong Kong back from the New Year holidays the place was busy. A big screen was showing football and they had to compete with the noise.

'Who?' said Kelvin.

'You remember – he was jailed a few years ago for a hit-and-run,' said Yannie.

'Vaguely,' said Alice. 'What's the big deal?'

'There were rumours at the time that he wasn't the driver. That it was a cover-up.'

'It's coming back to me now, sort of anyway,' said Kelvin. 'Something to do with Xinhua, if I remember. But nothing was ever proven, was it?'

'No, and the driver confessed, but it just struck me as odd. He got ten years but is out after three on medical grounds?'

'Well, fair enough I suppose, if he's ill,' said Alice.

'When did all this happen?' asked Emma.

'Four, no, maybe five years ago. Four and a bit. In '92, I think,' said Alice.

'So what were the rumours?'

'Like Yannie said, there was some gossip he was just a fall-guy and that the driver was a mainland official who left Hong Kong in a hurry. But it was just talk and, anyway, why would anyone admit to something like that if they didn't do it?'

Charles had finally succeeded in getting the attention of a passing waiter and ordered more drinks. Alice was leaning into Liang-bao, her right hand resting on his left. Their relationship seemed to be more open now, at least within the group. Emma wondered if Alice's parents knew.

'You okay, Emma? You look a little off-colour.'

'Fine. Perhaps I shouldn't have another drink though. It's a bit loud in here for me; I think I might get going.'

Back home, Emma was restless. Briefly she thought about ringing her parents before remembering that they were away on holiday. She knew there was no point in trying to get to sleep. Eventually she gave in to the temptation she had been trying to resist since getting back from the meeting and took a small photograph album down from a shelf. Making herself comfortable, she started to look through pages of memories: family holidays in Wales and Cornwall; visits to relatives in the Netherlands; children playing in the garden. She knew what she had to do in the morning.

***

Emma was already awake before the sound of the first tram made its way along the street; the ringing bell, the metal wheels grinding against the track. Slightly to her surprise there hadn't been a dream to disturb her that night, but even so she hadn't slept well. But at least she now had a plan and a sense of purpose, even if she had no great expectations of any results. She was glad she wasn't working today, that nothing would get in the way of what she wanted to do, and after breakfast she headed to the Central Library, an uninspiring 1960s concrete edifice near the Star Ferry.

Emma approached the information desk. 'Excuse me, I'm looking for back issues of newspapers. Where do I go?'

She was directed to a department on the floor above, where she found another desk.

'I'm looking for back editions of the *South China Morning Post* – can you help me?'

A young woman looked up from the filing cards she was organising.

'What years you want?'

'1992 and '93. Perhaps 1994 as well.'

'Up to 1992 we have microfiche, from 1993 onwards we have CD-ROMs. I show you.'

The assistant took Emma to a desk with a microfiche reader.

'These drawers have films for 1987 to 1992.' Showing Emma another cabinet, she added: 'Here you'll find the discs for 1993 onwards. There are few PC station around you can use. Are you familiar with using CD-ROM?'

'Yes.'

'Then I leave you. Come find me if need anything.'

Emma sat down at the microfiche reader and started to realise the enormity of her task. She didn't even know exactly what she expected to find, only that she hoped she might learn something. She was at least doing something productive, and on the plus side she knew where to start. It didn't take her long to find the *South China Morning Post* for 17 September 1992 and she soon came across the item she was looking for.

TOURIST KILLED IN HIT-AND-RUN

A tourist was killed last night in a hit-and-run accident in Wan Chai. According to the police, the victim, who has not been named, was killed by a car at the junction of Lockhart Road and Luard Road. Witnesses say that the man was hit by a silver Mercedes that stopped briefly and then drove off.

Emma had only read the reports in the British press

before, but this short paragraph didn't tell her anything new. She looked through the next few editions in case there was any further mention, but there was nothing until another brief item three days later:

VICTIM OF HIT-AND-RUN NAMED
Police have identified the victim of the hit-and-run incident on Wednesday night as British citizen Peter Janssen, 28. Mr Janssen was on holiday in Hong Kong at the time of his death. Police are still looking for information as to the driver of the car.

Emma continued to trawl through the microfiche slides looking for any follow-up article or anything she didn't already know, but there was nothing of interest until the next article, which came from 27 September 1992:

ARREST IN HIT-AND-RUN CASE
A man has been arrested in connection with the death of a tourist in a hit-and-run accident in Wan Chai on September 16th. Peter Janssen, 28, visiting Hong Kong from the United Kingdom, was killed when he was struck by a car at the junction of Lockhart Road and Luard Road. Chan Wah Man, aged 34, has been charged with death by dangerous driving and failing to report an accident. Chan Wah Man is believed to be employed by Xinhua News Agency as a driver. It

*is understood that nobody else was in the car at
the time of the accident.*

Emma hadn't known before that Chan Wah Man
was employed by Xinhua; that was news to her. She
remembered that Kelvin had said something about
Xinhua in the bar. Emma went through all the remaining editions for 1992 but there was nothing
else, so she replaced the microfiche slides in the
cabinet and switched to the CD-ROMs. Taking the
disc for 1993, she found a vacant PC and placed
the CD-ROM in the drive. A basic search function
installed on the disc allowed Emma to find what she
wanted quite quickly:

GUILTY PLEA IN HIT-AND-RUN TRIAL
 *Chan Wah Man, 34, has pleaded guilty to
causing death by dangerous driving and failing
to report an accident. Chan Wah Man admitted
causing the death of Peter Janssen, 28, a British
tourist, in September last year in a hit-and-run
incident in Wan Chai. Speaking in mitigation,
Gao Zhihua, a senior official at Xinhua News
Agency, said that Chan Wah Man was his regular
driver and was a conscientious and careful driver
and that the accident was out of character. Chan
Wah Man was remanded into custody and will
be sentenced at a later date.*

There were no other references to the story and

Emma didn't need to go any further, she knew the rest. Chan Wah Man was sentenced to ten years but now it seemed he had been released after only three. There was nothing in those brief reports to suggest the cover-up Yannie had suggested. Perhaps that might have been in the more scandal-filled Chinese press rather than the sober *SCMP*, but if so that wouldn't help her as she couldn't read Chinese and wouldn't know where to start looking. But if Yannie was right then what about Gao Zhihua? There was something vaguely familiar in the name. Had she heard it somewhere? Emma hadn't come to Hong Kong for the trial, but her parents had. Emma didn't recall them saying anything about a Gao Zhihua when they returned, but they had been so upset she hadn't asked them too much about what had happened. She puzzled over why the name rang a bell.

Emma realised that she had been in the library for longer than intended. There was little more she could do so she removed the disc from the computer and returned it to its place.

***

Emma flung her jacket on the bed and lay down wearily. She had agreed to meet Sam for a drink after work but wasn't in the mood. Getting up again before she got too comfortable, she picked up the telephone and called him. Her tinnitus was sometimes a useful excuse for getting out of things when she wasn't in the mood, and although she could hear the disappointment in Sam's voice there wasn't a problem and they agreed to rearrange sometime soon. She went to lie down again, but then stopped and picked up the phone once more. She called the number she used to get Alice at work, which took her through to the main reception. A voice answered saying something in Cantonese that Emma just ignored.

'Hello. I'd like to speak to Yannie Chan please.'

'Who?'

'Yannie Chan.'

'One moment. You hold on.'

There was a pause with the silence broken only by static on the line and the click of the call being put through. Finally a woman's voice answered in Cantonese and again Emma simply spoke in English.

'Is that Yannie? This is Emma, Alice's friend from the group.'

'Oh, hi Emma. Did you want Alice? She's around somewhere I think.'

'No, actually it was you I wanted to speak to. Do you have a minute?'

'Sure.'

'I was wondering if we could get together sometime. There's something I'd like to ask you about.'

'Of course. We can talk at the next meeting if you want.'

'No, I was thinking of just you and me, it's something private.' Emma didn't exactly know why she didn't want the rest of the group to know her problems, but she rarely told other people about Peter. Sometimes it was easier with strangers, but with friends and colleagues she was wary.

'You're sounding very mysterious, Emma, but okay, no problem. I can't do tonight but how about after work tomorrow?'

'That's good for me. When and where?'

'I finish about six, meet me in our reception and we'll go find somewhere.'

'Thanks. Oh, just one thing – please don't mention this to Alice.'

'Okay – I think she's in the Kowloon office tomorrow anyway.'

'Thanks again. See you tomorrow.'

'And you're not going to give me a clue what it's about?'

'Tomorrow, I promise.'

This time Emma allowed herself to lie down on the bed and although it was early she fell asleep still dressed.

***

Emma arrived at Yannie's office in Causeway Bay in good time and took a seat in reception. She didn't have to wait long before a lift door opened and Yannie walked over.

'Have you been waiting long?' Yannie asked.

'Just a few minutes, I didn't want to be late.'

'There's a new bubble tea place around the corner I've been wanting to try. Shall we give it a go?'

'Sure. Anywhere you like.'

The bubble tea shop was already busy with young Hongkongers. Emma suddenly felt very old; many of the customers barely looked out of their teens.

'What would you like?' asked Yannie.

'I've no idea.' Emma was bemused by the drinks list, which was only in Chinese, and the accompanying pictures of various multicoloured concoctions didn't help much. 'This is all new to me.'

'It's a Taiwanese thing. The tea is mixed with tapioca, milk and various fruit juices. Green tea with milk is my favourite.'

'Then I'll try that as well.'

Emma grabbed an empty Formica table while Yannie ordered at the counter. Shortly, Yannie returned with two alarmingly fluorescent green drinks. Emma sipped hers cautiously through the straw.

'What do you think?' asked Yannie.

'Not sure, if I'm honest. The tea itself is okay but the tapioca reminds me of school dinners.'

'Perhaps it's not for foreigners. What was it you wanted to talk about?'

Yannie played with her straw, stirring the tapioca so that it mixed with the tea. Emma put her drink down and took a deep breath.

'The other night in the bar you were talking about that guy being released from prison.'

'I remember.'

'You said something about rumours of a cover-up. That he hadn't been driving that night?'

'That's right.'

'Can you remember what the rumours were?' asked Emma.

'It's a while ago now, but I remember he was the driver for a mainland official and there was gossip that it was the bigwig himself who had been driving.'

'Do you remember a name? For the official?'

'No, I don't remember that, sorry.'

'Could it have been Gao Zhihua?'

'Possibly. I couldn't be sure though. Why are you asking this, Emma? You're acting like a police detective.'

'Okay, you deserve an answer.' Emma leaned across the table closer to Yannie and lowered her voice a little. 'It was my brother who was killed that night.'

'No!' exclaimed Yannie, before dropping her voice. 'In the hit-and-run? Oh God Emma, I'm sorry.'

'It's okay, it's been a few years now, but you can see why I needed to ask you about it.'

'Of course. I didn't know you had a brother. Where did you get that name from? Gao Zhihua?'

'I've been reading the press reports from the time. He was named as the driver's boss and gave a statement in mitigation. So I just wondered …' Emma's attempt at keeping her composure faltered. Yannie put a hand on her arm.

'Emma, it's alright. Here, take this …' Yannie fished out a clean tissue from her bag and passed it over. 'He was an older brother, I guess? What was his name?'

'Peter. He was three years older than me. I always looked up to him when we were young and he always looked after me. He was an English teacher. The newspapers said he was here on holiday, which is sort of true, but he was looking to move here. He loved Hong Kong.'

'And I've brought it all back with my big mouth,' said Yannie.

'You weren't to know, but I need to try and find out more. Can you remember anything else?'

'A lot of the gossip came from reporters in the newsroom at Eric's paper – Eric's my husband. If you like I can ask him if he remembers anything?'

'Would you? But please can you keep this between us? Don't tell the others.'

'Of course.'

'It's not that it's a secret, after all, if anybody goes back to the newspaper reports they'd spot the name, but I'd just like to keep it private if I can. For now, anyway.'

'No problem.'

Emma sniffled and blew her nose.

'Look at me,' she said, 'I'm supposed to be a grown woman.' She tried another taste of her bubble tea. 'Perhaps it's growing on me.'

'Don't feel you have to finish it. You've been through quite enough without being inflicted with strange Chinese drinks.'

'Would you like to have it?' Emma could see that Yannie had almost finished hers.

'Pass it over.' Yannie took the plastic cup and swapped Emma's straw for her own.

'What do you make of Alice's boyfriend?' asked Emma, looking to lighten the mood.

'I'm not sure. There's something odd about him. He's good looking though.'

'Has she told her parents yet?'

'Not as far as I know. I think she's scared. She was torn over the New Year. She wanted to spend time with him, but of course she had to do everything with her family.' Yannie looked at her watch. 'I'm sorry, Emma, I promised Eric I wouldn't be late home.'

They both stood up from the table and Yannie put her arms around Emma and held her for a moment.

'You take care, Emma. I'll be in touch.'

CHAPTER 10

THE TRAIN RATTLED THROUGH INTERMINABLE Shanghai suburbs until it reached the outskirts of Suzhou. There was a time when the sixty miles between the two cities was filled with villages and rice paddies, stereotypical images of rural China, but now a visitor would be hard-pressed to know where one city stopped and the other began. There was no longer any real country-side, only construction sites that had reached various stages of completion. Factories, apartment blocks, and indeterminate buildings that might become schools or hospitals; it was difficult to say which as most of them were being built in a standard vernacular that owed much to Lego. But the most obvious consequence of all this development, the most common sight from the train, was the enormous amount of litter and rubbish strewn along the side of the track. Canals and streams full of junk passed by with depressing frequency. Feral dogs hung around piles of waste, scrabbling for scraps of food. Was this the inevitable result of China's economic growth or just a disgrace? Kwok-wah wasn't exactly a card-carrying environmentalist but even for him it was a dismaying sight. It was hard to match the view from the train with the ever-present propaganda images of the bright new China.

It had been Susan's idea to visit Suzhou for the day. One of the oldest cities in the neighbourhood of Shanghai, it was famed for its classical gardens, canals and temples. A popular daytrip for both locals and visitors.

'I'd like to go,' she said one day, 'but friends tell me that Western women – even if they are Chinese – can get hassled. Would you like to come with me?' Kwok-wah had been ambivalent – Suzhou of all places – but increasingly he found he couldn't say no to Susan. He worried about that.

The journey lasted barely an hour. While Kwok-wah watched the fruits of economic expansion from the train, Susan read her guidebook.

'You know that Suzhou is known as a city of classical gardens? *The Humble Administrator's Garden* – I just love the name. So cute. Can he really have been that humble if he had an entire garden named after him? We have to see that. And the *Yunyan Pagoda* – apparently it leans over like the Leaning Tower of Pisa.' Susan realised that Kwok-wah wasn't paying much attention. 'You okay?'

'Sorry – yes – fine. I was just thinking. Then there's the *Retreat and Reflection Garden*, the *Lingering Garden* … loads of them …'

Susan was surprised at Kwok-wah's knowledge of Suzhou.

'Have you been there before?' she asked.

'No, but sometimes I feel as though I have.'

'What's that supposed to mean? You okay? You seem in a strange mood. It's not like you to come over all New Age.' Susan turned in her seat towards Kwok-wah and hooked her arm around his. 'Tell me. What's wrong? We may not have known each other long but I can tell that something's up.'

'Nothing – honestly. I was just thinking. My grand-mother came from Suzhou. She always used to talk about the place. How beautiful it was.'

'I didn't know, you should have said … Sorry, per-haps I shouldn't have asked you to come? Does it seem strange coming here?'

'A bit, but it's okay, she only had good memories of Suzhou. She just wished she could have come back sometime.'

'Is she still alive?'

'No – she died a few years ago. I was just thinking about her. Wondering what she'd think of me studying in China and coming here. She met my grandfather in Shanghai and they escaped to Hong Kong just before the Communists took control of the city. That's why my parents were so unhappy about me coming here.'

They lapsed into silence for the rest of the journey while Kwok-wah recalled the painful family arguments after he had announced his plans to come to China. His mother had been so angry, she told him he was betraying everything the family stood for, and his father refused to speak to him. For a time Kwok-wah wondered if he was making a mistake, but he was stubborn and even if they weren't happy about it, eventually his parents let him have his way.

Susan and Kwok-wah did the sights. Walked by the canals (also strewn with litter, they noted); explored the gardens; admired the temples and pagodas until they were all duly seen and ticked off. Susan and Kwok-wah were both hungry. They surprised themselves by admitting that they were both sick of the noodles and meat of doubtful provenance that was the main offering of the University cafeteria, so they took the chance to gorge themselves on McDonald's. While they sat at a red and yellow plastic table under the watchful gaze of Chairman Ronald, Susan took the opportunity to ask Kwok-wah about Professor Ye.

'So does he mainly do research in the same area as you?'

'Mainly, yes – but I think he may be moving on to some new areas.' Kwok-wah took a sip from his Diet Coke.

'What makes you say that?'

'I signed for a delivery of books the other day and they were all about cryptography. Codes and so on. I didn't know that was his thing but I guess he must be branching out.'

'Is that close to what you are working on?'

'Not really.' Kwok-wah thought about it for a moment. 'But I suppose I can see where he might be going with it.'

'How's that?'

'Well, I guess once you start sending data by your cell phone some people might be worried about security. You might want to encrypt it to make it more secure.'

'I suppose the other thing is that if stuff is secure some people might still want to be able to read it. Y'know, police and so on?'

'I hadn't thought of that,' Kwok-wah acknowledged, 'but yes, that too. Interesting. It's not something I'd given much thought to but the more I think about it the more it makes sense.'

Suddenly Susan giggled.

'What's funny?' Kwok-wah asked.

'Don't look now but the man sitting at the table behind you is wearing women's shoes. I don't know why I'm whispering, I don't suppose he speaks English. Drop your napkin on the floor and have a look when you bend down to pick it up.'

Kwok-wah did as he was told and tried hard to suppress a laugh but with limited success. The man was dressed fairly normally but there was no doubt about the shoes.

'Do you think he knows they're for women?' asked Kwok-wah.

'Stop laughing! You'll set me off again.' Susan gathered herself and then changed the subject. 'It'd be cool to see where you work. Any chance?'

'The department? I don't see why not. There's not much to see though. Just loads of computers.'

'Still, I've got a picture of what it's like in my head, I'd just like to see if I'm right. And I'd like to see where you spend your time when you're not with me.' Susan reached out and touched Kwok-wah's hand.

**

According to the rules Susan wasn't allowed in the computer science building. It was off-limits to anybody who wasn't a member of the department. In practice as long as you were accompanied it wasn't a problem, and Kwok-wah gestured his thanks to the security guard as he opened the door and ushered Susan through.

'Like I said, there's not much to see really,' he told her.

'I don't mind.'

Kwok-wah showed Susan his desk. Late winter sunshine was flooding through the window. He had discovered that the wooden window frame had swollen in the rain during the winter and now couldn't be opened, meaning that for several hours a day his desk was now too hot. In the research labs, Kwok-wah spotted a fellow PhD student.

'This might interest you,' he said to Susan. He switched from English to Putonghua. 'Xiao-Fan, are you running your graphics program at the moment?' Xiao-Fan was the only woman in the department above undergraduate level.

'Yes. You want to see?'

'Do you mind? I'm just showing my friend Susan around.' Kwok-wah and Susan gathered around the terminal where Xiao-Fan was working.

'Oh my God!' Susan's enthusiasm was genuine. On

the screen was a computer simulation of a street scene: buildings, cars, pedestrians. 'The level of detail is amazing,' she said in her Californian-accented Putonghua.

'You're American, right? Watch this.' Xiao-Fan used her keyboard to change the viewpoint and all at once the view was as if they were a bird flying above the scene. The transition had been seamless.

'That's really impressive. We have some CAD/CAM machines in building sciences, and some architectural software to help plan buildings, but I mean, nothing with the level of detail you have here. It would be really useful for us.'

'We're working on a new graphics chip,' explained Xiao-Fan. 'Faster than before so when you change the point of view it's smooth and quick. This street scene is just a demonstration of what it can do, the possible uses are endless. Games, of course, but sure, architects could use it as well. Anybody really.'

'Thanks, Xiao-Fan,' said Kwok-wah. 'What do you want to see next?' he asked Susan as they left Xiao-Fan to get on with her work.

'Professor Ye?' Susan paused and then laughed. 'The look on your face! Don't worry. If he doesn't even have time for you he's hardly going to want to be introduced to me. But I'm curious to see what he looks like. Do you think he's around?'

'I don't know, but his office is this way.' Kwok-wah led Susan down a corridor to Professor Ye's office. The door was closed. 'Looks like he's out somewhere. Or not receiving visitors.' He turned to the departmental secretary, who was collecting and sorting documents. 'Do you know where the professor is?' he asked.

'He's in a meeting in the administration building. He won't be back today,' she replied as she left her desk and headed for the photocopying room.

'It's like I told you,' Kwok-wah said to Susan. 'He's often not here.'

'Another time then. I guess I've probably taken up too much of your afternoon. But thanks, I like to see other parts of the university. And it's good to see where you work.'

'My pleasure.'

Susan looked at her watch. 'I've got to run, so I'll love you and leave you. Hang on though.' She looked worried. 'Where's my bag? Did I leave it on your desk? I think I might have done.'

'I'll go look. Just wait here for me.'

When Kwok-wah had gone Susan checked that the departmental secretary was still occupied with photocopying. Reassured that she was, Susan quickly opened the secretary's desk drawers one by one until she found what she wanted: a selection of keys on a keyring bearing the university crest. She pocketed the keys and closed the drawer before Kwok-wah returned.

'Here you go,' said Kwok-wah. 'As you thought, it was on my desk.'

Kwok-wah took Susan back to the main entrance and watched her head for the library. When she turned, looked back at him and smiled, Kwok-wah realised for the first time, and somewhat to his horror, that he was falling in love. He had come to Shanghai to devote himself to his research. To lose himself in mathematics and software. The last thing he had been expecting was love. This really wasn't what he was looking for in the slightest. He wished there was an algorithm he could follow that would tell him what to do next, because he hadn't a clue.

***

There was a time within living memory when dance halls and ballrooms were a defining feature of the social scene in Shanghai. In the years before the war, every night the city was full of waltzes and foxtrots. Dancing crossed social boundaries, for the young and old alike. Stylish young Chinese women, Russian émigrés, European and American expatriates, all shared a love of the tango and the quickstep; gangsters mixed with prostitutes, while debutantes waited to be asked to dance by young naval officers. This was within living memory, yes, but at the same time it had been another world. Now, for the most part, only an echo of those days persisted in the elderly couples who danced in the parks as an alternative to *tai chi*, and most of the dance halls never reopened after the revolution.

One of the remaining relics of Shanghai's golden age was the afternoon Tea Dance at the Majestic, a dance hall that had somehow managed to survive uninterrupted apart from a short hiatus during the Cultural Revolution. Dusty chandeliers provided a dim light that hid from sight the patches of damp on the ceiling and the places where the gilt was starting to come away from cornices and mouldings. The dim light also hid from view discreet assignations. There were stories that in her youth Madame Mao had once danced there, and even though she had fallen out of favour long ago, the glamour of the association hung around the Majestic like a faint perfume. A small band made up of piano, trumpet, bass and drums were playing a foxtrot on a raised dais at one end of the ballroom. The musicians looked old enough to have played for Madame Mao herself and were all dressed in black tie, but the jackets were developing threadbare patches and the players looked more like waiters from a restaurant that had seen better days. Nobody appeared to notice that the trumpet was slightly out of tune.

At four in the afternoon the room was busy, mainly with Chinese couples of an age for whom the foxtrot was natural but there were also some who were younger and a few Western tourists. Some were taking a rest, sitting at tables and watching the dancers. Others were sipping tea and eating delicate sandwiches and petits fours. Most of those on the dance floor were moving with grace and elegance. Susan was not one of those. She did not know the foxtrot and was relying on trying to follow her partner, a Western man in his sixties with greying hair, immaculately parted, and a distinguished, patrician bearing. His light grey suit was classically cut, with a crisp linen handkerchief in his breast pocket. He had suggested that Susan dress smartly, but even in a skirt and blouse, which she hardly ever wore, she still felt underdressed. The man held Susan properly, in a gentlemanly manner with his right hand resting lightly on her lower back, as he did his best to guide her among the dancing couples. When the music stopped they took a break and sat at a table in a booth. Two drinks and a bowl of peanuts were waiting for them on a silver tray.

'This is the most unlikely place to meet,' said Susan. 'What made you choose it?'

'You've just answered your own question, my dear,' the man replied. He had an accent straight out of *Gone With The Wind*. 'It's somewhere we can talk in private without being overheard, and it's a place where nobody thinks anything of seeing an older Caucasian man with a pretty young Chinese woman. And at least as importantly, I enjoy dancing. It reminds me of the balls I went to as a young man in Charlotte. Have I ever told you about those? One day I'll show you some old photographs. It may surprise you but I was quite the dashing beau back then.' He raised his whisky sour in Susan's direction. 'Your good health. So, tell me, how are we doing with our young man?'

'Making progress. I think he likes me.'

'I'm sure he does. He'd be a fool if he didn't. Tell me about him.'

'He's a geek. His only real interest is in computers. He's a decent guy though. I get the feeling he's struggled to adjust to life as a student in China. I don't think he has any local friends. I mean, he gets on alright with his room-mates and they'll go for a beer together. But I don't think he's close to any of them.'

'Family?'

'His parents. No siblings. Interestingly his grandparents came from Suzhou and Shanghai. There's a bit of history there we might be able to work on if we need to. He does have a cousin in Hong Kong – she's older than him – who appears to be more politically aware than he is. I don't know if that might be useful or not.'

'What about the target? Are we right about him?'

'Too early to say for certain but everything points that way.'

'Come,' said the man. 'Let's dance. You can tell me in three-quarter time.' The musicians had started a waltz. 'Nobody will pay us any attention.'

Susan realised that her companion was right. While they danced it was natural for her to talk directly into his ear. With couples swirling around them they were invisible to the rest of the room that afternoon.

'He's obviously doing something for the military. Kwok-wah has seen him showing round a uniform. Of course he has no idea who the guest was … Sorry.' Susan stumbled over her feet a little before recovering herself. 'Or even what part of the military he comes from.'

'We need to find out.'

'Agreed. It looks like it's something to do with data encryption though,' said Susan.

'Which is what we thought.'

'Quite.'

'But do we know what they are planning on doing with any encryption technology they develop?' he asked. 'The PLA must have whole units devoted to the subject. What is so special about working with Professor Ye?'

'I don't know.'

The music stopped and there was a ripple of applause.

'You're getting better, I think,' the man said.

'Y'know, they don't teach this at Langley. I'm pretty sure it wasn't part of my induction training.'

'More's the pity. I shall have to suggest it the next time I'm there. I think ballroom dancing is an essential life skill. You never know when it might be useful. Come. Let's take a break.' Seated back at their table, he continued. 'He has no suspicions, I assume? Kwok-wah, that is. About you I mean.'

'No,' Susan laughed. 'He's very innocent of the world. It would never cross his mind. All he wants to do is play with his toys. Quite sweet really.'

'Do you think he's being watched?'

'I am a little worried about that. I'm a little wary of one of his room-mates. His father's in the PLA. I've made friends with a girl who dated him a little. Apparently he's very devout. Could just be a coincidence, of course – I'm sure a good university is full of the children of high-ranking Party members – but then again it might not.'

'What do you propose to do next?'

'I don't know. There's only so much I can get out of Kwok-wah when he doesn't know himself what Ye

Zhang is up to. I need to get into his office.'

'Which won't be easy.'

'I have a key.'

'That's very resourceful, my dear. How did you manage that?'

'I got Kwok-wah to show me around. By chance the departmental secretary was away from her desk, so I got rid of Kwok-wah for a couple of minutes, went through the drawers and found a set of keys. I'm assuming one of them is for Ye Zhang's office. I don't know for certain, of course, but I'd be surprised if not.'

'Won't the keys have been missed?'

'I hope not. I had them copied and then I sort of found them, if you get my drift, and handed them in. I'm relying on the secretary having been too embarrassed to admit they had been missing in the first place. I don't think security is that tight. No matter what Ye Zhang is up to it is just a university department at the end of the day.'

'I expect she wouldn't want to lose face.'

'That's my theory. But there's still a problem …' Susan paused while a waiter passed their table. The band struck up another number with the trumpeter now not only out of tune but also a beat behind his colleagues. 'It's all very well having the key to his office, but I have to get into the department in the first place.'

'There's a security guard, I assume?'

'At all times.'

'Can you get your young man to help you get into

the building?'

'I'd rather avoid that if I can. I don't see a way of asking him to get me into the department out of hours without having to tell him something about who I was, and I'd rather not put Kwok-wah in any more danger than he already is.'

The man was thoughtful as he swirled the remains of his drink in the glass. 'What do you propose to do?'

'To be honest, I don't know.'

'I know this is your first operation in China, but we really need to know what he's up to. I wouldn't force you to do anything you're unwilling to, but how far are you prepared to go?' he asked.

'I don't know.'

There was a pause.

'One last dance before you go, my dear?'

***

Zhanyuan opened the window, leant out and carefully brought in the bottle of Tsingtao that had been standing on the window ledge for the past couple of hours. They weren't supposed to bring alcohol into the dorm. It was strictly against the rules and anyone who was caught would be fined. It would go on their academic record and would be an obstacle to a good job or Party membership, unless, that is, you had the right connections to get it removed. But students being the same everywhere, sometimes a rule was simply something that needed to be broken.

Getting the beer past Granny Sun was the easy

bit; the challenge was finding somewhere to keep it cool. There was a fridge in the communal kitchen but Granny Sun was known to check that from time to time, and anyway, keeping beer in the kitchen ran the risk that it would be stolen. Until the weather became too warm, the window ledge was the best option. Zhanyuan gripped the bottle in both hands to assess its temperature.

'Not too bad,' he concluded.

'What we need,' said Li Lao, 'is a bucket and some ice. Couldn't you pinch some liquid nitrogen from the solid-state physics lab?'

'Typical fucking Beijinger,' said Zhanyuan. 'You think this is one of your fucking Beijing restaurants? Perhaps you'd like to see the fucking wine list?'

Li Lao caught Kwok-wah's eye and smiled. 'Bad day in the lab, was it?'

'Crap, as it happens.' Zhanyuan poured three beers and passed the glasses round. 'My practical went completely wrong. We were supposed to be measuring the charge on the electron. It's a standard experiment but everything I did went balls up. So rather than start all over again, I thought: Well, we know what the answer should be so why not work backwards and invent some results that will give the right answer?'

'Sounds a sensible thing to do,' said Li Lao. 'I thought that was what all experimentalists did anyway?'

'So, I write up the experiment with my faked results and take it to the lab supervisor. As soon as he looks at it, I know something's wrong. He studies the results

I gave him and says: *"These can't be right, they're way out."* Then he turns to my calculations and of course I'd fucked up the maths so my faked results were even worse than the ones I'd got actually doing the experiment. Of course, he knew what I'd done. He refused to sign off the experiment and I'm going to have to do it all again.'

Kwok-wah and Li Lao both nearly choked on their beer with laughter.

'Yeah, very funny. Something you can tell your American girlfriend.'

'What's this?' asked Li Lao. 'Something I should know about?'

'You should ask our southern friend here. Real Chinese women aren't good enough for him. He has to screw an American banana.'

Kwok-wah was both embarrassed and angry at the same time.

'She's not my girlfriend and we certainly haven't had sex.'

'If you say so. But that hasn't stopped you going out with her. Day trips to Suzhou wandering along the canals hand in hand I expect. Going for runs together. Showing her round your department.' Kwok-wah was shocked and alarmed with how much Zhanyuan knew. He hadn't been keeping his friendship with Susan a secret as such, but he was certainly being discreet. At least he thought he had been.

'So what?' said Li Lao. 'Good for him.' To Kwok-wah: 'Don't take any notice of this jerk. He's just jealous because that girl in the football team he fancied turned him down. She told him that she had a lot of experience kicking balls and he took the hint.'

'Her loss.'

CHAPTER 11

EMMA TOOK A SEAT IN Yannie and Eric's tiny living room. The flat in Yuen Long was scarcely larger than Emma's studio but it was home to a family of three. Emma had met Yannie from work and they'd travelled together. Yuen Long was one of the new towns in Hong Kong and largely a dormitory suburb. It was a part of Hong Kong Emma had never been to before and largely off the expat radar. Yannie had warned her that she would never find the place on her own, and after travelling for over an hour using a combination of MTR, bus and light rail, before arriving at a flat on the twenty-third floor of Block G of a new development where all the buildings looked the same, Emma was glad to have had a guide.

'You do that journey every day?' she asked when they finally arrived.

'Unless I'm working in the Kowloon office when I can get a bus direct from Yuen Long. The bus isn't really any quicker but it doesn't involve having to change.

You get used to it though and we could never afford to buy anywhere closer into town. It's also near to where my mother lives and she helps with Thomas.'

'Have you lived here long?'

'We bought the place about eighteen months ago, just after I got pregnant.'

An older woman, who Emma took to be Yannie's mother, came into the room carrying a baby.

'*Mama, da goh jiu fu,* Emma,' said Yannie.

'*Nei ho,* Emma.'

'My mother doesn't have any English, I'm afraid.'

'No problem,' said Emma. '*Nei ho,*' she replied to Yannie's mother, using up a significant percentage of her conversational Cantonese. 'Can I see Thomas?'

'Of course.' Yannie took the baby from her mother and held him in her arms.

'He's cute,' said Emma, knowing that was the expected response regardless of what the child actually looked like.

'My mother thinks he takes after me, but I think he's closer to Eric. Lily thinks he's just a baby and they all look the same anyway. She's probably right.' Yannie passed Thomas back to her mother: '*Mama, nei ho yi tai tai bo bo hau, dong ngo dai suet wah?*'

'I've asked my mother to look after Thomas while we talk,' said Yannie. 'Eric should be home shortly. I don't know how much he'll be able to help but I know he's been looking in the archives.'

'I'm just grateful you've both tried. It's really appreciated.'

'And afterwards you'll stay for supper I hope? Ah, here's Eric.' The door opened and a good-looking thirty-something came in. He took off his jacket, put his case on the table, and greeted Emma.

'You must be Emma. It's a pleasure to meet you.'

'You too, Eric.'

The three of them chatted about the weather, children and family for a while, but Eric could tell that Emma was anxious to hear whether he had been able to discover anything.

'Let me get a beer from the kitchen and then I'll tell you what I found. Do either of you want anything?' They both declined and waited until Eric returned with a San Miguel.

'So, I went to talk to the people in the newsroom. It took a while to find out who had covered the story. It wasn't a big story at the time – sorry.' He looked at Emma. 'That may sound insensitive, obviously it was huge to you and your family but to the paper it was just another road traffic accident.'

'Of course, I understand that,' said Emma. 'Please, Eric, go on.'

'It turned out that the main person on the story was a relatively junior staff reporter, Brian Lo. He left us not long afterwards to move to Australia. Apparently he works for the *Sydney Morning Herald* these days.' Eric could see that Emma was starting to look crestfallen. 'But after he left, some of his notes were kept in the paper's archives.'

'How long do you keep things for?' asked Emma.

'Usually a few years, I think. I'm not sure if it's a consistent policy that's always followed, but sometimes they're kept in case there's any dispute over something that we've printed, especially after someone has left, or if a journalist needs to research something while working on a story. Sometimes things just get kept because nobody can decide what to do with them. I asked a favour from the chief archivist and got him to search around.'

'Was he happy to help?'

'Oh yes. One of the advantages of being a sports writer is that I can get tickets for things, access to inside information and so on. I expect he'll do well at Happy Valley next week ...'

'And did he find anything?' Yannie wanted to get Eric to stop rambling and get to the point.

'Yes. Some of Brian's original notes were there. I've got copies in my case.' Eric took out a sheaf of papers that he laid out on the dining table. 'I'd probably be getting the archivist into trouble if I gave these to you, Emma, and anyway, they're all in Chinese, but I can tell you what they are and what they say.'

'I understand.' Emma was watching Eric's lips intently, making sure she didn't miss a word. Her hands were clasped together, her fingers twisting and untwisting.

'Most of the stuff was pretty unremarkable: copies of the official police statements on the case, photographs of the scene ... I've left them out ... unless you'd like to ...?'

'No, I don't think so. Not yet anyway.'

'But there were also Brian's notes from interviews with eyewitnesses. He had terrible handwriting, you know … quite hard to make out in places. It's like he had his own personal shorthand …'

'Was there anything interesting in them?' Yannie prompted.

'I'm not sure. Most of the people Brian spoke to hadn't actually seen the accident. They just described the aftermath. The police arriving, the ambulance and so on. But there was one guy who did see it all. Most of what he said was unremarkable, but there was just one thing that stood out as being a little odd, which is that his description of the driver doesn't really tie in with the guy who was convicted. What was his name …?'

'Chan Wah Man,' filled in Yannie.

'Chan Wah Man, that's right. The eyewitness described the driver as being an older man but Chan Wah Man was thirty-four at the time.'

'So he can't have been the driver?' said Emma.

'Well, let's not get ahead of ourselves,' said Eric. 'You've got to remember that it was late at night in Wan Chai, so you can assume that any witness had probably been drinking. The driver never got out of the car so the witness can't have seen him fully, indeed the car barely stopped so it must all have happened very quickly. The possibility that he was simply wrong must be high.'

They all sat in silence for a moment until the spell was broken by the sound of Thomas crying. Yannie left the room to go see to him.

'But even so, Chan Wah Man might not have been the driver after all?' said Emma finally.

'Perhaps not, but as I said, you've got to remember it's quite possible the guy was wrong, and in the end Chan Wah Man pleaded guilty, didn't he?'

'Do the notes give the name of the witness?'

'Yes, but only a name and nothing else. Cheung Wing-ho. It's a pretty unremarkable Cantonese name, I couldn't even begin to imagine how you could find him if that's what you're thinking of doing.'

'Was there anything about Gao Zhihua in the notes?'

'Only what we already know. That Chan Wah Man was his driver.'

Yannie came back into the room carrying Thomas, who was quiet again.

'So Emma, what do you think?' she said.

'I don't know,' said Emma. 'I know you're right, Eric. Being realistic about it there's every chance the witness was wrong, but I don't know … it's tantalising … I can't explain it but there's something bugging me about all this. Something that says there's more to what happened than the official story but I've no idea what to do next.'

'What to do next is to have something to eat,' said Yannie. 'Mum's been preparing some food.'

They cleared the papers away to create some space and sat at the table, sharing a family supper that Yannie's mother brought out dish by dish. It was the first time that Emma had eaten at home with a local family and she was grateful for their kindness. She sat quietly with her own thoughts while the family chatted in Cantonese for a while.

'Emma,' said Yannie, turning to her, 'my sister was in Wan Chai the other week.'

'Lily?' Emma couldn't see the significance of Lily having been in Wan Chai.

'Yes. She was buying tickets for a movie and she thought she saw you come out of the cinema.' Yannie looked at Emma expectantly.

'Oh.' It suddenly dawned on Emma what Yannie was getting at. Lily must have seen her with Sam. Emma felt herself blush slightly.

'Anything you'd like to share with us?'

'There's not much to say really. He's a guy I worked for a couple of months ago. We'd been to see the new Maggie Cheung.'

'A boyfriend? Sorry if I'm being nosey, but we married women have to live through others.'

'Too early to say. We've only met up a couple of times. He's been busy with work, and to be honest I've been rather preoccupied with Peter's death.'

'I can understand that,' said Yannie. 'I shall say no more.'

'Why would anyone plead guilty to something they hadn't done, knowing they would get a heavy jail sentence?' asked Emma, still thinking about Peter and the accident.

'Well,' said Yannie cautiously, 'it does happen sometimes, even in the US and Britain. There could be any one of a number of reasons. A confession might be obtained by force. I'd like to think that was unlikely in Hong Kong but you never know.'

'Perhaps if someone was being framed and they knew they had no chance they might plead guilty to minimise the sentence?' suggested Eric.

'Possibly,' continued Yannie, 'or perhaps they may have been blackmailed with something worse? Or bribed with something that would make it worthwhile? Along with a promise of early release …' Yannie's voice tailed off as she realised what she had said.

'Which is exactly what has happened,' said Emma.

'Which is exactly what has happened. But Emma, I don't want to get your hopes up. Like Eric said, there's every chance the witness was wrong anyway and it's so little to go on. I almost wish I hadn't mentioned Chan Wah Man at all. Even if you did find out that someone else was the driver, what are you going to do? Nobody's going to be interested in reopening things at this stage.'

'I don't know,' said Emma. 'I know it sounds ridiculous, like something out of a movie, but I have to follow this as far as I can. I owe it to Peter.'

Travelling back home, Emma was lost in her thoughts. It was just as well that the return back to Hong Kong Island was easier than the way out or she might have ended up anywhere, but it wasn't until the final leg of her journey and she was on a bus heading along Queen's Road East that she had an idea. She was surprised it had taken so long to come to her and that she hadn't thought of it before. She was working for the next two weeks but after that she had nothing planned. Emma felt she was due a holiday, and she'd always liked Sydney.

***

That night it took Emma some time to fall sleep, her mind repeatedly going over what Eric had told her, back and forth, round and round, but ultimately getting nowhere. When she did finally sleep, Emma had a dream that she'd often had before but hadn't had for some time. In the dream she is seven, perhaps eight or nine, playing in an English country garden. There are roses, wisteria and a large magnolia bush. The sun is shining and it's obviously summer; July or August perhaps. Peter is in the dream as well, lying on the grass reading a book. Standing centrally on the lawn is a trampoline, her pride and joy, something that she had pestered her parents to buy. In the dream Emma is bouncing as high as she can, aiming for the sun and turning this way and that as she rises and falls. She is alternately laughing and screaming as she gets higher and higher. But then she overdoes it, and as she lands her right ankle strikes the trampoline frame. She falls, crying out in pain. Peter rushes across the lawn and helps her down from the trampoline. She turns to thank him but he's no longer there. Ignoring the pain in her ankle, she looks everywhere for her brother but can never find him.

***

It was an evening of surprises.

'You play the saxophone? How come you haven't told me this before?' Emma was taken aback when Sam told her that he was playing at the Fringe Club on Friday night. They were having dinner in a small Italian restaurant in SoHo when Sam came out with this revelation.

'I played in various jazz bands at school and university but not much since then. I've been trying to pick it up again. Get back into the groove as it were – if you'll forgive the pun. We've got a quartet together and done a few gigs playing in bars, but the Fringe Club is a step up for us. We're only a supporting act, but still …'

'How did you meet the others? I mean, corporate law and jazz? I'd have thought there wasn't much overlap between them?'

'You'd be surprised. Perhaps it's our desperate attempt to do something creative, perhaps we're just doing it to seem like normal people. The pianist is an Australian investment banker I met through work. He already had a trio with bass and drums but they were looking for a sax. So, can you come?'

'Try stopping me. Do you mind if I bring some friends?'

SoHo – South of Hollywood Road – was an up-and-coming area that was being gentrified, to the delight of some and the puzzlement of others. Almost as soon as the Mid-Levels escalator had been built, a multitude of restaurants and bars opened up in what used to be older walk-ups, all designed to tempt weary commuters on the way home from work. Every night the streets were busy with young professionals, expats and locals, couples and groups of friends, all enjoying the buzz. Meanwhile some of the older residents of the area were still wondering what had become of what was once a quiet traditional neighbourhood. Like most places along the street, the restaurant Sam and Emma had chosen was little more than a front room opening out onto the pavement; they watched as a *lap sap* woman pushed her cart piled high with flattened used cardboard boxes.

Over coffee, it was Emma's turn to surprise Sam.

'Sydney?'

'Just for a week,' she said. 'It's one of the good things about working as a temp – being able to go on holiday at short notice. Provided you've got the money, of course, and I've had some decent work recently.'

Sam was surprised that she was planning a holiday so suddenly. It had come out of the blue, not something she had mentioned before. Perhaps it just went to show how different they were. Sam could never imagine going on holiday without weeks of careful research and planning: reading guidebooks, considering possible itineraries and places to stay, making travel arrangements, organising inoculations. Sometimes he was amazed he ever managed to go anywhere at all.

A final surprise came at the end of the evening. Walking along the street before they went their separate ways home, Emma's fingers searched for and then found Sam's hand. He turned to face Emma, who was smiling at him. They stopped where they were, outside a laundry that was just closing up, and Emma leaned up towards Sam and kissed him. A kiss that was returned, Sam holding Emma with one arm while caressing her cheek. He could feel her slender body through the thin material of her dress. They stopped when they realised that they were getting in the way of everybody passing by. Emma was still smiling, Sam somewhat lost for words.

'You okay?' she asked. 'You look a bit … I hope I didn't presume …'

'No … that was lovely … just a bit of a surprise …'

'Well, I wasn't sure if you were ever going to kiss me so I thought …'

Sam took the rest of the sentence out of Emma's mouth by kissing her again. He'd forgotten how a woman's lips tasted.

***

The Fringe Club was always popular. The consciously distressed interior – rough plaster, visible plumbing – hosted regular exhibitions, plays and music, while the cheap drinks made it particularly popular with students. Emma and Alice found a table while Liang-bao went to the bar to get the drinks. When Emma had told Alice about Sam, she had been quick to suggest a double-date. While she had Alice to herself, Emma quizzed her.

'So, have you told your parents about Liang-bao yet?' she asked.

'Last week. They were getting suspicious of my late nights. I couldn't keep telling them I was out with you. They were starting to think you were a bad influence.'

'Very considerate of you. How did they take it?'

'Not too well if I'm honest, but they've calmed down a bit now. They think it's just a passing phase that won't last.'

'And will it? How serious are you two? Have you slept together yet?' asked Emma.

Alice was spared the embarrassment of having to answer by Liang-bao returning with the drinks.

'White wine for you Emma,' he said, passing her a glass, 'and red for you,' handing another to Alice. 'So, when are you off to Sydney?' he asked Emma.

'Sunday night.'

'Just a holiday?'

'Yep. I've been there a few times now. It's one of my favourite cities. The food, the wine, sunshine, beaches … The weather should still be good at this time of year, better than here at the moment, so what's not to like?'

The stars of the evening arrived in the bar. Sam spotted Emma and went over to her, leaving his bandmates to head for the stage.

'You've got a good table,' said Sam, giving Emma a kiss on the cheek. Alice caught Emma's eye and raised an eyebrow. Emma made the introductions before Sam left the three of them to go help his colleagues set up for the gig.

'So,' said Alice, 'the mystery man you've been keeping from us.'

'You're not in a position to comment on keeping things quiet,' said Emma. 'Pots, kettles and the colour black, you know?'

'Quite good looking I suppose. Nice eyes. But, I mean … a lawyer?' said Alice teasingly.

'A jazz-playing lawyer though, and anyway what's wrong with lawyers? Don't you want to become one?'

'Fair point. Is he any good? His playing, I mean?'

'I don't know,' admitted Emma. 'We'll find out soon.'

The room was starting to fill. All the tables were taken and it was standing room only at the bar. A young crowd, predominantly local but with a sprinkling of expats. Emma spotted Kate at the bar and waved her over.

'Are you on your own?' Emma asked. 'Why don't you join us?'

'Thanks. Yes, just me. I had to come and give Sam support. It's packed in here. I didn't realise it was going to be so popular. It's good to see you again though, it seems ages since you were working for us. I gather from Sam you're off to Sydney next week? Lucky you. It must be great to be able to just drop things and go off like that.'

Emma made more introductions. A scream of feedback told them the music would be starting soon and suddenly, without expecting it, Emma found herself somewhere else. No longer in Hong Kong in the Fringe Club watching Sam open with Sonny Rollins' 'St. Thomas' but in the Student Union bar at Exeter. She was seventeen, no, not even that, only sixteen and probably shouldn't have been there at all, but she was spending the weekend with Peter and he'd sneaked her in. They never told their parents, Peter would have been in big trouble had they found out. He was in his second year studying English, but music was his real passion and he played tenor sax in an R&B band. She remembered when he first took it up. She was only young at the time but she could still remember the strained wailing that used to come from his room, to the exasperation of the whole family. Thankfully he quickly got much better, he turned out to have a flair for the instrument, and that night at Exeter he would catch her eye between numbers and smile. She had felt so grown up. How long ago was it now? Emma did the calculation; thirteen, fourteen years? There were times it seemed much longer, but then other times when it felt like only yesterday.

Back in the present day the music stopped and the Fringe Club was full of cheering and clapping. Emma reluctantly came out of her thoughts and memories and joined in the applause, though she realised that she hadn't heard a note of the music.

***

'Wow! That was terrific, Sam. Come and sit down.' The set had finished and Kate created room for Sam to join them at the table. 'I didn't expect you to be that good.'

'Thank you … I think …' Sam was not quite sure if Kate was complimenting him or not. 'There were a few dodgy moments but on the whole it went pretty well.'

'Let me get you a drink. Beer?'

'Please.'

While Kate headed for the bar, Alice and Liang-bao added their own congratulations, but Emma was quiet and withdrawn.

'What did you think?' Sam asked her. 'Emma?' He wasn't sure if she had even heard him.

'Sorry? Oh, yes, very good.' There was a blankness to Emma's voice; Sam tried to hide his disappointment. Perhaps she was just trying to be polite, but it was as if she had hated the music. He hadn't realised until now just how much he was hoping to impress her.

'Emma, is there something wrong?' Alice asked.

'It's the noise, and the heat in here, it's so stuffy. Perhaps I'd better leave.' Emma got up and gathered her things together in a rush.

'Emma …?' Sam couldn't understand what was wrong and why she was so anxious to get away.

'Sam, I'll call you.' Emma started to head for the door just as Kate returned with Sam's beer.

'What's wrong?' Kate asked Sam, who was standing looking lost and confused. Kate then added a firm instruction: 'Go after her.' Sam took the advice and followed Emma, catching up with her at the entrance just as she emerged from the Fringe Club onto the street. It had started to rain.

'Emma … wait.' Not sure she could hear him, Sam reached out to her shoulder to get her attention. Emma stopped and turned, and he saw she was crying.

'Emma, what is it? Tell me. Please.'

'I'm sorry, Sam, I really am, but I can't stay ...'

'Is it the noise in there? Why are you crying?' Sam found a clean tissue in his pocket and passed it to Emma who dabbed her eyes, but the tears still came. 'Please, Emma, tell me. Have I done something, said something? It can't be just the noise or the heat. Not the way you're crying. Please tell me what's wrong. What can I do?' Emma's tears were starting to ease but her eyes were red. 'Emma?'

'I'm sorry ...' Emma spoke quietly and haltingly. Sam could only just hear her over the traffic. 'I've messed up your big night ... I didn't mean to ...' She took his hands in hers. 'I ...' The words dried up completely and Sam pulled her to him and held her tight. 'I'm ... I'm so alone,' she said forlornly.

'Alone?' Sam had no idea what Emma was going on about. Whatever was wrong, her being alone was not what he expected. 'You've got good friends like Alice. Family back home.' Sam sensed Emma shudder at those words and he hesitated before plucking up the courage to add: 'You've got me ... at least, I hope you know that?'

'I know, Sam, I know, but it's not the same.' The tears had started to come again, along with the continuing rain that was soaking them both as they stood there.

'Not the same as what?'

'I just miss him so much ...'

'Miss who?'

'I've got to go.' Emma broke away from Sam and

hurried down the street. Sam stood there for a moment, confused and hurt, until he realised that Kate was standing beside him.

'You okay?' she asked.

'I just don't understand. What happened?'

'Come on.' Kate hooked her arm around his. 'Let's go back inside. We're both getting wet and your band-mates are looking for you.'

CHAPTER 12

SPRING PROPER WAS STILL SOME time away, but Shanghai had broken the back of winter and there were now quite distinct signs of the coming change of season, and after grey cloud, rain and fog, the blue skies and sunshine caught everyone by surprise. The mornings were still cool but cherry blossom was starting to appear in the parks; the afternoons, if the sun was shining, could even give the impression of being warm.

It was such an afternoon that found Susan sitting on a bench in the rose garden outside the computer science department. If not quite T-shirt weather, Susan was able to get away with a blouse and a light sweater draped over her shoulders. A pair of sunglasses sat perched on her head for style rather than function. She had arrived a full hour before the time she had agreed to meet Kwok-wah, having discovered previously that the bench was very conveniently positioned for watching the entrance to the department. Susan prided herself on her ability to observe unobtrusively. Her instructors had taught her well. It wasn't always about hiding, sometimes it was quite the opposite and you were better being in plain sight. Today she was pretending to read a textbook, taking in the odd paragraph or two and turning the pages now and then, while throwing the occasional glance towards the entrance. To anyone else it looked as if she was intent on her study of reinforcing girders, but she saw everyone who entered or left the building, all the comings and goings.

Mainly they were teachers and students – she recognised some of them – and miscellaneous university staff. There were cleaners, technicians; the occasional delivery man. She paid them all little attention, noting them only in her subconscious as being of no interest, but when her eye was caught by the sight of a man in military dress leaving the building Susan was immediately alert. She made a mental note of the uniform. High-ranking PLA certainly. There was plenty of braid on the epaulettes and quite a number of medal ribbons, but she couldn't see enough detail to go beyond that. It must have been the guy Kwok-wah had told her about and she considered following him before deciding against it. He was unlikely to be here alone and she might be spotted. In any case, it was almost time to meet Kwok-wah.

He was a worry. She had been trained to avoid emotional attachments, to focus on the job in hand, to be cold and dispassionate at all times. She thought this was something that was easy to say in a classroom at Langley, but not always so easy to keep to in the field.

Susan was aware that she was becoming genuinely fond of Kwok-wah. She found his innocence and naivety endearing compared with the cynical world she inhabited. She knew there was no danger of actually falling in love with him, even if they'd met in more normal circumstances he wasn't really her type, and she had a job to do, but she was determined to do her best to make sure no harm came to him. She hoped he wasn't falling in love with her. That would be a nuisance.

Kwok-wah left the building soon after the PLA guy and she waved him over. When he reached the bench where she was sitting, Susan stood up and kissed him on the cheek. Kwok-wah blushed.

'I've just seen a guy in uniform leave your department. Was that Professor Ye's military friend?'

'I expect so. Certainly he's had a visitor all day.'

'Smart uniform, that's for sure.'

'Where do you want to go?' asked Kwok-wah.

'It's a nice afternoon still. It should be fine for a while yet, at least until the sun starts to go down. Let's take a walk by the lake. Do you think he's doing something for the army? Professor Ye, that is.'

'I don't know for sure, but it does look like it.'

'Would that bother you?' Susan asked. 'I mean – would you think less of him if he was working for the military?'

'Should it?' Kwok-wah looked puzzled.

'Well …' Susan hesitated. She didn't know how far to push Kwok-wah. 'It's just after Tiananmen some people might feel uncomfortable about it.'

'Perhaps. I don't know.'

They stopped to watch the family of ducks that lived on a small island in the middle of the lake. A small duck house had been built, and while other birds went south for the winter, these rarely left the island and the surrounding waters. It was as if they were conscious of their privileged position in the ever-changing city. Fearful perhaps that if they left their island it may have been redeveloped by the time they returned.

'I guess it might depend on what he was doing for them,' Susan continued to probe gently. 'Could be harmless I suppose.' She decided the seed had been sown and there was no need to press the point further for now. There'd be other times, better not to rush things. Slow and careful was what she had been taught. 'Enough about Professor Ye. How was your day?'

While they circled the lake they discussed lectures and research. Computer software and composite building materials. Tutorials and seminars. Kwok-wah tried to explain the advantages and disadvantages of two different algorithms, Susan countered with an explanation of pre-fabricated concrete panels and their role in manufacturing building components off-site. When they had exhausted talking about their studies Kwok-wah changed the subject.

'What did your family think about you coming to China?'

'I don't know …' Susan wondered where this question had suddenly come from. Was Kwok-wah having doubts about being in China? 'I guess they were a tad unhappy at first. I can still remember how obsessed they were with watching the TV news at the time of Tiananmen Square. I was only young but we talked about it a lot. When I got the place here I had to promise my parents I'd keep a low profile, y'know, and stay out of politics. Which is what I've tried to do while I've been here. Sometimes the other students try and get me to talk about stuff, ask me about America, ask me what I think about China, but I just tell them I'm not interested.'

'My cousin – Alice, I think I told you about her – did try to warn me about coming to China.'

'She's the one in a human rights group?'

'That's right. She tried to talk me out of coming here, and my parents were really unhappy about it. It caused quite a few arguments.'

'Are you starting to think they might have been right?' Susan wondered if Kwok-wah was becoming more realistic about China, if he was starting to lose his innocence.

'Sometimes … I don't know …' Kwok-wah stopped and looked at Susan. 'I keep thinking about Granny Sun.'

'Who?'

'She's the woman who looks after my dorm. She lives in a small room by the main door.'

'Oh, I know who you mean. She always gives me a funny look when she sees me.'

Kwok-wah laughed. 'I can believe that. She's very … well I was going to say protective, but I'm not sure who is being protected. Anyway, one way or another she keeps an eye on the dorm. Let's sit down.' They sat on the grass, looking over the lake.

'So why have you been thinking about her?'

'I got talking to her over the Lunar New Year. She told me her history, the things she's been through. She's had such a tough life.' Kwok-wah gave Susan a summary of what Granny Sun had told him.

'Jeez, that's terrible,' said Susan. 'I mean, things being so bad that you have to sell your own child? I don't think I can imagine what that must be like.'

'It makes me think about my grandparents.'

'The ones who escaped from Shanghai?'

'What if they hadn't? What would have happened to them? What would have happened to my parents? One thing's for sure, I probably wouldn't be here today.' Kwok-wah took Susan's hand in his and Susan let him. 'But surely somebody must know?'

'Sorry? Know what?' Susan was a little worried about where Kwok-wah was going with this. She had to try and keep a balance between making Kwok-wah question what Professor Ye was doing and complete disillusionment. The last thing she wanted was for him to leave just now and go back to Hong Kong. After all, Kwok-wah wouldn't be any use to her there.

'Shu-ming,' Kwok-wah continued. 'Somebody somewhere must know what happened to Shu-ming. There must be records that say what happened to him. Mustn't there?'

'I don't know. Perhaps. But it was a pretty chaotic time back then wasn't it? I guess a lot of stuff would

have been lost. Some of it might even have been deliberately destroyed. I mean, after the Cultural Revolution
I bet a lot of people probably wanted to hide what
they did.'

'Really?'

'That's what I've read anyway, but I don't know
much.' Susan remembered the hours in the classroom
studying all aspects of Chinese twentieth-century history. Her lecturers had been some of the best experts
in the States.

'I'd like to be able to find out what happened to
Shu-ming for Granny Sun's sake. She's always thinking
about him. But I haven't a clue as to how to go about it.'

Susan reached over to Kwok-wah and before she
could stop herself, before her training and better judgement kicked in, she kissed him.

***

It was a little after eleven that night when Susan left
her dorm. Her room-mates were getting ready for bed.

'Where are you off to at his hour?' said one of them.

'A boy?' asked another. 'Is it that Hongkonger you've
been seeing?'

'Maybe, maybe not. Perhaps I'm just going for a
late-night run.' Susan smiled. 'I like to keep some se-
crets to myself.'

'Just be careful,' said the first.

'And give us a blow-by-blow account later,' said the
second, causing the first to burst out laughing.

'See you later, girls,' said Susan.

Susan slipped out of her building without difficulty. Her own Granny Sun equivalent was nothing like as vigilant as the real thing and was already asleep. After the fine day the skies were still clear and a half-moon illuminated the campus in a way that was both a blessing and a curse. She knew the library and the main buildings would all have their own guards, but a previous reconnaissance had told her they were not especially watchful and could be easily avoided. More of a risk to her plans were the regular patrols of the campus that were the main form of security. She would just have to be careful.

Susan avoided the well-lit main paths and instead made her way through the grounds dotted with various large shrubs and trees that made conveniently dark resting points where she could pause and watch for the patrols, and listen for them as well. But in the darkness all sounds were amplified – traffic on the elevated expressway that ran past the university, the general background hum of the city. Shanghai quietened a little at night, but it never fell completely silent. A dog barked in the distance. The patrols didn't have dogs, did they? She didn't think so. Susan made her way around the back of the library, well out of sight of its guard, and waited – hidden in the moonlight shadow – while one of the regular patrols passed by, without a dog she was relieved to note. When the patrol had gone, and keeping again to the grounds, she worked her way across the campus to the computer science department where the ornate, almost baroque structure of the old building provided plenty of cover. Susan stopped in an archway from where she could see the main door and a small room just off the entrance, illuminated by a single bare light bulb. Two security guards sat at a table and shared a flask of something while they played cards. Susan watched them for thirty minutes until one of them left the room. Torchlight visible through a succession of windows told her that he had started a patrol of the department. Ten minutes later he was back and the guards began another hand.

With the clear skies, the mild temperature of the day had vanished and Susan wished she was wearing a warmer jacket. Holding her body close against a cold stone wall, she could feel the heat being sucked out of her. Her legs were stiffening. She wanted to jump up and down to get some feeling back into her limbs. Instead, she moved slowly, quietly, and staying in the shadow of the wall she crept away from the main entrance and towards the end of one wing of the department. When Susan was confident she was out of sight of the guards she made her way to the rear of the building. There was no path and she had to push her way through thick bushes; more than once her jacket snagged on branches and she cursed under her breath as thorns scratched her hands. To her relief the back of the building was clear of vegetation and more easily accessed, and importantly she was reassured that it wasn't overlooked. She explored the length of the back wall and came across a large door that appeared to be for deliveries. Probably no use to her. Then, a little way further along, she found what she hoped she would find. A fire escape with a door on the first floor and a metal staircase leading to the ground. She noted the relative position of the door compared to the windows on the first floor before retracing her route back to her dorm.

She crawled into her lower bunk bed, trying not to wake anyone.

'I hope you had a good workout,' said a voice from the bunk above her.

Laughter came from the rest of the room.

CHAPTER 13

THE PATHS THAT WEAVED THEIR way through the Botanical Gardens were full of joggers that morning, and more than once Emma – preoccupied with her lunchtime appointment – had to take avoiding action when a collision seemed inevitable. The Sydney sunshine suggested that Friday was going to be another fine day, and even at this early hour Emma could feel the warmth of the sun on her skin as she ran. The good weather that week, the blue skies and clean air, had all made a welcome change from Hong Kong where everything had been disappointingly grey and damp of late. If nothing else the change of scene had lifted her spirits, and at times she had even come close to forgetting her worries. The idea of moving here for good seemed very attractive and she was more than a little sorry to be going back to Hong Kong the next day.

Emma had arrived early Monday morning, after an overnight flight where a screaming child in the row behind her had made sure she didn't get any sleep, enabling her to spend the whole flight brooding over what had happened at the Fringe Club. Sam hadn't deserved that, and she couldn't stop herself thinking she had blown it with him. She had tried to call him before she went to the airport. She wanted to explain, but he was either not at home or not answering. Either way, she couldn't blame him. Reluctantly, she knew she had to put Sam to one side for the moment. She had come to Sydney for a reason and that had to take priority. She'd try explaining to him when she got home.

Emma had wasted no time in ringing the offices of the *Sydney Morning Herald* first thing Monday morning, only to be told that Brian Lo was not in the office that day and, no, they certainly wouldn't give a stranger his home number. He would be back at work on Tuesday if she wished to call again. This had been an unexpected setback and she was angry with herself for not having had the foresight to call in advance. She was lucky he was only away for the one day and not all week. In the meantime she tried her best to enjoy the city, but the reason why she was there was always at the back of her mind.

First thing Tuesday Emma had telephoned again, and after a short pause she was put through.

'Hello?' said a man's voice.

'Is that Brian Lo?'

'Yes. Who is this?'

'My name is Emma Janssen. You don't know me, but I live in Hong Kong and I was given your name by a friend of mine who works for the *Sing Pao Daily*. You worked there a few years ago, I think?'

'Yes. It was my first job in journalism.' His voice was wary. 'What can I do for you?'

Emma took a deep breath before getting to the point.

'I'd like to talk to you about a story you covered in Hong Kong. Back in 1992 or '93. It was a hit-and-run in Wan Chai. Do you remember it?'

There was silence on the line and Emma wondered if he was still there.

'Hello? Mr Lo?'

'Yes, I'm still here.'

'Do you remember the story?'

'Vaguely.' He had become more distant; if he had sounded wary before, his tone was even less friendly now.

'Would it be possible to meet up and have a chat about it?' asked Emma.

'I don't know. It was a long time ago, I don't remember much about it.'

'I'd still like to talk to you if I can.' Emma was becoming worried that her reason for coming to Sydney was falling at the first hurdle. 'Please.' An element of pleading entered her voice. Again there was a pause but Emma didn't want to press him. Finally he spoke.

'Why are you interested?' he asked.

'You didn't recognise my name?'

'Emma …'

'… Janssen.' She spelt out the name for him.

'Janssen … Oh, I see … Okay.'

He agreed to meet her at a small café near his office at 1 pm the next day. By half past he still hadn't arrived and Emma was struggling to make her long black and panini last long enough to pay rent on the table. She ordered a second coffee and decided to give him until two. Just before the hour, a Chinese man about her own age entered and looked around. Emma had given him a brief description of herself, but looks that were distinctive in Hong Kong were less so in Sydney and she waved him over.

'Brian Lo?' she asked.

'Miss Janssen?'

'Please, call me Emma.'

He sat down and ordered a coffee from a passing waitress. There was an uncomfortable silence between them as they each waited for the other to begin. It was Emma who spoke first.

'Thank you for agreeing to meet me, though I was wondering if I'd got the wrong place.'

'Yes … sorry about that, I was delayed.' He had an accent that somehow managed to be both unmistakably Australian and yet at the same time not that of a native speaker. His coffee arrived and he paused until the waitress had gone. 'I don't have long, I'm afraid.'

'I think you know the story I want to ask you about?' Emma prompted.

'I'm guessing he was your brother?'

'That's right.'

'My condolences, Miss Janssen, but I'm not sure what I can do for you?'

Emma hesitated. Although she had spent days re-hearsing this conversation, when it came to it she didn't know quite where to start. She sensed a reticence in him, a reluctance to talk that was not promising. Not encouraging. Emma also didn't want to risk getting Eric into any trouble by revealing how much he had helped.

'I understand that you reported on the accident?'

'Yes, I was the general duty reporter that night.'

'You interviewed various bystanders and witnesses?'

'Of course. What's this all about?'

'Do you remember one witness in particular?' Emma probed gently. 'I think his name was Cheung Wing-ho?'

'No, I don't think so, it was years ago now.' He had answered so quickly that Emma doubted whether he had given her question any thought.

'Are you sure? He was one of the few witnesses who had seen the accident itself. Not just the aftermath.'

'Quite certain. I know I spoke to a number of people but I can't remember them individually.'

Emma decided on a different approach.

'Did you follow the story all the way through to the trial?'

'Yes.'

'So you remember that Chan Wah Man was convicted?'

'He pleaded guilty, didn't he?'

'Yes, and now he's been released early.'

'Miss Janssen, sorry, I don't mean to be rude but I need to get back to work soon. Where's all this going?'

Emma decided to come to the point. 'Did you ever have any suspicions that Chan Wah Man was not the driver that night?'

A frown crossed Brian Lo's face. 'Not at all. Why on earth would I?'

'Because a man you interviewed, Cheung Wing-ho, gave a description of the driver that didn't match Mr Chan.'

'That's nonsense.' An agitated tone had entered his voice.

'Mr Lo, I've seen your notes. I know it's true.'

'You've seen my notes?' It was clear to Emma that he was surprised. 'How?'

'I'd rather not say,' said Emma, not wanting to name Eric. 'But I have seen them.'

'I don't remember anything like that. I'm sorry, Miss Janssen, but I really don't see how I can help and I do need to get back.' He started to rise from his seat and Emma feared her chance was slipping away.

'Please.' She leant over, placing her hand on his arm to stop him, and he paused for a moment. 'Please, just hear me out and then if you want to leave, go ahead.' He sat down again and Emma continued. She was angry with him for his disinterested attitude and she tried to use that anger constructively.

'Peter wasn't just my brother. He was my best friend, my confidante, protector. Not a day has gone by since his death that I haven't thought about him. Not a day that I haven't missed him desperately. I dream about him and then I have to wake up and I remember he's gone. I get a sickening feeling in the pit of my stomach, and sometimes I throw up. Have you ever lost someone close to you, Mr Lo? Do you know what it's like? Do you have any idea? I can't get him back but I need to know what happened. I don't think Chan Wah Man was driving that night. Someone else killed my brother and I think you can help.' Emma stopped, out of breath.

'Miss Janssen. I'm sorry, I really do have to go. Where are you staying? I'll try and see if I can remember anything. If I do I'll give you a call. How long are you here for?' His tone had softened slightly, offering Emma some suggestion that her trip hadn't been a complete waste of time. After finally getting to meet him she really didn't want to let Brian Lo out of her sight, but she couldn't force him to stay. She had to hope that she'd said enough to prey on his conscience.

'Until Saturday,' she said, giving him her hotel details.

'I'll see what I can do. I'm not promising anything though.'

'I understand,' said Emma, 'but thank you anyway.'

After that Emma had been reluctant to leave her hotel room at first, for fear of missing a call, before telling herself she was being ridiculous and she started to go out again. In the end she did miss the call, which came on Thursday afternoon, but he left a message and a home phone number. She rang him that evening and they arranged to meet Friday lunchtime at the same place. It was her last chance before her flight back to Hong Kong. Emma was early, and on this occasion he arrived at the agreed time.

'Do you mind if we go for a walk?' he asked. 'Quite a lot of my colleagues come in here. Somewhere quieter, more private, would be better.'

'Of course. No problem.' Emma paid for the tea she'd ordered and they headed to a nearby park. 'Have you found anything, remembered anything?'

'I'll be honest, Miss Janssen, I'm not at all sure I should be talking to you.'

'Why not?'

'Tell me, how long have you lived in Hong Kong?'

'Two years.'

'And will you stay after the handover?'

'I don't know. Why?'

'Do you think it will be safe then? When China takes over?'

'I don't know. I guess so.' Emma wondered where he was going with this.

'You're a Westerner. A *gweilo*. You've got your British passport and I suppose you can just get up and go whenever you like. Whenever you need to. Hong Kong is just a passing phase of your life.' He paused and looked directly at Emma. 'Hong Kong was home for me. I was born there. Went to school and university there. My family are still there, so are most of my friends. In a way it is still home for me, I suppose it always will be, but I've never been back since I left.

Not even when my grandmother died and my parents wanted me to come back for the funeral. They were so angry with me when I said I couldn't. Do you understand, Miss Janssen?'

'Yes,' said Emma, not really sure that she did.

'Miss Janssen, I need to know whether I can trust you or not.'

'Trust me? In what way?'

'Does anybody know you've come to see me?'

'No,' said Emma. 'A few friends know I've come to Sydney, but I often come here. Nobody knows that this time I was coming to try and find you.'

'Good. Can we keep it that way?'

'Sure, no problem,' said Emma, puzzled.

'Yes, I remember Cheung Wing-ho, I spoke to him several times. Perhaps you've seen the notes I kept of my meetings with him?'

'Well, just the one interview.'

'Just one? No that's not right, I must have interviewed him five or six times. He was insistent that the police had got the wrong man, even when he pleaded guilty.'

'How could he be so sure?' asked Emma.

'He saw the pictures of Chan Wah Man in the papers and knew it wasn't the man he'd seen driving the car. It's as simple as that. He went to the police but they weren't interested. After a while they told him to stop bothering them. They threatened to arrest him for wasting their time.'

'What about Mr Chan's lawyers? Did he go to them?'

'Yes. He told me that he'd tried to speak to the solicitor but he was even less interested than the police. He was just a young legal aid lawyer. I think as far as he was concerned Chan Wah Man had confessed. He'd get his standard fee anyway. It just wasn't worth his time to follow up.'

They sat down on a bench. Office workers filled the park, enjoying lunch in the sunshine, chatting and laughing. A group of students were playing Frisbee.

'What about you?' asked Emma. 'Did you cover these doubts in a story?'

'Of course. For a young reporter like me a possible miscarriage of justice was a godsend. A chance to make my name.'

'So what happened after the story was printed?'

'That's simple. It was never printed.'

'Why on earth not?' asked Emma.

'I was given various excuses. At first the news editor was very interested, but then some Cantopop starlet had split from her boyfriend. There was a corruption case involving a local businessman. All sorts of things were considered to be more newsworthy. There was always some excuse as to why there wasn't space. But I kept pressing for the story and I must have made a nuisance of myself because in the end I was summoned to the office of the editor-in-chief. I don't think we'd so much as passed the time of day before.'

'What did he want?'

'In short I was told to drop the story if I wanted my career to go anywhere.'

'He said that?'

'Well not in those words, of course, but that was what it amounted to.' Emma could hear the bitterness in Brian's voice. She took a moment to take in the implications of what he had said. There was none of this in the papers Eric had found in the archives.

'You were silenced and your notes were destroyed?' said Emma.

'So it seems. I'm surprised some of my notes are still around. They must have been overlooked.'

'Was that why you left Hong Kong?'

'Not at first, no. Let's walk on a bit.' They started walking along a path leading towards a coffee stall. 'Can I get you something?' he asked. Emma declined and he bought himself a drink. Emma suspected he had more to say and was gathering his thoughts.

'Miss Janssen, I know this is important to you, but if you want my advice you should drop this now. Don't pursue it any further. You said yourself that you can't bring your brother back.'

'I've told you. I can't do that. You know that so why are you saying this?'

'It was only a few years ago but I am much more cynical about the world these days. Then I was young and like most new journalists very idealistic. I was angry. I told my editor that if I couldn't get my stories printed what was the point of continuing? I said I would quit and take the story somewhere else.'

'And did you?'

'I thought about it for a few days. I was torn between my principles and the practical reality that I had a good job at a major newspaper that many of my contemporaries would have killed for. In the end, though, you might say I was given a helping hand in coming to a decision.'

Emma thought he was becoming unnecessarily cryptic.

'How?' she asked.

'I was walking home one night, quite late as I'd been on an evening duty roster, when two men came up behind me. They grabbed my arms and pulled me into an alleyway, forced me against a wall. I thought I was being robbed and hoped it was just money they were after, but it wasn't a robbery at all. There was another guy in the alleyway waiting for me. He said he wanted to give me some advice. That I should drop a certain story, that I knew the story he meant, and if I didn't he knew where I lived. They suggested I might want to broaden my horizons and pursue a career abroad.'

'You were being threatened?'

'Not just me, my family as well.'

'Do you know who they were?'

'No, but they were just paid thugs. The one who spoke did so in a very vulgar rough Cantonese. No doubt they were triad members but it doesn't really matter who they were, they were just the hired mouthpiece.'

'Jesus. I'm sorry,' said Emma. 'I don't know what to say. Who do you think put them up to it?'

'I don't know, I didn't want to find out to be honest. But that was when my ideals took second place. I resigned and moved here, and haven't been back to Hong Kong since.'

They walked on a little way in silence.

'Tell me more about Cheung Wing-ho,' said Emma.

'Don't you understand what I've been saying? Just because you're a *gweilo*, it won't give you any protection.'

'Please. Tell me about him.'

'There's not a lot to say. A decent guy in his fifties. He ran a convenience store in the area.'

'Do you think he'd talk to me if I found him?' asked Emma.

Brian stopped and turned to face her. 'Not unless you know how to conduct a séance. A few weeks later he fell from a window twenty floors up. They said it was suicide.'

CHAPTER 14

THE SWAN-SHAPED PEDALO EDGED AWAY from the jetty and moved out towards the middle of the boating lake. The swan had seen better days. The white paint was peeling and it had lost one eye. The lake was crowded with families and few of them had much control over their direction of travel. The two passengers on this particular bird were trying to keep the vessel in a straight line while watching out for any errant swans that might be heading their way. When they reached a good distance from the edge of the lake they stopped pedalling and let the swan bob and drift, only taking evasive action when a collision seemed possible.

'Every time we meet you surprise me,' said Susan. 'Always a new adventure.'

'I like to keep things fresh,' said her companion. 'So, you wanted to talk? Has something happened? Have you been able to get in to his office?'

'Not yet no, but I will soon. Leave that to me.'

'Then what is it?'

'I wanted to ask you something. I wanted to ask you a favour.' Susan, nervous, paused, but when he said nothing in reply she was forced to continue. 'Would it be possible to find out what happened to a child who was adopted during the Great Famine? I say adopted, but sold would be a more accurate description.'

'Sold? By the parents?'

'His mother, yes.'

'Well, my dear, that's not something I get asked every day. Before I come to the "why", what information do you have about this person?'

'I can get you the name, age, home village and the year.'

'We're drifting back to the shore. Let's move out again.' They pedalled for a few minutes in silence. 'You know how incomplete the records are?'

'Of course, but assuming what I'm looking for is in the records somewhere, do we have the ability to find out?'

'In principle, yes. Now on to the "why". Why do you need this information?'

'If I'm honest, I don't know that I do. But Kwok-wah would like it and I'd like to be able to give it to him.'

'Is this his price?'

'No. He hasn't asked for it, and anyway, I don't think I'm going to need to ask him to help. At least no more than he has unwittingly helped already. I'd just like to be able to give this to him.'

'Is it a family member?'

'No. It's the son of the old woman who looks after the building where Kwok-wah lives. He's very fond of her and knows it would mean a lot to her.'

'Susan, we're not talking sentiment here, are we?'

She flinched at his cold tone of voice. 'Ah, the S-word,' she said. 'I know, I shouldn't have any. I know I've no right to ask this.'

'Let me get this straight. You want me to risk an asset for something like that? Just to get information – which, by the way, may not even exist – for you to give to your young man so he can be kind to an old woman? Without any operational benefit or justification whatsoever? You do realise just how crazy that is? What's more – how do you plan on giving this information to him? How are you going to explain to him where it came from?'

'I don't know.'

'It's madness and completely against all the rules. Even this meeting is a quite unnecessary risk. I'm disappointed in you, Susan.'

'I know I've no right to ask. It was just … never mind. Forget I asked. Let's go back to the shore and pretend we never had this conversation.' Susan knew he was right in every regard and was embarrassed with herself for even asking. She hoped her faux pas wouldn't be reported back to her boss. They were silent as they pedalled the swan back to the jetty and returned it to the old man who was in charge of the fleet that afternoon.

'God, I'm getting as bad as you, young lady,' said Susan's companion. 'This sentiment crap must be contagious. Get me the information on the target, and I'll think about it. Just think about it, mind, no promises, and only because I'm unaccountably fond of you.'

***

'She's after something and it isn't your dick.'

Kwok-wah was waiting for Susan in the cafeteria and Zhanyuan's words from their argument still haunted him. The two of them had almost come to blows and probably would have if Li Lao hadn't intervened. Kwok-wah was angry at the insult, to both himself and Susan, but what nagged at him during the night, what stopped him from sleeping in the early hours, was the question that annoyed him like a persistent mosquito: *What if Zhanyuan was right?* Kwok-wah couldn't imagine what Susan saw in him when she must have the pick of admirers back in California. He was flattered, of course he was, but what could she possibly want from him? What did he have that she might be after? Other than an ability to fix laptops, Kwok-wah couldn't think of anything he had to offer.

Susan arrived and joined Kwok-wah at the table he had chosen. A table in as quiet a corner as was possible in the busy cafeteria. Kwok-wah stood when Susan arrived – he had been well-taught by his parents – and she kissed him on the cheek. They exchanged pleasantries and talked about their studies, but it was soon obvious to Susan that Kwok-wah wasn't really listening.

'Of course,' she said, 'when the spaceship lands things will be very different.'

'Yes.'

'And when ET takes over …'

'Yes … sorry, what?'

'Phone home, Kwok-wah, phone home. I knew you weren't listening to me. What's the matter? Is something wrong? Something bothering you?'

'Sorry, Susan – no, nothing's wrong. Not really. It's just that one of the guys in my dorm has been talking about us.'

'Who?'

'Zhanyuan – I don't know if you know him.'

'Only by reputation. Some of the girls I know have come across him. But what's he been saying?'

'Nothing I could repeat in front of you,' said Kwok-wah. 'He's very crude.'

'I see.'

They were both quiet for a couple of minutes while they picked at their food. It was Susan who broke the silence in the end.

'Does it bother you? Being talked about?' she asked.

'I'm just not used to it, I guess. I've never been the subject of gossip before. Mind you, I've never known someone as good looking as you before.'

Susan laughed. A genuine unforced laugh that surprised everybody on the neighbouring tables so that they stopped what they were doing and looked at Kwok-wah and Susan.

'Sorry,' said Susan when she had calmed down. 'I didn't mean to laugh like that, but really ... you're such a charmer. Like they don't say, flattery will get you everywhere, y'know.'

'I ...' Kwok-wah began.

'I think I know what the problem is,' she said, sparing Kwok-wah the embarrassment of continuing with whatever he was going to say. 'You shouldn't run yourself down, y'know? Zhanyuan is just jealous. Like I said, he's tried it on with a few girls I know and always been turned down because he's a cocky little so-and-so who's too full of himself.'

'Perhaps. Take no notice of me. I'm just being stupid.' Kwok-wah relaxed, feeling more comfortable than he had been earlier.

'I think it's sweet,' said Susan. 'Look, I've got lectures this afternoon, but why don't we go do something later? How about that new gelato place we saw on Nanjing Road? Are you going to be in the department this afternoon?'

'Yes, I expect so.'

'Good. I'll come and meet you there after class.'

After lunch Susan sat at the back of the lecture theatre. It was as good a place as any to sit and think. Alarm bells were ringing in her head. She knew who Zhanyuan was and who his father was. She had been worried about him ever since she had discovered he was in Kwok-wah's dorm. She hoped it was just sexual jealousy but couldn't rely on that. She had to consider the possibility that time was running out. She would have to act fast before it was too late.

***

Susan gave the guard on the computer science building one of her most winning smiles. He repulsed her. He was overweight and had a prominent wart just above his upper lip, but she made a point of flirting with him every time she came to the department. Susan needed the guard to feel comfortable letting her into the building; if he made her wait for Kwok-wah to collect her at the entrance, she'd have no other reason to go inside. Her efforts over the weeks had clearly been successful and he waved her past with a gap-toothed smile that was no doubt meant to be endearing but only caused Susan to flinch inwardly. Even from a safe distance she could smell his body odour and his breath. The things she had to do; dating Kwok-wah was a positive joy in comparison.

'Hi there, handsome,' she said to Kwok-wah in Cantonese. 'I've been practising,' she continued in English. 'I should learn more Cantonese, then we could say what we like and nobody round here would have a clue what we were on about.'

'Your accent's good,' said Kwok-wah when he had recovered his composure. 'I'm nearly finished, if you just give me a minute or two.'

'No problem, I need to go to the bathroom anyway.'

'You know where it is?'

'Down the corridor then right at the end?'

'Yes.'

'Won't be long.' Susan slung her bag over her shoulder and headed down the corridor. When she reached the end she checked that nobody was behind her and then turned left. She'd been that way before on a previous visit when she had deliberately got lost looking for the toilet. In fact, over the weeks Susan had explored most of the department while trying to find the bathroom. Anybody more suspicious than Kwok-wah might have thought she had a bladder problem. She counted the number of windows she passed until at the expected point she came to a door that opened on to a stairwell connecting the floors at the back of the building. The number of dead cockroaches on the stairs suggested nobody had been that way recently. She paused for a moment and listened for footsteps. When she heard nothing she skipped down one flight to the first floor where the stairs opened out onto a small landing with two doors. One of the doors had a *Fire Escape* sign confirming that Susan had found what she was looking for, and she assumed the other door led to a corridor on the first floor matching the one on the floor above.

Susan took a small rubber wedge from her bag and used it to jam closed the door to the corridor. It wouldn't be enough to stop it from opening, but on the off-chance someone wanted to come through it would at least give her a moment's warning. Turning her attention to the fire escape, she was encouraged to find it was a standard design; a simple push-bar linked to a single vertical rod locked the door in place. Susan pressed on the bar to release the rod and then pushed the door open a few inches. Looking through the gap, she checked that, as she thought, the door opened onto the external staircase that led down to the rear garden. She allowed the door to close again while keeping the push-bar in the unlocked position. From a distance everything looked normal. If anybody looked closely they would see the door wasn't locked, but Susan had to hope that nobody checked the fire escape that frequently. The cockroaches suggested that this was not an unreasonable hope. Anyway, it didn't have to be for long. After retrieving her rubber wedge, she headed back to Kwok-wah.

'You okay?' he asked. 'You've been a while.'

'It always takes us girls longer, y'know. Just one of those mysteries that men will never understand. Come on, let's get going.'

***

This time it was later when Susan left the dorm, and her room-mates were all sleeping. One of them was snoring, and together with the sound of heavy rain this helped mask any noise Susan made. With the rain it was darker than before and she took a moment to allow her eyes to adjust and to calm her nerves. She'd done this kind of thing countless times in training, but this was the first time for real, where the stakes were more than just a rap on the knuckles from her instructors. She could have done without the rain. It had started earlier in the evening when she was sharing an ice cream with Kwok-wah, but now it seemed like a bad omen and only increased her anxiety, even though the rational part of her knew the rain would be a help; for a start, it would reduce the chance of her encountering anyone else.

Susan retraced the route she took previously. This time there were no shadows to hide in, but there were no signs of any patrols either. She stopped to check on the guards at the computer science department. The same two. One of them was reading a magazine while the other had his head down on the table either asleep or drunk. Again Susan worked her way round to the rear, making a better job than before of finding her way through the vegetation. She took a moment to check that nobody was around. From the back of the building she could see a light in one of the rooms on the second floor. Susan watched for a while but there was no sign of anyone or any suggestion of movement in the room; the light must have been left on by accident, at least she hoped so, but as a precaution she made a mental note of where that room was.

She climbed the fire escape to the first floor and tried the fire door. This was the first critical moment. The first thing not under her control. If the door had been locked again then she was stuck with no alternative plan. The door opened. She slipped inside, stopping the door from swinging shut behind her and allowing it to close gently. Quietly. She stood on the stairwell landing where she had been only a few hours ago. It hadn't been so frightening then. She took a moment to let her eyes adjust to the dark, to allow her breath to quieten and her heart to relax. She listened for human sounds. The sound of rain made it difficult to be certain, but there was nothing obvious. Standing still Susan felt the rainwater dripping off her onto the floor, and she realised her trainers were muddy from the wet ground. *Damn,* she thought, knowing she mustn't leave an obvious trail of footprints, grateful at least that she'd noticed in time. That would have been a rookie mistake. She looked for somewhere to put her shoes where they wouldn't be seen in the unlikely event that someone should come this way. Nowhere seemed suitable so she had no choice other than to open the fire escape door again and leave the shoes outside. *Great, I'll have soaking wet feet later.*

She climbed the stairs to the next floor and stood by the door to the corridor and listened. Nothing. She opened the door a couple of inches and looked through the narrow gap. Nothing. She listened again. Still nothing. As confident as she could be that nobody was around, but not feeling confident at all, Susan opened the door fully and stepped out into the corridor, again taking care to stop the door from banging shut behind her. Light was spilling out from one office further down the corridor, the room she had seen from outside, but she realised that thankfully she didn't have to go past the light. Instead she turned right and made her way towards Kwok-wah's room in her stockinged feet. There was less light here and she laughed to herself as she wished she'd asked him to leave a light on for her. She did have a torch but decided against using it. Her previous visits to the department were paying dividends; she knew the layout of the floor as well as anyone and found Professor Ye's office with no difficulty.

Susan tried the door just in case (*You never know*) but it was indeed locked, so she took out the copied stolen keys from her pocket. Most were obviously the wrong type at a glance, but there were still several candidates. *I'm screwed if none of these work.* The fourth key worked, the lock turned and she opened the door and went in, closing the door behind her. She didn't dare turn on a light but this time she did use her torch. The window had a blind that she drew closed to be on the safe side, though she knew the guards couldn't see the window from their room. She looked around. It was much as she had expected from Kwok-wah's description. Shelves of textbooks, piles of papers on every spare surface. There was a computer, which she considered turning on, but doing so would make more noise than she was happy with and, anyway, surely Professor Ye of all people would have set a password. The computer would be her last resort.

The desk drawers turned out to be unlocked and Susan quickly went through them finding nothing of interest, except in one drawer where she found a pornographic magazine and a photograph of a familiar looking young woman; a woman who was not the one in the silver-framed wedding photograph that sat on the desk. *Interesting*. Something to come back to later perhaps. Finished with the desk, she turned to the two filing cabinets in the corner of the room, which seemed to be more likely prospects. They were both locked and none of her keys were the right type. Obviously Professor Ye didn't trust his secretary with these cabinets, a fact that encouraged her, but they were only standard commercial filing cabinets; she learnt how to pick those in her first month of training and within five minutes they were both open.

Susan pulled out folders to examine. *What am I looking for?* She didn't really know. Not exactly, anyway. She hoped it would be one of those things that jumped out at her when she saw it. The first files she looked at turned out to be research papers, some that had been published, others still in preparation, but there was nothing out of the ordinary in any of them. She knew more about Professor Ye's work than Kwok-wah could have imagined, possibly even more than Kwok-wah himself. There were files on each of his students. She skimmed through most of them but looked more closely at the one on Kwok-wah. It didn't tell Susan anything she didn't already know, but she was interested to read Professor Ye's comments that academically Kwok-wah was nothing special but that *'a friend in Hong Kong may be useful one day'.*

While Susan examined folder after folder, one part of her was still on alert and she stopped when she heard footsteps in the corridor outside the office. She turned off her torch and stood still. She hoped the sound of her heart beating was not as loud the other side of the door as it was in her ears. The footsteps came closer but then receded. Based on previous observations she knew she'd have at least an hour before the guard did another round. *Plenty of time. Hopefully.*

In the end, it took her another forty minutes to find what she was looking for. An unmarked folder of correspondence, technical proposals, procurement requests. She took out a small camera, turned on the desk lamp (*No choice*) and speed read the papers as she photographed them. She didn't understand every detail, some of the technical language in Chinese was beyond her, but enough to get the gist. When she finished she replaced the folder and decided she had time to return to the photograph in the desk drawer. Why was the face so familiar? It had been bothering her. Susan was sure she should know who it was. Looking at the picture again it still took a moment before recognition kicked in; the woman was a well-known news anchor on Shanghai TV, in her mid-twenties and a regular on the celebrity circuit. *Very interesting.* Also in the drawer was a black appointment diary that Susan had missed the first time. On an impulse, she decided to take it with her, figuring it would be thought lost rather than stolen.

Time to leave. Susan took a last look round the office in case she has missed anything, but nothing else seemed remarkable. It was time to make a move but the guard hadn't yet been back on his round (*He must be due soon surely?*) so Susan decided to wait until she has heard him pass. A wise decision, as it was only a couple of minutes before there were footsteps. Once more they came closer before fading into the distance. When all was quiet again she looked around the office one last time, making sure everything was left as it was, and then left, remembering to lock the door behind her.

Susan made her way back to the stairwell and saw that the room where the light had been was now in darkness. *Did the guard turn it off or had someone been there?* She hurried down the one flight of stairs to the fire escape only to find that the door was closed with the bolt in place. *Shit.* That wasn't supposed to have happened. Not part of the plan at all. Adrenalin took over and her heart began to race. She stopped for a moment, knowing this was when she needed to be in control of her emotions. *Calm down, Susan. There's no sign of anybody around.* She pushed the bar down to unlock the door again and slowly, very carefully, she pushed the door open while saying a silent prayer as she did so. To her relief there was nobody on the other side and her shoes were where she left them. *What are the odds of someone, just now – in the middle of the night – noticing that the fire escape wasn't closed properly?* The answer didn't really matter, she was where she was and there was nothing she could do about it now.

It was still raining. She put on her shoes and in her fear didn't notice how wet they were.

CHAPTER 15

'CAN I COME ROUND TONIGHT?' Emma had rung Sam the Sunday morning after getting back from Sydney. 'We need to talk. At least, I need to talk. Somewhere private.'

Sam had been surprised when she called him; he was far from sure she would. Following that night at the Fringe Club he had lost himself in work, spending most of his time in the office. Kate had taken him for lunch the Saturday immediately after, but she had a date of her own that night. His emotions were all over the place and they included more than a little anger. He wasn't proud of that but the Fringe Club had been, or at least should have been, a special night, and it had been ruined. Above all, though, his dominant feeling was one of complete confusion. He went over all the conversations he'd had with Emma, trying to remember anything he might have said to upset her. Or for that matter anything he hadn't said but should have. Nothing stood out. Nothing at all.

I'm just so alone. Sam could still hear those words and the desperate tone they'd been said in, but he was no closer to making any sense of them. Emma seemed to have plenty of friends. He knew she had split with her fiancé before coming to Hong Kong, but that was two and a bit years ago. Was she really still thinking of him? Sam and Emma may only have been dating for a few weeks, but the way Emma had kissed him after that Italian in SoHo surely meant something?

They agreed she would come round that evening for dinner. Sam spent the morning tidying the flat to make it presentable, wishing for once that he had a maid. In the afternoon he went shopping to get the ingredients for lasagne; one of the few things he could cook really well – his signature dish. He found the preparation therapeutic and listened to Coltrane while he worked; making the roux and the béchamel took his mind off worrying about what Emma wanted to talk about. He couldn't imagine it was going to be anything good. He remembered being dumped in London. As the evening approached he lit some candles, and then the doorbell rang.

Emma looked tired. He'd even go as far as to say weary, more than simply the effects of the flight. He would be the first to admit he wasn't the most empathetic of people, but even to him it was as if she had the troubles of the world on her shoulders. Her hair was tied back in a ponytail and Sam could see she was using her hearing aid, something he knew she only did when necessary, and then usually only in private, rarely in public. Seeing her like that Sam felt his anger evaporating. Tonight she was a combination of highly desirable and vulnerable at the same time.

'Hi Sam. Are you going to invite me in?'

Sam realised he had been standing silently like an idiot, momentarily lost for words. 'Of course, sorry, come in.'

'Something smells good.'

'Lasagne. I hope that's okay?'

'Of course. A man who can cook, I'm impressed.' Emma looked around. 'And a man who can clean.'

Emma shook off her shoes before making herself comfortable on the couch, while Sam poured a couple of glasses of wine.

'How was Sydney?' he asked.

Emma ignored his question. 'How long until dinner is ready?'

'Thirty minutes or so. Are you hungry?'

'No, it's not that, I'd like to talk to you before we eat. Explain things. Apologise. We'll enjoy the evening more when I get this off my chest.'

'It's only lasagne, it can keep warm if necessary.' Sam sat down next to her. He was still confused but her words were promising. Perhaps things were going to be okay after all. Emma had some of her wine and then put the glass down and turned to face Sam.

'First of all I have to apologise for the Fringe Club. You were terrific, I let you down.'

'I'm sure …' Sam started to say before Emma stopped him.

'Please, Sam, let me say my bit. Hopefully you'll understand then. You asked me once about my family, I think it was that time in Tai Mei Tuk after we'd been hiking. You asked about brothers or sisters and I said that I didn't have any. That was true but not the whole story. I did have a brother, an older brother, but he was killed.' Sam started to speak but again Emma stopped him. 'Please. This is difficult for me to talk about. He – Peter – was killed in a hit-and-run in Wan Chai back in 1992.' Emma paused and took another sip of wine.

'Was anybody caught?'

'Yes, and jailed, and I thought that was the end of it, and until recently it was.' Emma told Sam the full story: her suspicions, what she had learnt and why she had gone to Sydney.

'I don't know what to say,' said Sam when Emma had finished. 'What are you going to do now?'

'I have no idea. I seem to be at a dead end. It may be there's nothing more I can do. I need to think about that some more, but I needed to tell you this. It was time I told you. Well if I'm honest with myself, I guess I should have told you before. I'm sorry now I didn't. Really sorry.'

'You and Peter must have been very close?'

'Very. I don't think I could explain just how close. The thing is, Peter also played the saxophone, and it sounds stupid but hearing you play at the Fringe just brought everything flooding back.'

'I wish you'd told me this before.'

'I know. Like I said, I should have, I'm really sorry, but it's not something I find easy to talk about. Most of my friends don't know. I can't explain why, I don't really understand it myself, but it's something I prefer to keep quiet about. Perhaps I don't want to be pitied or felt sorry for. I don't know.'

'So when you said you were lonely and you missed him, you were talking about Peter? Not your fiancé?'

'Mike?!' Emma laughed in surprise. 'Certainly not. You didn't think I meant him, did you?'

'Well …'

'But do you understand now? It still doesn't excuse my behaviour, nothing does, but does it sort of explain it? You must have hated me.'

'Hate, no. Upset, yes, and confused. I couldn't work it out. I thought there must have been something I'd said or done, or not done. Now I'm not sure quite what to think. I'm relieved it wasn't me – well, more than just relieved, but I can't be too happy knowing what you've been through and … I'm perhaps also a little upset that you didn't think you could tell me this?'

'If I could turn the clock back, I would. I can't explain it.'

'Come here.'

Emma moved closer and Sam took her in his arms. They kissed, uncertainly at first and not quite in sync as they rediscovered each other, and then with increasing abandon as Emma lay back and Sam plucked up the courage to let a hand find its way under her dress.

'You're not quite as shy as I thought you were,' said Emma. 'Does this mean I'm forgiven?'

'Nothing to forgive.' They kissed again until Sam realised the curtains weren't drawn and they were putting on a performance for the world to see. 'I should close the curtains,' he said.

***

Emma stood over the road from the Xinhua building in Wan Chai. There was a nominative irony that the de facto communist embassy was located on Queen's Road East opposite the Queen Elizabeth Stadium. The weather was cool for March and she held a small umbrella to shield her from the light drizzle that had started to fall. The building itself was completely unremarkable and there was nothing to distinguish it from any other office building other than the discreet nameplate by the door. It would be easy to imagine that it was the head office of a small trading company. Perhaps a business that imported cheap household goods from China before sending them round the world.

Emma wasn't completely sure what she was doing there. She didn't know what she hoped to achieve, but talking it over with Sam the night before it was the only thing they could think of. The trail led to Xinhua so she had to follow it, but now she was there, standing across the road on a damp Monday morning, second thoughts and doubts were not just creeping in; they were shouting at her to turn round and go home. Forget this obsession; concentrate on enjoying the here and now, her future with Sam. And what if Brian Lo was right? Would she be in danger if she pursued this any further? Sam had offered to come with her but Emma felt a single woman was less suspicious. She was glad she had explained everything to him last night, that she had someone she could trust and confide in, relieved he hadn't sounded sceptical or doubtful. She didn't understand why she hadn't told him before; why she insisted on keeping everything to herself. She certainly wasn't doing herself any favours that way. Perhaps it was something she could work on changing.

In the meantime here she was, opposite Xinhua, plucking up courage to cross the road and go inside. What was she thinking? As Sam had pointed out, it was unlikely Gao Zhihua was still working there. Even without anything happening that might precipitate an early departure, Xinhua staff were probably rotated anyway. Nor did she have any idea of what position he had held when he was there, and anyway, in the exceedingly unlikely event that he was still working there, what was she going to do? What if the receptionist actually said *'Yes of course, one moment, I'll get him for you'*? Would she be able to look him in the face or would she turn and run? But still, what else could she do? She had no other link to Peter's killer beyond where he worked, and *'Peter's killer'* was how she thought of him now. She was certain of that much.

A knot of anxiety was growing and Emma was starting to feel sick. She had decided on a cover story: she was a student doing a dissertation on the role of Xinhua in pre-handover Hong Kong and had been given Gao Zhihua's name as someone she should talk to. If, as was likely, it turned out Gao Zhihua was no longer there, she would simply say that she must have been mistaken, apologise for the inconvenience and leave. She was wearing her hearing aid and could always use that as an excuse if need be. Emma decided she would count to ten and then come what may she would cross the road and go in. After all, what was the worst that could happen? They'd simply ask her to leave. Unless, of course, the worst thing that could happen was that he might still be there after all.

She got as far as eight when her eye was caught by a momentary glimpse of a man leaving the Xinhua building before her view was blocked by a passing bus. A young Chinese man, uncharacteristically tall. Wasn't that Liang-bao? Emma pressed the button on the pedestrian crossing and waited impatiently for the signal to change. Once across she walked briskly in the direction the man had gone, but the delay had been too long and whoever it had been was now lost in the crowds.

***

'But you did go in, in the end?' asked Sam. They were back in his flat later that day. Emma had been recounting her visit to Xinhua, their conversation accompanied by the sound of a child crying from across the corridor.

'Yes. Eventually. I finally forced myself to go in. But it was much as you said it would be. There was nobody with that name working there. The receptionist obviously didn't recognise the name at all, but she was only young and had probably only been there a short while. So, a dead end.'

'But at least you tried.' Sam stroked her forearm. 'Do you think it was Liang-bao?'

'I don't suppose so.' Emma had been worrying about this all evening. Why on earth would Liang-bao be visiting Xinhua? She had told herself she must have been mistaken. 'There was just something about the man's height and build, but I only got the briefest of looks.'

'So what are you going to do next? About Peter.'

'I don't know. I could ask some of the group if they have any ideas. I don't know if any of them have any contacts in China who might know where Gao Zhihua went to, what he's doing now. But I still don't think I want to tell them about Peter. Yannie knows, of course, but she's promised to keep it quiet. And anyway, even if they did know something, so what? What would I do? I've no real evidence, and like everybody keeps telling me, nobody is going to be interested in reopening something that was settled years ago. I think the only thing that matters is that I've done the best I can for Peter and at least I know what really happened that night.'

'Have you told your parents any of this?'

'No, not yet.'

'Are you going to?'

Emma hesitated before answering. 'I don't know. I think probably not. It will only bring back bad memories for no real purpose. But I did speak to them last night after getting back to my place.' Her face brightened. 'And I told them I wasn't coming back for Easter, so we can spend it together.'

'You told them about me?'

'Well … no.' Emma looked sheepish. 'If I did that they'd be planning the wedding. I just said I didn't have the money for the flight, which after Sydney isn't far wrong.'

'I think my mum's greatest ambition in life is to be able to say the words "my daughter-in-law". Anyway, what would you like to do at Easter? Any thoughts?'

'I was wondering about going away somewhere. Not far, I really can't afford much, perhaps Macau? We could go, stay over and have lunch somewhere, then come back?'

'I'll see what I can organise.'

Emma looked at her watch and saw that it was gone ten. 'I should be making a move. I'm working tomorrow.' She saw the look of disappointment on Sam's face. 'Next weekend you can have me all to yourself.'

Things were well again. This time nothing was going to get in the way.

CHAPTER 16

'THIS IS MORE CONVENTIONAL THAN usual,' said Susan to her companion. 'If I'm honest I'm a little disappointed. I was hoping for something a bit more out of the ordinary.' They were in a room on the twenty-first floor of an anonymous mid-range Pudong hotel. The carpet was beige, the curtains brown. A strong smell of cigarettes seemed to be ingrained in the fabric of the room, and the curtains looked as if they might once have been a different colour. Susan was sitting on the edge of a not particularly clean bed. Her companion had taken the room at short notice so he thought it should be clear, but he checked anyway and drew the curtains as a precaution.

'I rather got the impression that it was urgent, my dear. And again, it's not an unusual place for an older man to meet a young woman. At least so my straight friends tell me.'

'It is – urgent, I mean.'

'I assume you have news for me? Good or bad?'

'Both. Which do you want first?'

'Good, I think. Do you want something?' He was exploring the minibar.

'Something strong.'

'That's not like you,' he said, finding two miniatures of whisky and a can of ginger ale. He looked at the label on the whisky and frowned. He mixed two drinks and passed one to Susan before taking a seat in a faded armchair. He turned on the TV with the volume fairly high. 'So? What do you have for me?'

'Here's what you wanted.' Susan took a roll of film from her bag and placed it on the bed. 'It's all there.'

'Excellent work. Quick precis?'

'He's developing software that will be encrypted and preloaded onto mobile phones. If anyone has one of those phones, it will be possible to hack in and monitor anything they do or say. Who they call, message, everything. They also hope to be able to record conversations when the phone is switched on even if the phone isn't in use. It will just be a microphone picking everything up. The user won't even know it's happening. The information will just be automatically sent back to Shanghai. It's all in there. Details of the PLA intelligence units that will run the hacking. How they plan to deploy the technology. The funding. Everything. You'll need to get this to Hong Kong as well. They'll need to know.'

'Excellent, my dear. I knew I could count on you to come through. How far advanced are they?'

'They're not there yet. They need the new facilities and new equipment that's being planned. I'm guessing it could be a couple of years still before they can begin hacking people. But I don't need to tell you that once they start something they're certain to finish it. It's a matter of when, not if. Oh, and I almost forgot. He's having an affair.'

'Who is?'

'Professor Ye.'

'Really?'

'Better than that, it's with a TV news anchor. The one who's on TV1 in the morning. I also stole his diary.' Susan took the diary out of her bag and passed it to him. 'I've had a look through it. It's a social diary – nothing to do with his work – but he's been seeing her for several months now. I don't see how he could afford a mistress like that on a university salary. She must be very high maintenance. He's presumably getting money from the PLA.'

Her companion was looking through the diary. 'Expensive restaurants, I see. I don't know. The PLA doesn't normally pay that well either. You're supposed to work for them out of love of the Party and the Motherland. Well, that and the fear of a bullet in the back of the head. I do hope he's not siphoning off university funds, or worse still, PLA money intended for the project. Now that would be risky ...'

'Surely he wouldn't be that stupid, would he?' asked Susan.

'You never know. Men sometimes do the strangest things for beautiful women. Apparently. I wouldn't know myself. I suppose the other possibility is that they know all about the affair. Perhaps they even initiated it so they had something on him? It could be a useful way to control the good professor. But that works both ways, of course. I wonder if we could do the same thing? I don't normally watch the local TV, to be honest. It's all too noisy and hectoring. But I must find out more about this woman.' He fell silent, waiting for Susan to continue. She downed her drink in one go.

'I may need out.'

'Are they on to you?'

'I think so. I don't know for certain but there have been warning signs.'

'A pity. I'm sure there's more you could get if you stayed there. Close to your young man. If you just vanish without warning, then if they were watching you they'll know for sure.'

'But we've got everything we need, haven't we? What more is there to get?'

'If you go now we'll never know. We don't know what we don't know, if you see what I mean. And what about Kwok-wah? What is he going to think if you just disappear off the face of the earth? More to the point, what will they think about him if you leave suspiciously? Have you thought about that? I can't make you stay, that was the deal, but can I persuade you to stick it out for just a little longer? I'll get everything prepared so we can get you out of the country quickly if we need to. Perhaps you should prepare a cover story as well?

You might want to drop hints about sick parents or something.'

Susan was not keen on the idea of staying on. If she was honest with herself she was scared, but she wouldn't risk admitting that. She was conscious that as one of her first overseas assignments it wouldn't look good if she bailed out too quickly. Plus, his warnings about Kwok-wah had hit a chord. If she left suddenly suspicions could fall on him. What would they think about him? Would they think he was involved? Perhaps if she stayed on and played it carefully for a few weeks, not going near the computer science department, she could keep an eye on Zhanyuan. It wasn't long until the end of term. She could stay until then at least.

'Okay, you win. I'll stay. For the time being anyway. I'll keep a low profile for a while until I can get a better sense of whether they know about me or not.' Susan reached into her bag one more time and pulled out an envelope. 'We had an agreement. In here is the name of a young man who was sold by his mother in Liaoning in 1960. There's his date of birth, the names of his parents, and the village he lived in.' She passed the envelope to him.

'What other surprises do you have in that bag? A rabbit? I'm a man of my word so I'll see what I can do, but you know I can't promise anything. It's going to take quite a while as well so don't expect anything back too quickly.'

***

'This is really not good enough, Mr Yang. Quite unacceptable.' Professor Ye threw the papers back across the desk. Sheaves of paper scattered and fell in different directions and Kwok-wah scrabbled around to gather them. 'What have you been doing the last six months? Your literature review is superficial and the preliminary data completely unreliable.' He was shouting now. Kwok-wah had never heard him like this before.

'I'm sorry, I … I didn't think the results were that bad?'

'No, you're right. You didn't think. Never mind being sorry, you need to get some serious meaningful work done and stop wasting your time here. Otherwise clear off back to Hong Kong. Now why don't you just get out of my sight.'

Kwok-wah closed the door behind him in a state of shock. The departmental secretary looked up from her desk. There was no doubt she must have heard. Most of the department would have heard.

'Don't take it personally,' she said under her breath. 'He's been like that with everyone today. I don't know what the matter is. He was fine when he came in this morning but since then he's been slamming drawers, shouting and swearing at everybody. He's …' She stopped as Professor Ye came out of his office.

'Did I ask you to gossip with my secretary, Mr Yang?'

'No, sorry, I'll … be going.' Kwok-wah hurried down the corridor to his office as fast as he could without actually running. He had no idea what had just happened. The storm had come without warning. His results had been reasonable, he thought. It was only early days but he felt he was making progress. His literature review, well, it was only a first draft but Kwok-wah had been pleased with it. He knew it needed polishing but even so, it didn't deserve that sort of response. He sat at his desk, staring at the papers in front of him but unable to take anything in.

He wanted to see Susan. One of her classmates had sent him a message saying she had some sort of bug and was laid up in her room. He also wanted to be back home. He decided to make plans to go back to Hong Kong for a break. He had started to dream about proper Cantonese *dim sum*. Hong Kong milk tea. He wanted to play basketball with his old school friends. See the latest Jackie Chan film. He longed to see Susan. Take the ferry to Cheung Chau for seafood. Go hiking. Spend time with his parents, his cousin. Waste away a Saturday afternoon seeing what was new in the computer shops in Shamshuipo. Go fishing for squid off Sai Kung. Mess about on a Lantau beach. He wanted to sing in a Tsimshatsui karaoke bar. He wanted to sleep in his own bedroom.

He ached to see Susan.

***

Kwok-wah heard the sirens from the library. He took no notice at first. They weren't unusual given the nearby hospital and the ambulances and emergency vehicles that often tore along the elevated expressway at speed.

Just part of the city soundscape that he absorbed without paying any attention. But when the sirens became louder, closer, and it was obvious that they were somewhere on the campus, he took more notice. Was there a fire? Had someone been taken sick? Curiously, the possibility that they might be police didn't occur to him. When he was sure there was nothing wrong in the library itself, he put any thought of the sirens to one side and went back to his work, until the level of nearby conversations slowly increased to the point they couldn't be ignored. The normal quiet bookish murmurings and whispers had become steadily louder until all library conventions had vanished and everyone except Kwok-wah had put their books to one side and were talking about the police and what on earth they were doing at the university.

When work became impossible Kwok-wah left the library to try and find out what was happening. Crowds of students were milling around and the rumours were already spreading. There had been a fight between two men over a woman. One of the cafeteria cooks was wanted for theft. They were searching for drugs. This last explanation was the story Kwok-wah was told when he came across Li Lao, and it soon became the established version that everyone accepted, though nobody could have said why and nobody knew anyone who took drugs anyway.

'Apparently they've been searching all the women's dorms,' Li Lao said.

'Not the men's?' Kwok-wah was puzzled. If anybody

had drugs – which was unlikely – surely it would be a man?

'So it seems.'

Kwok-wah wanted to go and find Susan to see if she knew what was going on, but the police were keeping everybody away from that part of the campus. From a distance he could see three police cars and two vans parked in front of Susan's building. He watched as police began to disperse the students and most of them slowly disappeared into the late afternoon. He had no idea why but a feeling of cold dread and sickening foreboding started to spread through him. She was in trouble. He remembered all the things Zhanyuan had said about her. He knew something was wrong, horribly wrong, but he also knew there was nothing he could do. He should go back to the library or his room, but he felt as if leaving his lookout was abandoning Susan and he had to stay to keep her safe. As if he could keep disaster away by the act of keeping guard for her. He moved away a little to keep the police happy but still found a spot where he could see what was happening. But he couldn't keep her safe and after he had been watching for an hour he saw several women being led from the building and into the back of one of the police vans. One of them was clearly taller than the others. Her hair in a ponytail.

The next few days were hell. The other women taken away by the police had all come back, but not Susan. He scarcely slept and couldn't do any work. His be-loved algorithms seemed an irrelevance. Most of the department looked at him askance and largely ignored him. Zhanyuan was quiet and didn't say much, but Kwok-wah more than once caught him looking his way with an irritatingly smug expression that said 'I told you'. Li Lao was more sympathetic but didn't seem to know what to say so he mostly kept away. Kwok-wah tried speaking to Susan's room-mates but none of them wanted to talk to him. They certainly didn't want to talk about Susan. A collective amnesia was settling in and Kwok-wah suspected that soon they would deny having known Susan at all. Before long it was as though she had never been at the university in the first place; almost as if she had never existed. Had he imagined her? Had he dreamt her?

After six days it was Granny Sun who broke the silence. She called out to Kwok-wah one morning as he was leaving the building.

'Xiaoyang. Come and have some tea.' Kwok-wah was in no mood for work and didn't need any encouragement to skip a seminar and join Granny Sun. She gestured for him to take her single chair. Neither of them spoke while she made the tea. When it was ready she poured two cups and took her seat on the bed. 'So,' she said at last, 'your young woman has gone.' It was a simple statement of fact.

'So it seems.'

'You've heard nothing, I suppose?'

'No, nothing. When I ask people who knew her they clam up. It's ridiculous. These are people who only last week were laughing and joking with her. They shared a room. Now they don't even want to hear her name. I'm just so angry with them. Do they think I'm stupid or something?'

'No Xiaoyang, but it's not ridiculous. It's perfectly sensible. It's their survival mechanism. It's how it is here. You do what you need to do to survive. These young women are thinking about the rest of their lives, not the here and now. They're thinking about their studies. Getting a job later. Getting a husband. Cause trouble now, get thrown out of the university, a black mark on their record and that's it. Life over and done with before it has even started.'

'You think it's okay for them to act like that?' Kwok-wah was a little surprised at Granny Sun's attitude.

'No Xiaoyang, I don't. But I understand them. That's what you have to do in this country. We've all done it at one time or another. All I'm saying is just don't be too hard on them. Perhaps when the fuss has died down they'll talk to you about her. Quietly when nobody is listening. Don't go on at them too much now, give them a chance and see what happens.'

'I can't believe she was involved with drugs. I just can't. It doesn't make any sense.' Kwok-wah was fighting hard with himself trying not to cry. A fight he was in danger of losing. 'I never saw anything to make me think she was. And why would she be? Such a dangerous thing to do – especially here.'

'Xiaoyang, Susan came to see me two weeks ago—'

'She did?' Kwok-wah interrupted.

'Shut up and just listen to me. She sat where you're sitting now, drinking tea out of the same cup.' Kwok-wah looked at the cup as if it could tell him something.

'She seemed to me to be a good girl. I'd seen her around with you, of course, but I hadn't spoken to her before. Nothing more than a polite greeting anyway. But this time we had a good long talk. She's a nice girl, I could tell. But …' Granny Sun paused for a moment and took a sip of her tea. 'But there was something about her I couldn't put my finger on. There was something she wasn't telling me. When you get to my age you develop a sense for these things.'

'You think she was involved in drugs?' Kwok-wah couldn't believe what he was hearing.

'Drugs? No. Like you say she'd have to be an idiot and she wasn't stupid. No – it's something else but I don't know what. The thing is, we talked for quite a while, an hour or so, and when she left she said something strange.' Granny Sun broke off to give free rein to a hacking cough.

'What did she say?'

'She said,' continued the old woman, when she was ready and not before, 'that if something was to happen to her I was to tell you not to believe anything they said about her.'

Kwok-wah didn't know what was going on or what to make of this message. He was silent for a moment while he tried to work out the implications of what Granny Sun was telling him.

'She expected something like this to happen?' It wasn't really a question.

'I suppose so. I didn't really understand what she was saying at the time but now … yes, I think she must have known. The thing is, Xiaoyang, she obviously wanted you to know that whatever happened, or whatever they say happened, it wasn't true. She didn't want you to think badly of her.'

'The worst of it is I feel useless. I really want to do something. Find out where she is. Get in touch with her family. The American Embassy must know something, maybe I should speak to them?'

'You're a good boy, Xiaoyang, but take my advice: don't. Leave it be. If they don't want you to know what has happened to her there's no way you'll find out anything. You'll just be putting yourself at risk. I don't know – I must be getting soft myself in my old age – but something tells me that if you're meant to meet again, you will.'

It had started to rain and raindrops were collecting on the window before forming tracks of water that ran down the glass. Kwok-wah watched as sometimes two tracks would come together only for the combined stream to part again and form two paths that went their own way. Now and then – just occasionally – they would come back together.

CHAPTER 17

'THE BAD NEWS IS THAT he's still under arrest. The even worse news is that there are rumours he's going to be charged.'

Good Friday and Kelvin was updating the group with the latest information on Yan Xiao-ling. The medical researcher with his unwelcome opinions on infectious diseases was still one of their main concerns. Kelvin had been using his university connections to keep in touch with Yan's family and find out what was going on. The news wasn't good. According to his wife, Yan had been followed by two plainclothes policemen for weeks; his arrest had come after he had applied for permission to travel to a conference in Singapore where he was going to present a paper reporting his concerns about the increase in outbreaks of bird flu in China.

'Charged with what?' asked Lily.

'Spreading false rumours, causing public anxiety, anything like that. I'm sure they can think of something. The question is, what do we do next? I was thinking of going to the conference myself and saying something there about him. I'm not sure what I'd say though or even if the organisers would let me. You know what Singapore can be like at the best of times, they're not likely to be keen on making a fuss.'

'Wasn't it a little foolhardy?' asked Liang-bao. 'Wanting to go abroad to talk about an outbreak of bird flu in China was asking for trouble, surely? He must have known they'd never let him.'

'Foolhardy? Perhaps you could say that – or perhaps he was just being brave. One of the two anyway. Or both. Who knows? I've been trying to persuade some of my colleagues to help me smuggle copies of his paper into Hong Kong so we can publish it here, but none of them have been particularly keen to get involved. The trouble is they all have their own research projects, many of which rely on collaborations with people and institutions in China. I think they're worried that if they help then their own work is at risk. I was thinking of going to Shanghai myself to see if I could get to speak to Yan Xiao-ling, but now he's been arrested I don't know that I could do any good. I might be able to see his wife, but unless she has a copy of his work there wouldn't be much point. It's a possibility though.'

'Wouldn't that be a bit dangerous? Putting yourself at risk like that?' asked Alice. She was sitting next to Liang-bao on Kelvin's sofa. 'I mean, they are bound to be watching her and who she meets. They'd know if you met her and then they'd just put two and two together. You'd be certain to be stopped from bringing anything back. Couldn't she just post it to you, or is that too simple?'

'If I could get my address to her – and, of course, assuming she has a copy of the paper anyway – but they may be listening to her calls and checking her mail.'

'How about your cousin?' Emma asked Alice. 'Could he help, do you think?'

'Kwok-wah? I don't know … perhaps, but I wouldn't want to put him in any danger.'

'Who's this?' asked Kelvin.

'My cousin. He's studying in Shanghai at the moment. If you were to write a letter, I could send it to him to post in Shanghai. That would have a better chance of getting through than anything with a Hong Kong stamp.'

'Well, let's think about it some more and come back to it later. We seem to be going round in circles getting nowhere and none of the options are very good. Let's move on to something else.'

'Do you think we're doing any good?' asked Lily. 'Or are we only making things worse?'

'What do you mean, Lily?' asked Alice. Lily was always one of the quieter members in the group, often letting her sister speak for the pair of them. But for once Yannie wasn't there; expecting a second child, she had decided to give the meeting a miss.

'I don't know. I just wonder if by making a fuss we're just provoking China. Sometimes it's like the more we go on about something, the more Beijing gets really heavy-handed. Perhaps we should turn it down a bit?

There's a limit to what we can do, maybe we need to realise that? Concentrate on fights we can win. Suppose Kelvin can get a copy of this research paper and gets it published here – will that help Yan Xiao-ling or just put him in more danger? He might find himself in even more trouble because they'll say that he's been collaborating with people from outside of China. They might even accuse him of spying for imperialist powers – you know the sort of thing they say.'

'You think it's our fault?' said Emma, staring at Lily.

'Well, I—'

'We can't just let these bullies get away with this sort of thing,' Emma continued, animated now and looking around the room. 'That's what they are – bullies. Thugs. You've got to stand up to them or they'll just think they can do what they like and they'll just carry on like that – or worse. That's what happened to me at school; I used to get picked on because of my hearing. At first it was just words – the other children liked to think I was stupid, I got called a retard, a spastic and so on – but then it got worse, became more physical. They liked to play this game where they would creep up behind me, quietly so that I wouldn't hear them, then pull my hair or hit me in the back. It went on for ages until Pete ... until someone showed me how to stand up for myself.

'School playground or Chinese politics, it's just a question of scale. Give one person power over another and the one thing you know for sure is they'll abuse it. It's the mentality of these people that really pisses me off. The way they push everybody else out of the way to get what they want. It doesn't matter to them who they hurt in the process, the lives they ruin and destroy, the little people they trample over. And what do we do about it? Nothing. We might just as well sit at home and watch TV all day. Let them do whatever they want while we eat pizza and soak up mindless pap.

'And what about after the handover? It's all very well when it's somewhere else. Somewhere far away that doesn't affect us. But soon they'll be here, and you can bet they'll be in charge no matter what any agreement says. Bit by bit, they'll change things. I expect we won't notice it at first. *"Look,"* we'll all say, *"everything's just the same,"* and people will relax. Then there'll be some small changes, but that will be okay, we'll tell ourselves, *"We can live with that, the important things haven't changed."* Who knows, we might even believe it. But slowly, bit by bit, everything will be different and then what are we going to do about it? Say that we shouldn't create a stir? We don't want to upset people in case things get worse? But it will get worse. You know what they say about frogs and boiling water? Drop a frog into hot water and it will try and get out, but put a frog in cold water and slowly bring it to the boil … Well, that's what will happen to Hong Kong unless we stand up and do something.

'And Lily' – Lily was looking down at her hands – 'what about your nephew, what future is Thomas going to have? Don't you want him to live in a place where he can feel free to do and say what he likes? Pursue his dreams and ambitions in whatever way he wants? Or would you rather he lived a life where he was always having to watch his back? Making sure he doesn't say the wrong thing? Doesn't upset the wrong people? Come on, everyone, isn't that why we're all here? Otherwise why bother? Let's just give up now and do something else with our lives.'

There was silence in the room interrupted only by Charles clearing his throat. Emma began to think that perhaps she'd gone too far.

'Sorry, I'm not getting at any of you – especially not you, Lily – it's just that … Oh, I don't know. Take no notice of me.'

'No need to apologise, Emma,' said Kelvin. 'But let's take a break. I've got some food ready in the kitchen. I'll go get everything.'

Emma fiddled nervously with her hearing aid. Perhaps she should think about leaving after that outburst. What must the others think of her? None of them would have had a clue what had brought it on. Only Yannie might have understood if she was there. Emma's reaction had surprised even herself, though she knew where it had come from. She thought about how Brian Lo had been forced to move abroad, leaving family and friends behind, too scared even to come back for a funeral, and she thought about Cheung Wing-ho. Twenty floors was a long way to fall. She'd been thinking about him ever since she got back from Sydney. She wondered if he'd had time to understand why he was being killed. Did whoever killed him say anything? Did they explain? Did he have time to regret making a fuss? What thoughts went through his head in those final seconds before he hit the pavement?

Was she making a nuisance of herself that she might one day come to regret? What would Peter say? That was something Emma often asked herself when she didn't know what to do. She remembered how he always used to stand up for things that he thought were right; she hoped he'd be proud of her, though she suspected he'd also be more than a little bit surprised that his baby sister was becoming so forceful.

'Perhaps I'd better leave …' she began.

'Why?' asked Alice. 'That was magnificent but, well, not exactly like you … Are you okay?'

'I should apologise to Lily, I wasn't meaning to get at her, or any of you, and I'm no better really. I mean, what do I do? I come to these meetings, write a few letters, and that's it. It makes me feel better about myself, but I don't suppose anything I do makes a blind bit of difference one way or the other. Who knows – Lily may be right. In the end perhaps all we do is make things worse.'

'You don't really mean that,' said Alice.

'Don't I? Sometimes I wonder, but then …'

Kelvin was bringing plates of this and that into the living room.

'I'm sorry, Kelvin, I think I might make a move if you don't mind.'

'Really, Emma? Do you have to?'

'My hearing, you know …' Emma's gaze fell on Liang-bao still sitting on the sofa. He seemed to be looking at her with interest. Emma remembered the man she saw leaving the Xinhua building. 'Oh, Liang-bao,' she said, 'there was something I meant to ask you. A couple of weeks ago I was coming out of the Queen Elizabeth Stadium after playing badminton' (this was a story Emma had prepared earlier, ready for the opportunity to ask Liang-bao) 'when I saw a man coming out of Xinhua who looked just like you. Did you know you have a doppelganger? Or a *dubbelganger* as my father would have said in Dutch.'

'A doppelganger? What's a doppelganger?' asked Liang-bao.

'Sorry. A double. A lookalike. Someone who looks just like you.'

'Ah, I see. No, it might have been me. What day was it?'

'It was a Monday, what – two weeks ago? Really? It might have been you?'

'I was there a few weeks ago … Let me think, was that on a Monday? Yes, I think it was. Yes, it must have been a Monday because that's the one day of the week I don't have classes.'

'Why were you at Xinhua?' asked Alice. 'What on earth were you doing there?'

'I was delivering the petition.'

'What petition?'

'You know – the one we talked about? The petition about academic freedom after the handover? I was getting some of my fellow Masters students to sign it?'

'I suppose so …' Alice looked doubtful.

'You're getting forgetful. Come on, let's see what Kelvin has made for us. You too, Emma, stay and have something to eat.'

***

The ferry pulled away from the terminal in the morning sunshine of Easter Saturday. The vessel moved slowly at first while it negotiated the crowded waters of the inner harbour, and then once it reached the main fairway it picked up speed, raising its body on submerged hydrofoils until the hull was completely out of the water by the time it was moving smoothly past Green Island and Peng Chau, and then on through the channel separating Cheung Chau from Lantau. The ferry was packed. Sam and Emma evidently not the only ones who had decided on an Easter weekend in Macau.

Sam was slightly hungover. The night before while Emma was at her meeting, he'd made the mistake of joining Kate and Rob for dinner to celebrate the conclusion of a deal they'd all been working on, following which a gang of them had hit the bars. Sam had been one of the first to leave, but even so he hadn't made it to bed until three. He had taken a masochistic delight in being interrogated by Rob and Kate as to why he was going to Macau for Easter. He took pleasure in being the subject of sexual speculation for once. Emma, on the other hand, appeared to Sam to be in a very exuberant mood. *('Oh dear, you look … Am I speaking too loud? Late night I guess?')* The seating was airline style and they had been lucky to get a couple of seats by a window. Sam gazed out at the passing view. He had offered Emma the window but she had hastily declined it. (*'No thanks, I'm not that good on boats, I'd rather pretend I'm on a plane.'*) He wasn't exactly seasick, but in his fragile state, and even though the hydrofoil rode above the swell, he could have done without the vibrations from the engines, the smell of diesel, and the loud laughter and chatter of the other passengers. He tried to concentrate on the horizon. This was only partly to help quell any sense of queasiness but it also distracted him from thoughts of the night ahead. He wondered if Emma was as nervous as he was. If so she wasn't showing it, her head buried in a newspaper.

'Where did you decide for dinner tonight?' she asked, setting aside the letters page and interrupting Sam's reverie.

'Sorry? Oh, A Lorcha. Do you know it? It's a classic Macanese place near the Maritime Museum.'

'No, but it sounds good.'

'Anything you'd particularly like to do this afternoon?' Sam always especially enjoyed the calm of the Old Protestant Cemetery with its history and the fascinating stories told by the gravestones of sailors and Victorian adventurers, but given what Emma had been through in recent weeks perhaps a graveyard wouldn't be the most appropriate suggestion. Certainly not the most seductive. 'We could trawl some of the antique shops perhaps?'

'I don't really mind, just a wander round is fine for me.

I might see if I can find something small to send to my parents. Sort of to make up for not having been back at Christmas. In fact, at the moment I don't have any plans to go back. Not in the near future anyway.' Emma hooked her arm around his and rested her head on his shoulder.

'Are you feeling guilty?' he asked.

'Well, I suppose if I'm honest,' continued Emma, 'perhaps I do feel a little guilty. A bit. Last year was the first Christmas since Peter died that I hadn't been at home. Even when I was with Mike we used to spend Christmas with Mum and Dad.'

'Would they come out to see you?'

'I don't think so. The only time they've been here was for the trial after Peter's death so they've no good memories or feelings about Hong Kong. For them it's a place with only bad associations.'

'But not for you?'

'I don't know. Perhaps a bit, when I first arrived.' Emma thought about Sam's question. 'I certainly had mixed feelings when I came here but at least I hadn't been here for the trial. I hadn't originally planned on visiting Hong Kong let alone living here, that was something of an accident and my parents weren't happy about it at all. But I knew how much Peter loved this place so I think I stayed on to try and understand what it was that he liked, and, of course, soon enough I was happy here as well. I think Peter would have wanted me to see and experience all the great things about Hong Kong that he did. What about you? You weren't home at Christmas either, were you? Do you have any plans to go see your parents?'

'Not really, I'll have to make a visit back some time, of course, but I've nothing lined up at the moment,' said Sam.

'I'll go back for a visit when I've got the money. But I can't keep going there for the rest of my life. What is it people say about "time to move on"? I've always thought that was an irritating expression, but now I think I know what it means. Something like it anyway.'

'How about "closure"?'

'Another horrible term ... one of those American things I suppose, but again there's some truth in it. I do feel better now for knowing what happened to Peter even if I can't do anything more. Mind you, I am still pissed off that Gao Zhihua got away with it like that.' Sam was more than a little shocked. He hadn't heard Emma swear before. 'Did you notice the bag I've got with me?' Emma gestured to the battered holdall she had placed in the overhead rack. 'Peter bought it for me when I went to university. It's been a few places now but it's still hanging on in there. A bit like me.'

***

They spent the afternoon sightseeing. Four hundred and fifty years of Portuguese rule always made Macau seem a little like a Mediterranean escape compared with Hong Kong. They stood at the top of the Fortaleza do Monte where the old cannons still stood guard over the town defending them from any unlikely invasions. The sun was bright and Sam was glad of his sunglasses. He placed a hand against Emma's back and gently caressed her through the fabric of her T-shirt. She turned and smiled.

Looking down they could see the maze of streets and *travessas* they had been lost in only an hour before. Streets that were lined with old shophouses full of everything from gold jewellery to antiques, and the *pastelerias* with queues round the block for their egg tarts, almond biscuits, cakes and delicacies. Narrow lanes that would open out into old squares with churches that breathed the air of a different time. Alleyways tessellated in black and white; buildings rendered in yellow, green and ochre, sometimes with the paint faded and peeling, but always telling their history. Looking from the fort across the inner harbour there was China. So close you could almost read the road signs. It looked very shabby but it was the future. Macau was due to return to China in three years' time.

'I wonder how many people escaped from China across that stretch of water,' said Emma, not so much asking a question as simply thinking out loud. 'It's so short it would be easy to swim across.'

'I don't know. I guess the challenge would have been getting there in the first place.'

They were enjoying playing the part of tourists. Emma found a small antique bowl for her parents. They bought custard tarts from the Lord Stow bakery and then drank *vinho verde* sitting in the shade at an outdoor table in a Coloane bar. From where they sat they could see the Chapel of St. Francis Xavier that

dominated the village square. The church was decorated with Easter palms and inside a giant portrait of the
Madonna took pride of place; a Virgin Mary with an
undeniably Oriental, Japanese even, look about her.
At the same time, reflecting the duality of Macau that
made it so delightful, by the entrance to the bar there
was a small Chinese altar with a figurine of A-Ma,
the goddess of seafarers and a particular favourite in
Macau. Two sticks of incense were burning and the
sweet aroma drifted over to their table.

Emma fixed her sunglasses on top of her head. In the
past Sam had always thought this was an affectation;
now he found it very attractive. 'I'm glad we came
here,' she said. 'It's a breath of fresh air. Getting away
from everything. I've been so preoccupied with Peter's
death I've not been able to concentrate on much else.'

'That's understandable surely?'

'Perhaps, but not healthy.' Emma slipped off one of
the sandals she was wearing and allowed her foot to
stroke Sam's leg. 'And not always fair to those around
me either.' Emma looked at her watch. 'Should we be
making a move if we want to get ready for this evening?
Get a taxi back to the hotel?'

***

Sam held open the door for Emma. Earlier they had
passed through only briefly to drop off their bags, now
they had time to contemplate the large double bed that
dominated the room. They unpacked in an awkward
silence, bumping into each other in the bathroom as

they laid out their toiletries.

'Do you want to shower first?' asked Sam.

'If you don't mind … Do you need …?'

'No I'm fine, you go ahead.'

Sam lay on the bed and started to browse the TV channels. He heard the sound of running water and turned up the volume on the TV a little so as to drown out thoughts of Emma naked in the shower. She emerged a little later wearing only the hotel bath-robe. 'The bathroom's all yours,' she said and Sam got to his feet, turning away from her so as to hide the embarrassment of his erection. When Sam was also showered he found Emma wearing a black dress that came to an inch above the knee, cut just low enough to allow her necklace to rest against her skin. A hint of make-up but not overdone, hair pulled back in her favourite ponytail.

'How do I look?' she asked.

For a moment Sam was silent. 'Fabulous,' he finally managed.

Dinner went in a blur. The white-walled restaurant was noisily alive; with families, with couples, with locals, with tourists. Three Russian men sat at a nearby table, sharing a bottle of vodka between them. Emma struggled with the background noise, the sound of animated conversations, orders being shouted to the kitchen by waiters. She went to the ladies and returned wearing her hearing aid. They ordered samosas, chori-zo, prawns, African chicken and then more prawns just in case they hadn't had enough. Sam hadn't seen Emma so relaxed before, the resolution of Peter's death, the change of scene, all brought out a lightness to her, a gaiety almost, that was new to him. He began to relax as well, aided by a beer to start with and then a bottle of Portuguese wine. He declined the waiter's suggestion of port, thinking it inadvisable. Dutch courage was one thing, but too much of it would not be a good idea.

***

For the third time that day Sam held open the door to their room. They paused for a moment before they kissed.

'Let me take this out,' said Emma, removing her hearing aid. 'It's not very romantic.' She slipped off her shoes, removed her necklace and loosened her hair, and they stood facing each other, hesitating before taking the next step. It was Emma who broke the silence.

'Why don't you undress me?'

INTERLUDE

Liver spots decorate his face, and with only a wisp of hair pretending to cover his head he looks older than his sixty-two years. He's been in the business for forty-five of them and has worked on this spot since the sixties. His pitch is on a covered walkway and like all the best real estate in the city the location is key; he is on the main thoroughfare between the office blocks of Central and the shops, hotels and restaurants of Admiralty, and from first thing in the morning to late at night they pass his shoe-shining stall.

Best of all he is under cover. This not only protects him from the sun and rain, but also encourages people to stop no matter what the weather. If anything, business is even better when the rain is heavy or the sun is too strong and passers-by look for a reason to stay under shelter for that little bit longer. They have an excuse to escape from the heat and noise when they take the worn wooden seat. A small chest holds his brushes, cloths, wax and polishes. A flask of tea and a Styrofoam lunchbox see him through the day.

He doesn't have much time for modern-day fashions. They're bad for business. He prefers the old styles. Young people in trainers? What use are they to him? He has a sideline repairing women's shoes, but his real interest lies in the traditional Oxfords and brogues; the choice of lawyers, bankers and businessmen. Thankfully there are still plenty of those passing by and enough of them stop to get their shoes polished to a jewel-like finish. He doesn't need much. His wife died of cancer a few years ago and his two sons are now grown up. One is a waiter, still living at home; the other is in Toronto, doing well, something in advertising apparently. He hasn't seen him in years. But do any of his scuffed-shoe clients pay attention to him while he works his magic? While his brushes and cloths move at speed, applying polish, buffing to a shine, back and forth across the toes, around the heel? Do they say hello? Do they thank him or pass the time of day as they hand him a twenty dollar note? No, they do not.

They read the newspaper while he works. They talk to each other while they wait their turn. They discuss mergers and takeovers. Land sales and new property developments. Sometimes he listens, thinking he might get an inside tip on a stock to buy. And sometimes – but only sometimes – they talk of the handover.

There are times when history changes direction. When a river changes course. Often nobody notices this until after it has happened. Sometimes it only becomes clear years later. Decades even. Rarely can it be scheduled, planned for, put in the diary, but Hong Kong in June 1997 is such a time and place.

In some ways the signs are easy to see. The city has been spruced up. Streets scrubbed clean ready for the world to admire. Flowers planted in the parks, illuminated dragon lanterns on the Tsimshatsui waterfront. *HMS Chatham* a sentry moored in the harbour. Foreign reporters in the taxi queue at Kai Tak, film crews blocking pavements as they record vox pops. Everybody getting their fifteen minutes of fame. Other indicators are more subtle. The pizza chain offering $97 handover specials. Official and not-so-official souvenirs. Bottles of Reunification Cabernet Sauvignon. The flags appearing on taxi dashboards, bauhinia next to the five golden stars on red. Farewell dinners and retirements.

And yet.

And yet the horses still race at Happy Valley and Shatin.

Fortunes are still told at the night markets and incense sticks burnt at Wong Tai Sin.

The Star Ferry still carries tourists and locals across the harbour, weaving its drunken way between the tugs and barges; the crew in bell-bottoms as they have been for decades, using billhooks to moor at the pier, passengers streaming ashore as the ferry rises and falls on the swell. Fishing boats still trawl the waters, nets hanging from their sides like a cormorant drying its wings. Old women play mah-jong all day long, the click of tiles competing with the gossip.

And yet children still go to school, lunch boxes in hand; backpacks full of textbooks so heavy they threaten to pull them over backwards.

And yet people continue to go to work and he still polishes their shoes.

CHAPTER 18

HONG KONG, JUNE 1997

EVEN AT THE BEST OF times it never took much to cause gridlock in Central on a Monday morning. By the time the police had determined that the suspicious looking package was not in fact a bomb but a shoebox full of sand with a wire sticking out of one corner, traffic was blocked everywhere. Connaught Road was solid back to Western, and cars were queuing all the way up Garden Road. Sam was stuck in a taxi with the meter ticking over remorselessly, but he refused to allow the traffic to spoil his good mood. He would be late for work but so be it. Emma had moved into his flat at the weekend. She'd worried it was a bit soon in their relationship but her lease was up so it made sense, and they'd alternated between lingering in bed and bringing things over from her place. It wasn't long though before Emma had started to put her own stamp on things.

'This lamp,' she said, eyeing a table lamp with a yellow and green ceramic base and a dusty shade that was beyond cleaning, 'are you very attached to it?'

'I hadn't particularly thought about it.' In truth Sam was fond of the lamp, but he was fonder still of Emma. 'Why do you ask?'

'I was just thinking it might look better in the spare bedroom.'

Sam knew things were going to change and he was happy with that. In fact he was happier than he had been in a long time. Emma was changing his life for the better. He was eating healthily, dressing more stylishly. She was even getting him to try playing tennis. He was relaxed and comfortable at work, enjoying more than ever turning down Rob's invitations to nights out in Wan Chai; why waste his time like that when he had Emma? If he missed the heart-to-heart conversations he used to have with Kate, then he was reminded every time he woke up next to Emma, her arm thrown across his chest, that it was a price worth paying.

The traffic was finally moving again and he was soon at the office only a hundred dollars out of pocket.

'Paul was looking for you,' said his secretary, Annie, after Sam had settled at his desk. It was, of course, inevitable his boss would have been looking for him the one day in the year he was late for work.

'Did he say what he wanted?'

'He asked if you could arrange a meeting with Mr Leung. Apparently Bright Talk have another deal in the pipeline.'

'Why can't his own secretary do that?'

'I don't know.' Annie shrugged. She thought that it didn't really matter because she'd end up doing the work anyway. 'I took the liberty of checking on Paul's diary and I've arranged a meeting for a week on Wednesday. Hope that's okay?'

'Of course.' In fact Sam had no idea if that was a good date or not but he assumed correctly that Annie would have checked his own diary. 'I guess I should refresh my memory about Bright Talk. Can you get me the file when you have a chance?'

'Already done. It's there on your desk in front of you.'

When Annie had left, Sam started to scan through the file, reminding himself of the details of the deal they'd done last year. Mr Leung's original instructions; his shareholding; the money from the BVI company, the unimaginatively named Golden Profit Limited; and the directors of Golden Profit. The structure of the transaction started to come back to him. He remembered the rumours about the BVI company. The stories of mainland money. He looked at the list of Golden Profit directors although he knew most were just nominees – accountants and company secretarial people, nobody who was actually involved in the business. Finished with the file he put it to one side and took out the papers for the client he was currently working for, but soon he stopped. He was finding it difficult to concentrate, reading the same paragraphs over and over without taking anything in. Something was troubling him, something about Bright Talk that he couldn't identify. Something was wrong, something he hadn't noticed when the deal was first done, more than simply the question of the BVI company. He felt a chill, memories of London hovering in his subconscious.

But he had absolutely no idea what was wrong.

***

The calm contentment in Sam's private life was in contrast to the mood in the city, the bomb scare being just one example of the rising tensions. The handover had always seemed something for the far distance. Something to worry about tomorrow, not today. When Sam was a boy, important dates used to come round so slowly; the run up to Christmas or his birthday always seemed interminable. Two weeks or two months, either way the longed-for day was always far off in the distance. When he'd arrived in Hong Kong, back in 1993, the handover also seemed remote. Something that could be safely ignored. Of course he hadn't been blind to the future, quite the opposite. The idea of being in Hong Kong for June 1997 had been part of the attraction of making the move. He didn't think he was alone in that.

But the closer the date approached there was an increased hedonism in the city, certainly among the expats anyway, as if everybody was trying to squeeze the last possible amount of pleasure from the time that was left. Trying to ignore the approaching date as if by partying as loudly and frequently as possible it might not happen. Drowning out thoughts of the inevitable changes ahead. But now tomorrow was almost here, the phoney war was coming to an end. People tried to disregard it, tried to carry on normal lives, but it was becoming increasingly difficult. Foreign journalists and TV crews were starting to arrive, stopping innocent civilians in the street and pressing a camera in their face. Hotels were full, restaurants booked solid.

Sam was starting to look nostalgically at the colonial flag he could see from his office. He guessed it had always been there, but he hadn't paid it much attention before. Now it had only a few weeks before its expiry date. He wondered what would become of it? Did someone already have their eyes on it? Probably. There might be a market for colonial memorabilia in the future. Details of the new Hong Kong flag had been announced some time back, along with the rules on how it should be flown, in particular its relative size compared with China's five-starred red. Smaller, inevitably. There was no news other than the handover, and distinguishing between hard facts and speculation became increasingly difficult. Rumours were rife. Streets were to be renamed and Queen's Road would be the first to go. Roads would be reconfigured so that cars could drive on the right. Nothing was too ridiculous that it couldn't be suggested and believed by some.

Sam had once assumed he would return to the UK after the handover. That had been the original plan anyway. A couple of years in Hong Kong, a little experience abroad never did anyone any harm he thought. Witness the change of sovereignty. Then back to London and a job in a City firm when memories

of his less than stellar pre-Hong Kong career had perhaps faded and people had forgotten. But after initially
finding it difficult to adjust, he had become settled in
Hong Kong. When he'd first arrived Sam had been
warned that the first year would be the hardest, that
he might struggle once the novelty and excitement of
the new environment had passed. First year blues it
was called, and Sam had found it to be very true. He
could still remember when he came back to Hong
Kong after his first trip home. It had felt like being
returned to prison after day release. But then, like a
runner going through the wall, things looked up again.
He made a positive decision to stick with it and work
his way through the difficult patch. More and more
Hong Kong had started to feel like home to him and
not just somewhere to spend a couple of years. In spite
of the uncertain future, Sam increasingly saw himself
living in Hong Kong for the long term.

Some weeks back Paul had asked him about his
future plans and suggested that if he did stay then
partnership was likely. It was a conversation Sam had
thought was coming, indeed he had hoped it was
coming, and yet somehow it still managed to catch
him by surprise. Like a good lawyer his answers had
been non-committal. Sam knew that if he was going
to go back to the UK then he needed to do so sooner
rather than later if he wanted to get a job in London.
Any more than three or four years away and what
seemed to him to be good experience would to an
employer simply mean time out of his normal career

progression.

And then there was Emma. Sam was starting to get beyond his insecurities. The constant wondering of what a woman like her was doing with a man like him. The conviction that she would find somebody better soon enough. To his surprise Sam was discovering that their relationship was only strengthening. The one thing they hadn't really talked about, the elephant in the room, was the question of Emma's visa. The rules were changing and in the future they would both need work visas. That was never going to be a problem for Sam, a lawyer in a large firm would have no trouble, but a temp who flitted from job to job? Who spoke no Cantonese and had a hearing problem? That wouldn't be straightforward. What argument could there be to justify Emma having a work visa? What job could she do that couldn't be done by a local? So far Sam had only mentioned it to Emma in passing, but it seemed to him the best chance would be if she could get a full-time position with McShane Adams. It wouldn't change the fundamental problem, but working for a firm of that size and with some clout might count for something. So Sam thought anyway.

The fact that today was June 4th was in his mind as well, though the date was apparently not in the consciousness of all of his colleagues.

'Are you on for a drink after work?' Rob had asked.

'No. I'm going to the vigil with Emma.'

'What vigil?'

'You know. The June 4th vigil.'

'June 4th?'

Sam was astonished that Rob seemed to have no idea what he was talking about.

'Tiananmen Square.'

'Oh, that.'

***

Victoria Park had been slowly filling since early afternoon, the crowds unconcerned by the rain. The basketball courts had been cleared and a stage set up at one end. A large screen dominated the rear of the stage with the sound system on either side. The effect was more rock concert than political rally. Early arrivals got the prime spaces at the front with a good view of the stage, and as the numbers swelled the concrete of the basketball courts steadily disappeared, hidden beneath the ever-growing multitude.

They were all ages: families with children; young and old; high-school students; others perhaps at university. Many were wearing black T-shirts, often with white bandanas tied round their heads. Some carried placards and banners. Almost everybody had a candle, and as dusk turned into evening the scene was illuminated with flickering points of light. There was discipline and order. Everyone gave each other room where they could. The very young and the very old were helped to find some space to sit. It was the most orderly, good-natured demonstration Sam could imagine – not that he had much experience to base his judgement on. A row of police vans were parked nearby and uniformed police officers kept a respectful watching brief. Everyone assumed that plainclothes police mingled with the crowds.

By the time Sam and Emma arrived in the early evening, the rain had eased off but it was still horribly humid. It was the first time Sam had been to any form of political demonstration and if it hadn't been for Emma he knew that he wouldn't have been there. Certainly, as far as he knew, none of his colleagues were coming. Sam couldn't remember the last time he had seen such a large number of people in one place apart from the rugby sevens. He had no yardstick to judge the numbers by, but knew it must have been tens of thousands. The mood was surprisingly upbeat. He had expected it to be more sombre. More serious. Although it wasn't exactly a party, there was a spirit of optimism. A sense that with collective action all would work out in the end.

'How on earth are we going to find them in this crowd?' Sam asked Emma. They had arranged to meet Alice and Liang-bao.

'They said they'd try and save some space. But even so you're right, there's no way we're going to find them. Let's just find somewhere to sit.'

The first speaker had already started as Sam and Emma picked their way through the seated crowds, apologising as they went. Eventually they found a space off to the right, most of the way back but it was the best they could do. The speech was in Cantonese.

'I hope it's not all going to be in Cantonese,' said Sam.

'I was planning on Alice translating for us.'

While the speaker continued, Sam took in the scene on the stage. Five men and a woman sat to one side listening, while the screen at the back of the stage showed the iconic image of the lone protestor standing in front of a tank. Tank-man. Sam recognised the woman as a leading pro-democracy politician, but he had no idea who the others were. When the first speaker finally came to an end there was a huge cheer from the crowd as one of the five men took to the microphone.

'Someone famous?'

'I think he might be an actor.'

Whoever he was, to the relief of both of them he didn't speak for long in Cantonese and after a short while he switched to heavily accented English.

'We all know why we are here tonight,' he said. 'We are here to remember the victims of Tiananmen. To honour those who died. To hear from the heroes of that night. I am immensely proud to introduce to you Wang Bao!' With a flourish, the speaker gestured to one of the men on stage who stood and walked to the microphone. The screen at the back of the stage started to show video footage of June 1989. Students camped in Tiananmen Square. Police. Soldiers. Tanks. More soldiers.

'I think I've heard of Wang Bao,' Emma whispered to Sam. 'He was one of the student leaders.'

Wang Bao was slightly built, gaunt almost, somewhere in his late twenties, thirty at most, but looked older. He spoke in English with a mainland accent.

Hesitantly at first, apologising for not speaking Cantonese, he spoke with increasing confidence as he began to tell his story. Wang Bao had been in Tiananmen Square that night. A chemistry student at Tsinghua University, he had been one of the early protestors and had gone to the square in early May. A week later he was joined by his girlfriend from college, Xiao-mei. The crowds listened intently as Wang Bao told them of the early optimism. Of how Party officials said that they understood their concerns. Of how there were promises of change and reform. Wang Bao told of the songs they sang. Of poems that were written. Friendships made.

The numbers of Tiananmen protestors rose steadily through the month of May and the mood changed. The hopes of the early days started to fade and a sense of anxiety began to fill the square. Everybody knew something was going to happen but nobody knew what or when. In spite of that foreknowledge, when the crackdown did come the ferocity of it still caught them by surprise. Wang Bao's voice started to falter as he began to describe the events of that night. His audience, already rapt, fell into an even deeper silence and Emma reached out for Sam's hand. The city that continued its life around them disappeared from their consciousness.

'They say,' continued Wang Bao, 'the Chinese Communist Party say, nobody died in Tiananmen Square that night. They may be right.' A puzzled mutter ran through the crowd. 'They may be right because most people died in the streets around the square as they tried to flee. That's what happened to us. When we saw tanks break down the barricades, I told Xiao-mei "follow me". We headed out of the square and down Qianmendajie. Hope to disappear in the hutongs. But they were waiting for us. A line of soldiers across the road blocking our escape. They opened fire. Can you believe? Chinese troops fire on Chinese people. We saw protestors in front of us fall to the ground. We turned down a narrow alleyway. But they followed and soon caught us. Xiao-mei was struck on the head with a club.' Wang Bao's voice faltered for a moment before he gathered himself and continued. 'It was so sudden she didn't have time to cry out. Just a little gasp and then she collapsed, blood coming from her ear. I crouched over Xiao-mei hoping to protect her from more blows, but then something or somebody hit me and after that … nothing.' The crowd was silent and yet only a short distance away the shops and restaurants of Causeway Bay were thronged.

'I woke up in hospital. They told me later I had been in a coma for three weeks. Nobody would answer my questions about Xiao-mei. When the doctors said I was okay the police took me. I spent two years in a re-education camp and when I was released I searched for Xiao-mei but nobody knew if she was alive or dead. Her parents had moved to another city and refused to talk to me. Years later I still do not know what happened to Xiao-mei.' Wang Bao was briefly silenced by a police helicopter that flew low overhead. Sam looked up and could see cameras pointing down at the crowds.

He wondered what Paul Ridgeway would think if he could see him here.

'And now,' Wang Bao resumed, 'Hong Kong is about to become part of China again. Many of you will welcome that. You are Chinese. But you must never forget Tiananmen Square. Never forget June 4th. Never forget democracy. Never forget those who were in the square. Even now people are rewriting history. You must remember the truth. In Hong Kong you have freedoms that nobody in China is even allowed to dream. You must look after those freedoms. Protect them. They will be threatened bit by bit. Slice by slice.'

After Wang Bao had finished, singing broke out in the crowd. Voices swelled, filling the evening air and overwhelming the sound of traffic and city life. Sam was surprised to find himself welling up a little. Unable to join in with the singing in Cantonese he still found that he was feeling at one with everyone else. It was the first time he had ever felt like a Hongkonger rather than an expat.

CHAPTER 19

'HE'S WITH PAUL AT THE moment,' said Kate.

Friday morning and Emma was in Central. Not having any work on, she'd decided to drop in on Sam unannounced. See if he was free to take her to lunch. Emma hadn't considered the possibility that he might be busy and she was a little nonplussed. Perhaps she should have asked him at breakfast rather than turning up out of the blue.

'But I don't think he's going to be long,' Kate continued. 'Come, sit down and I'll get us some coffee.' Emma waited in Kate's office with the uncomfortable feeling that she was interrupting a busy morning.

'Sorry, I must be stopping you from working,' she said when Kate returned with two cups.

'No problem, I could do with a break. This is so tedious.' Kate gestured to the papers on her desk. 'I seem to be the departmental dogsbody at the moment while Sam gets the glamorous mainland deals ... Sorry – I probably shouldn't have said that. Take no notice of

me. Thank God we've got a long weekend tomorrow.'
Monday was the Dragon Boat Festival and a public
holiday. 'Sam's says you're not coming on the junk
on Monday? Is that right? It would be a shame if you
weren't there. It's one of the best things about working
for a firm like this, having a junk.'

'I'm afraid I don't get on that well with boats and
water.'

'Pity. So how is it now you're sharing a flat? Sorry if
I'm being nosey. I've reached this ripe old age and I've
never actually shared a home with a man. You know,
week in, week out. Is he housebroken? Does he put
the toilet seat down? Do the washing up? That sort
of thing.'

'He's pretty good on the whole. He just has some
strange ideas on interior design ... But then it's his flat
after all. I don't want to change things too radically, I
might scare him off.'

'Oh, there's no danger of that, Emma. I don't think
I've ever seen him so happy. You're good for him.'

'Well it works both ways but I'm glad you think so.
You know ... I was jealous of you when I first met Sam.'

'Jealous? Of me?'

'You had – still have I guess – such a close relationship with Sam. I suppose I thought there must have
been something between you ...'

'I don't know ... it's funny, there's always been a
connection between us, but don't worry – never in that
way. More like brother and sister, I suppose. Mind you
I'd never tell my brother half the things I tell Sam, if

only because it'd get back to my parents. Do you have a brother or sister?'

'Me? No ... no, I don't.' No matter how many times Emma was asked that question she was never comfortable answering. But Emma was very pleased that Sam clearly did not tell Kate everything. 'Is Sam with a client at the moment?' Emma looked to change the subject. 'Perhaps I should be going.'

'I think he is, yes. I think he's with the people from Bright Talk at the moment. I don't think he'll ... Speak of the devil.' Sam had appeared at the door to Kate's office.

'Emma, sorry ... you've caught me by surprise. Were we supposed to be meeting?'

'No. I just called in to say hello. Kate and I were just having a chat. I can see you're both busy. I should leave you to it.'

'I'm just with a client at the moment. Kate, do you know where Annie is? I can't find her and there's a file I need.'

'Sorry. If she's not at her desk I've no idea.'

'Can I help?' asked Emma. 'Unless Annie has changed things, I do sort of remember her system.'

'Actually, you probably can. Thanks. It's one of the files you helped me with last year, Bright Talk Telecommunications. Do you remember it?'

'I think so. Give me a moment.' Emma left Sam and Kate and went over to Annie's workspace. She opened the top drawer in a filing cabinet and rifled through the files until she found the one Sam needed. 'Here it is.'

'That's the one. Sorry, I may be a little while …'

'Don't worry, I'll see you at home later. I'd just dropped by on the off-chance.'

It wasn't until after Sam had left that Emma saw the sheet of paper that had slipped from the file and drifted under Annie's desk. She bent down to pick it up and looked at it to make sure that it was indeed from that file and not something else altogether. Emma recognised it as being from a document she'd typed last September. There was a typo in one line and she remembered being grateful that nobody had noticed the misspelt 'Directorrs' heading the list of officers of Bright Talk Telecommunications Limited. Last year this had been just a list of names of no significance, but this time her eyes fell on the one name in the list that did mean something to her: Gao Zhihua.

***

Back in the flat, Emma had no memory of how she got home. Probably a taxi but it might have been the bus for all she knew. Travelling on autopilot while she recovered from the shock. She wasn't sure what, if anything, she'd said to Kate.

The questions came quickly but without answer. Was it the same man? How common was the name Gao Zhihua? Could it be a coincidence? Somebody with the same name but nothing more than that? How could she possibly find out? Should she tell Sam? Her thoughts finally settled on one question that soon started to obsess her: had she in fact already seen Gao

Zhihua? Had she smiled at him while asking him to take a seat in reception? Did she make him tea or coffee while he waited? Had she taken his coat? The thought that she might have made polite pleasantries with the man appalled her. What about Sam? Had he met Gao Zhihua? Had they had lunch or dinner together? Did she share a bed with someone who had laughed with the man who killed her brother? Had the hand that caressed her breast once shaken his hand?

She tried to remember the clients she had seen come to the office when she worked for Sam, but none of them had left any impression.

Later, that evening, conversation with Sam was stilted, Emma's mind elsewhere.

'When are you going to tell me what's wrong?' Sam finally asked.

'Wrong? Nothing. Honestly. It's just that my hearing is playing up again.' Much as Emma wished her hearing was normal there were times when it was useful. She had spent some time earlier wondering whether she should tell Sam that one of his clients might be her brother's killer. She couldn't even imagine what words she would use. *By the way, Sam, that client of yours, did you know he was a killer?'* Or perhaps: *'You know that client of yours, Sam? The one you did that big deal for? Well, I thought you might like to know he's a murdering bastard.'* Emma had just gone round and round in circles. The last thing she wanted to do was to interfere with Sam's work or do anything that might put him in an awkward position.

And – as she had to remind herself – she had no idea if this was the same man or not. She had come to the conclusion that since anything she said couldn't be unsaid it would be better to say nothing. For the moment anyway. Not until she knew more. Not that she would stop trying to get what she could from Sam, even if she felt bad for not being open about her questions.

'How did you're meeting go?' Emma asked. 'Sorry for turning up out of the blue like that.'

'No need to apologise, I'm just sorry I was busy. We could have grabbed a coffee or something. The meeting was fine, and thanks for finding the file.'

'What did they want?'

'They're looking to buy a factory in Shenzhen that makes mobile phones. They already own a major share of a network so I think they want to get into the hardware as well. I guess they can clean up if they make money both from selling people the phones and then getting them to sign up to their network.'

'I suppose so.' Emma would have felt better if Sam's firm working for Bright Talk had been a one-off thing, but it seemed the company was going to be a continuing source of business.

'Sorry, I forgot to ask, Kate said something about you feeling unwell? She said you looked pale when you left. Are you okay?'

'Oh, it was nothing. I didn't mean to worry her, I just felt a little dizzy. It happens sometime with my ears.' Again the excuse. 'It was fine when I got some fresh air.'

***

There were several stories for the origin of Tuen Ng – the Dragon Boat Festival. The most popular was that the festival commemorated the death of Qu Yuan, a poet and official of the Chu state in the time of the so-called Warring States. The story went that when the Chu capital fell Qu Yuan drowned himself in a nearby river and the local people raced out in their boats, either to scare the fish away or to retrieve his body. Whatever the truth of that, or any of the other explanations, it was unlikely that the beginnings of the festival involved large numbers of partying expatriates mixing alcohol and sunshine in a very unhealthy combination.

The McShane Adams junk was crowded. In truth it probably had more people on it than its legal capacity, but then since it was moored and tied between two other boats perhaps that didn't matter. The boat certainly wasn't going anywhere anytime soon.

Junks were a feature of expat life and working for a firm like McShane Adams that had its own boat was a privilege that made Sam and his colleagues very popular with friends who were not so lucky. There was always a waiting list for the boat at weekends, but Sam preferred the midweek evening outings to Lamma for seafood. Sitting on the top deck after good food and a few beers, the lights of Aberdeen glittering as they sailed back to Hong Kong Island, always made Sam realise just how lucky he was.

Other parts of Hong Kong held more serious Dragon Boat races. In Shatin and on the island of Cheung Chau fiercely competitive crews, often made up of young men from the same families and villages through the generations, raced fast and hard. Stanley, however, was for the expat racers. Not that it wasn't competitive, especially between the law firms and the banks, but it had nothing of the skill and speed of the real thing. Sam wasn't interested in taking part but he was more than happy to cheer on his colleagues. But it was a shame Emma hadn't wanted to come. He had once persuaded her to go on an evening trip to Lamma, but she had been very reluctant and seemed uncomfortable on the boat. He hadn't pushed it again.

The spectator boats were moored in two lines along the side of the race course, each tied tightly to its neighbours. Sam had no idea what time of the morning the boats had taken up their positions, but it must have been early. Like everyone else he'd had to take a sampan from the beach to get to the McShane Adams junk, and the Hakka boatwomen were doing very good business with overcharged fares. What choice did people have? They either had to pay or swim.

'Here you are,' said Sam, passing Kate a beer fresh from the icebox. Kate was in a bikini and a wide-brimmed hat, making the most of the sun that had decided to grace the day, and Sam tried not to look too obviously at the flower tattoo on her upper left thigh. He was dressed rather more conservatively in a polo shirt and long shorts. He was conscious of how pale his legs were compared with everyone else.

'Thanks. How many more races to go?' asked Kate.

'Just three, I think. The two semi-finals and then the final. You getting bored?'

'A little. It depends on the men in the boat.'

'I see. You're perusing them with an experienced eye? Their paddling technique? Stroke rate? Whether they're together or not?'

'Something like that.'

'Something like that …'

'Don't tell me you don't do the same, Sam. All those athletic young women in wet T-shirts. I mean, I'm straight, but even I get turned on by some of them. But of course, I forget, you're taken.' Sam wondered if he detected a slightly bitter tone in Kate's voice. Not that she was jealous of Emma, more that she was angry with Sam for breaking their shared single status. The bond they shared had been damaged. Perhaps irrevocably.

'What happened to the guy you were seeing?'

'Scumbag. Dumped me for some compliant little Filipina.'

'Oh … First semi-final coming up. Are we in this one?' Sam asked to the boat at large. The McShane Adams dragon boat had been doing surprisingly well given that most of its members had spent the majority of their practice sessions discussing strategy and techniques in the Stanley bars rather than practising on the water.

'No. Next one.' The voice of one of the litigation department.

Sam had never got over just how noisy a dragon boat race was: the drummers on each boat setting a tempo; the less-than-coordinated thrashing of the paddles in the water; all topped off with the descant screams of the spectators. All conversation stopped while six boats stormed along the course, the top three going into the final.

'Did you not want to be in the boat, Sam?' Paul Ridgeway had appeared alongside Sam and Kate. His combination of sneakers, chinos and an Oxford shirt with buttoned down collar made Sam feel under-dressed. Kate pulled on a T-shirt. 'I can't say I blame you,' he continued, 'it was never my sort of thing either.'

'Too much work to do,' said Sam.

'Ha! Good answer!' Paul laughed. That rarest of things. 'Speaking of which, Mr Leung has invited us to dinner at the Jockey Club on July 5th.'

'Including me?' Sam was surprised.

'Including you, Sam. Mr Leung likes you and … well, I'm not going to be around forever. It's as much a post-handover social thing as anything. Not directly work-related. A bit of a pain, I know, but he's a good client. Some of his colleagues will be there I expect, but Elizabeth will be coming with me. Is there anyone …? Mr Leung tells me you have a partner?'

'Yes. Emma. You may remember her. She worked for me as a temp last September.'

'Sort of, I think. I'm not sure how Mr Leung knows more about your personal life than I do, but anyway, if she's available he thought perhaps you would like to ask her to join us. Ah, it looks like they're getting ready for the next semi-final. If you'll excuse me I need to go and make myself visible.'

'*Sort of*,' said Kate who had been listening attentively. '*Sort of remembers her*. Everybody remembers Emma. Every man, anyway. Still, flavour of the month, aren't you? Dinner with a client at the Jockey Club?'

In spite of screams and shouts of encouragement, the McShane Adams dragon boat came only fifth in the second semi-final.

'I hope that's not an omen,' said Kate.

***

Emma felt guilty about not wanting to join Sam on the McShane Adams junk. Many people would have jumped at the chance to spend a day watching the races from a boat with a well-stocked drinks cabinet. But she really didn't like being on junks. She'd tried a few when she first came to Hong Kong. After all, it was what everybody did at the weekend. At least that's what she was told. Pile on board with a chiller full of drinks and food, perhaps the Sunday paper, and spend the day moored in a quiet bay. But she didn't go in for water sports and soon started to feel trapped, especially when some banker tried to hit on her, and the bottom line was that she simply didn't care for being on the water. Even when she needed to cross the harbour she always took the MTR rather than the ferry, and the Easter trip to Macau had been a nightmare she'd had to hide from Sam. Anyway, today she had something else to do.

Emma was grateful that the library was open on a public holiday. She felt a sense of déjà vu as she sat down at the microfiche reader. Her life had changed immeasurably since she was in the same library just a few short months ago; she was in love, living with her boyfriend. And yet here she was again, still looking for answers to the same question. A question that didn't seem to want to go away.

She had spent the weekend wondering what to do, trying to behave normally and not let Sam think anything was wrong. Not that anything was wrong as such, but Emma sensed a storm might be coming, as if the No. 1 typhoon signal had been raised. She wished it was like a real typhoon where you could plot the expected path and when it was going to hit. She couldn't see anything good that was likely to come out of what she was doing, but it was as if she had no choice in the matter. She was being taken down this path whether she liked it or not. So here she was shortly after the library opened for the day with a pile of microfiches for 1992 editions of the *South China Morning Post*. What was she looking for? Any story that might have mentioned Gao Zhihua in a context that gave her some clue as to what his role had been in Xinhua.

She wished the microfiches had some sort of search facility. Within an hour her eyesight was tiring and she had barely reached the end of January. She leant back in her chair and rubbed her eyes. She opened them as wide as she could then shut them for a moment. She had been scanning pages for any stories that made reference to Xinhua or the New China News Agency. There were plenty but she could quickly dismiss them all as irrelevant; most of them being to do with politics and the handover. They rarely mentioned individuals. At most there was reference to 'a Xinhua spokesman', and certainly not Gao Zhihua.

By midday Emma had reached July and she was more than ready to take a break. Leaving the rest of the microfiches by the reader, she went to get some fresh air and walked towards Queen's Pier. She bought an iced tea from a vendor and sat looking over to Kowloon trying to let her mind go blank.

'Emma?' A man's voice behind her. She turned to see who it was.

'Liang-bao? Hi … what are you doing here?'

'Nothing much. Since it's a holiday, I've no classes today. I was thinking of going over Kowloon side. What about you?'

'What about me?' Emma was disoriented for a moment. Wondering what Liang-bao was doing there.

'What are you doing sitting on a bench by the harbour with a carton of iced tea?'

'Just taking a break.' She didn't want to explain why she'd been in the library, so she changed the conversation. 'How's Alice? I've not seen her for a while.'

'She's excited her cousin's going to be back in town soon. She's planning loads of things for them to do together.'

'Is that the cousin who's studying in Shanghai?'

'Kwok-wah. Yes.'

'How's he doing there?'

'I don't really know. I haven't met him myself yet. When he's back we should all get together – Alice and myself, Kwok-wah, you and Sam … I'll have a word with Alice. Try and fix something up.'

They sat in silence for a while. Emma wasn't ready to go back to her microfiches just yet, but she wished Liang-bao would go away and leave her in peace. Instead he sat looking across the harbour towards the Peninsula Hotel and the Cultural Centre until he spoke again.

'I do envy Alice – the way she's so close to her cousin. They're almost brother and sister. Of course not many people in China have a sibling. You know about the one-child policy?'

'Yes.'

'I mean, I do understand the need for it, why we have it, but sometimes I think it is strange. Several generations growing up without any brothers or sisters. Which means the next generation won't have any aunts or uncles, so there won't be any cousins in the future either. Well, there will be some. There are some cases where two children are allowed. But not for most people. It's going to be peculiar, I think. What about you? Do you have a brother?'

Emma hadn't been paying particularly close attention to what Liang-bao had been saying, but his question made her sit up and take notice.

'No, I don't.' She said. Not a lie but not quite the whole truth either. She didn't feel the need to expand on it.

'So that's something we have in common,' he said. 'Do you ever wish you did? Have a brother, that is?'

Uneasy at the direction the conversation had taken, Emma had difficulty in knowing what to say.

'I've never really thought about it,' she lied, before adding brusquely, 'I've got to be going.'

Back in the library Emma found was she shaking. She took the opportunity to go into the toilets to throw some water on her face and gather her thoughts before returning to her research. Her head told her it was just chance that Liang-bao had talked about families. That it was a natural conversation in view of Alice and her cousin. But there was also something odd about the conversation, she was sure of it, but she didn't know what. Emma dried her face with a paper towel, screwed it up into a ball and threw it into the bin, determined to forget about Liang-bao and get back to Gao Zhihua and his role in Xinhua.

Searching through the microfiches was proving both fruitless and tiring. She concluded that she really hadn't thought through just how much time it would take and how remote the likelihood of finding anything was. Things improved when she moved on to the CD-ROMs with their search facility. It was limited in scope, not a full text, but she could at least search for keywords in headlines. She looked for 'Xinhua', 'New

China News Agency' and 'Gao Zhihua' himself. His name itself found nothing but the other two inevitably gave a string of results. She started to go through them one by one: stories about Hong Kong after the handover; criticisms of Chris Patten (*'sinner of a thousand years, whore of the East'*); stories about how wonderful China was and the good works of the Communist Party; rebuttals of Western criticism. Most could be quickly eliminated and none made any reference to Gao Zhihua.

Emma was close to giving up when she found it. A report in the business section about the twelfth Asian Telecommunications Industry Conference. A report on a speech given about the future of the telecommunications industry in China. A speech given by a representative from Xinhua. A speech given by Gao Zhihua.

***

That night Emma slept fitfully. Her tinnitus was particularly bad. The usual low-pitched roaring in her right ear was especially loud, and there was a new sound: a high-pitched whine in her left. It had been a particularly hot and clammy night and even Emma, who generally didn't mind the heat as much as Sam did, found herself throwing off the bed sheet to allow the ceiling fan to caress her skin. There was a distant sound of thunder and Emma looked over at Sam to see if he was awake, but he slept on. Emma started thinking back over the day and knew there was no chance of getting back to sleep any time soon. Not wanting to disturb Sam, she got out of bed and went into the living room and looked out at the night scene. Lights sparkled on the container ships moored in the western harbour approaches, and even at this hour – in the middle of the night – she could see barges coming and going, loading and unloading. Business, trade, stopped for nothing. Not the clock, not the weather, not for politics. Certainly not for politics. But that was Hong Kong. Business, finance, profit, deals were what the city was all about. What the city had always been about and what would always come first. She was never quite sure whether that was a good or bad thing. In the distance, beyond Lantau, she could see lightning.

She thought about Gao Zhihua and what she had learnt today. She knew she couldn't be certain – perhaps she could never be completely sure – but it seemed more likely than not that the Gao Zhihua who had killed Peter was one of Sam's clients. So, what was she supposed to do with this information? Should she tell Sam? And if she did what did she expect him to do about it anyway? Emma went to the bedroom door and watched Sam sleeping. He had discarded the sheet completely and lay there naked in the heat. He'd come back from a day on the junk more than a little the worse for wear, and pink from the sun. He'd be painfully burnt in places by the morning. He looked vulnerable. Here was the man who had brought her not only happiness but even more importantly a stability. The possibility of a future. She knew she loved him.

She knew that he loved her. She knew she couldn't do anything, or ask him to do anything, that would jeopardise his career. But she also knew that she had to do something for Peter. If only she had the faintest idea of what.

Emma made herself tea and sat on the sofa, propping up the cushions so she could still see the lightning, which was now visibly closer. The storm was to the west, over Lantau, heading her way. One, two, three … Emma counted the seconds between the flash of light and the thunder. The gap was narrowing and the lightning getting closer, but then she could see that for herself without counting. She watched a particularly impressive strike hit the sea off Cheung Chau. The moment frozen in time by the illumination. That was when she suddenly realised what had been strange about her conversation with Liang-bao: why had he only asked if she had a brother? Not a sister?

CHAPTER 20

SUSAN INSPECTED HER FACE IN the mirror of the hotel bathroom. The bruises around her eyes were healing, the scar on her left cheek had faded and was a little less obvious than before. The judicious use of some concealer and letting her hair fall more forward than usual should be enough to cover the remaining discoloration. Not that she had anything to hide, but she would prefer it if people didn't stare the way they had on the plane. Now all that she needed was for the nightmares to stop.

Susan had been surprised when they struck her in the face. She had expected them to be more subtle than that. To not leave visible evidence. She wasn't sure if that meant that her interrogators were amateurs, or whether they hadn't expected her to be released so quickly that the bruising was still visible. Either way she was both relieved and at the same time in a curious way almost a little disappointed. Relieved that the physical pain had not been unbearable, relieved that she had been released after only two months, her ego disappointed that she wasn't thought to be a big player. Not worthy of high-level operatives.

After being taken from the university, Susan had spent three nights in a cold and damp police cell. She had been stripped and left in just her underwear for the first night until they gave her a grey prison overall. Other than the guard who brought her food, she was left alone until the fourth day. Alone except for the cockroaches. She had been in a shallow sleep when the door opened and she was dragged out by two young soldiers, thrown in the back of a van and then driven for several hours to what she assumed to be a military prison. Her first interrogator was an older man who seemed bored with the whole thing and uninterested in anything she said. After a few days he disappeared to be replaced by a younger man who took more pleasure in his work. Days of beatings, interposed with threats of sexual assault, until without warning or expectation, she was released.

Susan guessed that strings had been pulled. She had expected at least a year or two in jail before being kicked out. No doubt, she thought, with the world watching China as the handover approached, they had decided that this wasn't a good time to pick a fight with the United States. Whatever the reason, she had been taken from her cell in the early hours one Tuesday morning, and although she had feared the worst she had been driven to the airport and put on a plane to Hong Kong.

That had been a surprise at first – why Hong Kong and not the States?

'To watch you, to see who you meet here.'

That was the explanation given by the consular official who met her off the plane at Kai Tak. 'Be careful who you talk to while you're here, if not for your sake then for theirs. It's probably best if you don't stay in Hong Kong too long.' He was right, of course, and it didn't take long for Susan to start spotting the same two or three people who always seemed to be in her vicinity. They made her uneasy even though her rational mind knew that nothing was going to happen to her in Hong Kong. In theory there was nobody that she had to see here and nobody would have complained if she had simply taken a flight back home. Indeed, she sensed that the Consulate would have preferred that, but she had an envelope to deliver somehow. She had been given it in the car from the airport.

'I'm told this is what you wanted.'

Susan had taken the envelope, puzzled. The last two months had taken their toll, but when she opened the envelope and looked at its contents she smiled.

'Thank you,' she said. 'Yes. This is just what I wanted.' How to get it to its intended recipient was the only problem.

***

Hong Kong was a contradiction to Susan. Familiar and unfamiliar at the same time. Starbucks and McDonalds next to Chinese medicine shops. The city was gearing up for the handover and she wondered if everybody would have been so relaxed about the change if they had spent the last few weeks in a Chinese prison, but she knew better than to discuss it with anyone she encountered. The Consulate itself was one place where Susan could talk freely. She was followed there, of course, but there were countless practical reasons why she might visit the Consulate so it shouldn't seem suspicious. If it did, well, tough. They knew who and what she was anyway. She passed through the security barrier into the high-walled compound that occupied a prestigious spot near the cathedral. The Head of Station was expecting her. He was younger than Susan had expected, dressed casually, a West Coast university professor perhaps, and seemed to consider Susan an irritation that he could do without.

'When are you planning on leaving for the States?' had been his opening gambit when they were seated in his office. Very unsubtle, thought Susan.

'Soon. I just have one thing to do here and then I'll be out of your hair. I promise.'

'Which is?'

'I have to get in touch with someone in Hong Kong and give them an envelope.'

'Have you tried the postal service? It's quite efficient here, you know.'

'Her name is Alice Chan.' Susan was irritated by the man's sarcasm and tried to ignore it. 'She's the cousin of a student I knew in Shanghai. She's involved with a human rights group here in Hong Kong.'

The Head of Station sighed. 'Miss Khoo, as you can imagine we are rather busy at the moment. Busy all the time, in fact, but with the handover approaching even more so. However, much as I may not like it, I do have instructions from Shanghai to help you in this. Alice Chan … Do you have a Chinese given name?'

'No.' Susan was embarrassed that she hadn't thought to ask Kwok-wah this and she only knew the family name. 'Sorry.'

'I believe there are probably quite a few Alice Chans in Hong Kong. One moment.' The Head of Section got up from his desk and spoke to a colleague in an outer room. He returned to Susan. 'But we do keep a watching brief on local political activists. Nothing special, we don't get involved and leave that to the Brits if they want to, but we like to know who they are and what they're up to.' A man entered the room carrying a file that he passed to the Head of Section.

'Will you have been watching Alice Chan?' Susan asked.

'Possibly. Give me a moment.' Susan let her eyes wander around the office while he started to go through the file. Portraits of past US presidents hung on the walls. She tried to remember who they all were, but she couldn't go back any further than JFK. 'How many Alice Chans do you need? We have three on our books. One of them is fifty-eight and a schoolteacher. Another is a forty-four-year-old barrister, and the third – which I'm guessing may be the one you are looking for – is twenty-eight and a secretary in a trading company. Have a look.' He handed Susan the file.

'That sounds like her. Do you have contact details? It just gives here the company she works for.'

'Then that's probably all we have. If you contact her, be discreet. They're probably watching her.'

Susan bit her tongue. She wasn't that green, and besides, another name in the file had caught her attention.

'What do you know about this woman? Emma Janssen. It says here that she's another member of the group.'

'Here, let me see.' He took back the file. 'Not much. I think she's a friend of your Alice Chan.'

'No contact details?'

'Nothing here … Oh, I see, that's why there's nothing. She's a temp floating from job to job. She has – or at least had at the time this note was taken – a boyfriend. A lawyer working for McShane Adams, one of the big Hong Kong law firms. Why do you ask?'

'I used to know an Emma Janssen. It may not be the same one, of course. The Emma Janssen I knew certainly wasn't interested in politics at all, and if it is the same person I didn't know she was in Hong Kong.'

It didn't take Susan long before she was able to telephone Alice at her work. Susan thought it unlikely that a regular office number would be monitored.

'Hi, I'm Susan Khoo, I'm a friend of your cousin Kwok-wah, studying at the same university in Shanghai.' Susan had decided to assume from the start that she was speaking with the right Alice Chan. If not, no harm would have been done. 'I was wondering if we could meet. There's something I need to talk to you about.'

'What is it? Is he okay?' Susan could hear the anxiety in Alice's voice.

'Yes, of course ... Sorry, I didn't mean to alarm you. He's fine but I'm not sure when I will be back in Shanghai and there's something I would like him to have. I was hoping that if I gave it to you then you could pass it on to him the next time you see him.'

'I suppose so ...' Susan could tell that Alice was still a little wary.

'I was wondering if I could come to where you work?' Susan had been giving some thought as to how she could meet Alice without her minders knowing. The best that she had been able to come up with was that by meeting within the offices of a large company they wouldn't know for certain who Susan was meeting. Of course, they might put two and two together if they were watching, but then again her minders might be quite different from whoever was keeping an eye on Alice. Nothing was without risk. The only way of being safe was to do nothing. Susan was relieved when in spite of some obvious uncertainty and reluctance, Alice agreed to meet her.

When Susan found the building where Alice worked, she waited in reception until a woman, about thirty and almost as tall as Susan was herself, came over to her.

'Susan?'

'Yes. You must be Alice? Thanks for seeing me.'

'I'll admit that I'm puzzled … What can I do for you?'

'Is there somewhere more private?'

Alice took Susan into an empty meeting room where they both sat at a table. Uncomfortable with each other, it was Alice who spoke first.

'Forgive me, Miss …?'

'It's Khoo, Susan Khoo, but please, just Susan.'

'I'll be honest and say that Kwok-wah has never mentioned you. How do you know him?'

'We were friends …' Susan was a little unsure how far she could answer honestly. She didn't want to lie to Alice. 'But I had to leave suddenly – a family illness – and I'm not sure when I'll be able to get back.' Susan knew that she would be going nowhere near Shanghai any time soon, but she could hardly say that without raising even more suspicions. Susan pulled out an envelope from the bag she had with her. 'It's just that I need to get this to Kwok-wah.' She placed the envelope on the table between them.

'May I ask what it is?' Susan thought that Alice sounded suspicious. She couldn't really blame her.

'It's just something I know he would like … Some information that he wanted.' Again Susan hesitated, not knowing how far she should go, before deciding that the less she said the more suspicious she must sound. 'Has he mentioned Granny Sun to you?'

'The woman who looks after his dorm building?'

'That's right. I don't know if he's told you this but

Kwok-wah has become quite friendly with her. The thing is, she had to give away her son and she never found out what happened to him. The answer is in that envelope.'

Alice picked up the envelope and went to open it before stopping herself and putting the envelope back down on the table.

'So how did you get this information?'

'I'm sorry. I can't tell you that.'

'Who are you, Miss Khoo?'

'I'm sorry ... I wish ...'

'Kwok-wah will be back home soon. If you like you could give this to him yourself,' said Alice.

Susan wasn't expecting that. Term hadn't finished yet in Shanghai. She'd like to see him, try to explain things. But what could she tell him? That his supervisor was in cahoots with the army? She knew that she shouldn't see him.

'I expect I'll have left Hong Kong by then. Which is a pity. I'd have liked the chance to explain things to him.' Susan paused, still tempted to tell Alice more but knowing that she shouldn't. 'Can I ask one last favour of you before I leave? Can you please tell him something from me?'

***

Kwok-wah almost stumbled backwards under the weight of Alice's embrace. They were in the hallway of his parents' apartment. His mother was in the kitchen.

'It's lovely to see you again. Home safe and sound,' said Alice, when she had finally finished hugging him and ruffling his hair. 'Let me have a look at you. You seem older. More grown up somehow. Must be the travel. Being away from home.'

'I expect so.'

'Yes, travel does wonders. Broadens the mind ...' said Alice. 'Unless there's something you're not telling me.'

'What are you getting at?'

'You know very well, Kwok-wah. Just because you are several hundred miles away doesn't mean that Cousin Alice doesn't know what's going on.'

'You do? I wish you'd tell me ...'

Alice lowered her voice to a whisper. 'Susan.'

'What about her? How do you know about Susan!' Kwok-wah said in a louder than normal voice.

'Shhh!' Alice gestured to the kitchen. She continued to whisper. 'I've something for you. We need to talk in private somewhere. Let's go get a coffee.' Then in a raised voice: 'Hello, Auntie! How are you? I'm just taking Kwok-wah out to get a coffee. Bye-bye, Auntie! I'll bring him back soon.'

They spoke only of mundane matters until they were sitting with two cappuccinos in a quiet corner of a coffee shop.

'So, it's a routine day at work, a couple of days ago,' started Alice, 'when I get a call from a young woman asking to meet me, American by the sound of her accent, and she comes round to the office. American-Chinese it turns out. *Very* good looking, I might add. I've no idea who she is or what she wants but she says that she's a friend of yours in Shanghai?'

'Yes, she is. Or at least I thought so.'

'That sounds mysterious, but then she was mysterious as well. Anyway, she said that she had something you would want to see.' Alice took the envelope from the plastic supermarket bag she had with her and passed it over to Kwok-wah. 'Desperately curious though I am, I haven't opened it. I've no idea what it contains except that she said it was something to do with Granny Sun and her son.'

'Granny Sun? I've no idea what's in here,' said Kwok-wah as he turned the plain unmarked envelope over looking for clues but failing to find anything.

'Then perhaps you'd better open it and find out?'

Alice watched as Kwok-wah opened the envelope and took out a sheaf of papers. He started to look through them. Alice gave him some time.

'Well?' she asked, when her patience was at its limit.

'I don't understand. How did she get this stuff? Is she still in Hong Kong? Did she say where she was staying?'

'No, she didn't. She said she wasn't likely to be in Hong Kong for long and she didn't know when she would be back in Shanghai either. What is it? What's in the papers?'

Kwok-wah continued to look though them before answering.

'So, he's probably dead.'

'Who is? Her son?'

'Shu-ming, yes. Did Susan tell you the story? Granny Sun always wanted to know what happened to him, but the records seem to stop a few years after she lost him.' Kwok-wah thought for a moment. 'What do I do? Do I tell her? I don't know if knowing for certain is better or worse than living with the hope that he might be alive somewhere. What do you think?'

'I don't know either. Here, let me have a look.' Kwok-wah passed the papers over to Alice. 'These are very official looking documents. Extracts from school records, hospital records …' Alice leafed through the pages. 'Where did she get these from?'

'I've absolutely no idea.'

'Tell me about her.'

When Kwok-wah had finished telling Alice about Susan and her disappearance, she moved her chair so as to be next to him and put an arm around his shoulder.

'You loved her, didn't you?'

'Yes. I think she was the first girl I've loved. Really loved, you know? Not just dated and gone out with.'

'I know.' Alice passed Kwok-wah a tissue. 'There's one other thing that she asked me to tell you.'

'What's that?'

'She said to say that she was sorry.'

***

The rain had started last Friday and continued over the weekend. It had scarcely relented since, and when he left for work that morning Sam had cursed the weather for making such a crappy start to the week. Without a job to go to, Emma was left to deal with the consequences of the rain in their apartment. There was a damp patch in the bedroom that was growing, and when the rain came in on the wind, the water forced itself around the living room window, leaving a puddle on the sill. Emma had started leaving an old towel there to soak up the water. She sat wrapped in her dressing gown and stared out the window, watching a stream of water tumbling from a broken gutter.

Emma was restless. She didn't know what to do about the dinner with Sam's client. It was still some time away, but it was already starting to preoccupy her. She desperately didn't want to go, she didn't want to have anything to do with his client, but she knew how important it was to Sam, how much he wanted to take her as his other half. At the same time she was still completely undecided as to what, if anything, she should do about Gao Zhihua being one of his clients. She had some work lined up for later in the week, which would help take her mind off things, but for the moment she was going stir-crazy indoors. Rain or no rain, she needed to get out. To be lost among other people, to be distracted from her thoughts.

She dressed lightly. There was no point worrying about the weather. The rain was warm and her skin would dry faster than any clothes. Although she was no great lover of shops, Emma thought that even on a Monday morning the best place to find other people was a shopping mall so she headed to Pacific Place. Mid-morning it wasn't as crowded and busy as she had hoped and now that she was there she had no idea of what to do; there was nothing that she wanted or needed and she wondered how Alice managed to spend whole days in these places. Anyway, she could scarcely afford most of the shops, which catered exclusively to the well-heeled. Emma had a momentary image of a future life when Sam was a partner and she would be an expat wife: lunching with other expat wives and gossiping about who was sleeping with who before a little retail therapy or perhaps an afternoon at a spa. She laughed at the image; not so much a fantasy as a nightmare.

Emma saw him while she was half-heartedly trying on a pair of tennis shoes. While Emma tried to ignore the brusque entreaties of the salesgirl, she noticed Liang-bao looking into the shop and trying to catch her attention. She wondered why she seemed to keep bumping into him. Emma wasn't in the mood to talk to Liang-bao. Their conversation at Queen's Pier still troubled her, but she was trapped in the shop with no way of escape that would avoid him. Besides, she had to be civil to him for Alice's sake. She decided that she might as well get it over with, and to the ill-disguised disgust of the shop assistant Emma abandoned any pretence of being interested in the shoes and left the shop.

'Small world,' she said to Liang-bao.

'Sorry?'

'It's a small world. A surprise … seeing you here … a colloquialism.'

'Ah, I see. That's a new one for me. I must remember it.'

They stood to one side, keeping out of the way of

the shoppers.

'What brings you here? Apart from keeping out of the rain, that is,' asked Emma.

'Looking for a present for Alice,' he replied.

Alice's birthday was on Friday. She must get something herself.

'Have you found anything yet?'

'I saw some earrings that I think are her sort of thing. I may go back later and get them. How's Sam?'

Emma started to walk towards a stylish boutique and looked in the window. She hoped that Liang-bao might get the message. She wondered what she might wear to the dinner with Sam's client.

'Good, thanks,' she said eventually. Liang-bao failed to take the hint and suggested that they sit on a bench.

'Have you made plans for the handover yet?' he asked. This was a major topic of conversation as the date approached. *What are you doing? Where will you be?* Many of the best restaurants and clubs had been booked up months ago. People seemed more concerned about dining options than history.

'We found a restaurant in Causeway Bay that still had places. Sam, me and a couple of his friends from work.'

'Sam's doing well at work, isn't he?'

'Yes, I guess so. There's talk of partnership.'

'Wow. That is good. So, he is staying on after the handover?'

'That's the plan.'

'And you too, I guess?'

'So it seems.' In truth Emma didn't know. She and Sam hadn't discussed it much. They were going to have to sometime though. She would need a job that gave her a visa, and without any special skills it wasn't obvious how she would get one. Unless of course they were married, but then she didn't want to get married just to be able to stay in Hong Kong, and she certainly didn't want to pressure Sam into some kind of immigration-related shotgun marriage. If they were ever to get married it had to be for the right reason, not just to solve some bureaucratic problem.

'Of course, whether we like it or not things are going to be different. Even for Sam. Perhaps especially for Sam.'

'In what way?' Emma was puzzled as to what Liang-bao was getting at.

'In the future more and more of his work is going to involve China. Chinese companies, Chinese investors. Even the Chinese government sometimes. There will be times when he has to be discreet. Careful with his words.'

'I'm sure he knows that.'

'I expect he does, Emma. Of course, he will also need people around him that he can trust. People he can rely on not to let him down.'

Emma wondered if she'd heard correctly. 'Sorry?'

'Sam doesn't need people who might embarrass him.'

'Embarrass him? What are you talking about?' Emma suspected that she knew exactly what Liang-bao was talking about but she had no idea how he knew. She tried to read him. How much did he know? Did he know about Gao Zhihua and Peter? Emma couldn't see any way that he could. She certainly hadn't told Alice. Had Yannie said something? It seemed unlikely. It was months ago that Emma had talked about Peter to Yannie and Eric.

'Emma, I like you. You're a friend and I hope you think of me as a friend as well. I'm just saying that if you want what's best for Sam, then be careful what you say and who you say it in front of.'

'I'm sorry, Liang-bao, my hearing is playing up today. I've no idea what you're talking about. Perhaps I'd better be going.' Flustered, Emma started to gather her things.

'Forgive me if I've upset you, Emma, but think about what I said will you?'

Emma spent the rest of the day thinking about little else. She replayed the conversation in her head repeatedly as if on a loop. How can Liang-bao know about Gao Zhihua, and why did she keeping meeting him unexpectedly? Outside the library might have been coincidence – but again? Getting nowhere with this chain of thinking, Emma tried to put it out of her mind when another thought came in its place: what was Liang-bao doing in Pacific Place in the middle of the day anyway? Okay, he said that he was looking for a present for Alice, and it was true that her birthday was soon, but surely he would have had classes or something at the university? And how would he afford jewellery from one of those shops? But if he wasn't there by coincidence, buying a present for Alice, why was he there? Emma realised that the only other explanation was that he was hoping to meet her, to talk to her. But then Emma was hardly a regular visitor to Pacific Place, she didn't even know herself that morning that she would be going there. Which left only one possibility. That she had been followed. More than that, he had been watching the flat.

A ridiculous idea. Emma told herself to stop being so stupid. She was starting to obsess about Peter and Gao Zhihua so much that she seemed to be losing the power of rational thought. All this speculating about cover-ups was turning her into some crazed conspiracy theorist. Coincidences did happen, that's why the word existed. After all, wasn't it just a coincidence that a few months ago she'd seen someone who looked a bit like Liang-bao come out of the Xinhua building?

CHAPTER 21

SUSAN LOOKED AT HER TICKET again. A Cathay Pacific flight to Los Angeles leaving Saturday, 21st June 1997. Tomorrow night. The plan was for her to have some R & R with her parents in California before flying to Langley and returning to duty. She was looking forward to seeing Mom and Dad and spending some time just chilling. She'd telephoned them from Hong Kong to let them know where she was. Not that they knew exactly what she did. They thought that she worked for the State Department on international aid projects, so they were used to her turning up in unlikely places. The whole idea of being back in California was very tempting, so why was she thinking of staying on?

Her hotel had been prepaid by the Consulate until tomorrow. She had a little money of her own, the Consulate had given her an advance on her salary, so if she could change the ticket and find somewhere cheaper to stay there wasn't really an immediate need to leave Hong Kong, was there?

Why did she want to stay? Susan wasn't really sure herself. Unfinished business perhaps? She remembered Emma Janssen. She hadn't followed that up. If it was the same person, they'd become quite close in a short period of time. It was a couple of years ago but it would be good to see her again, have a few drinks and catch up, and if it was the same Emma Janssen and she was a friend of Alice Chan, then who knew? She might be useful. Susan figured that if she was a temp dating a lawyer there was a chance that she was working for the same firm. A call to McShane Adams quickly revealed that she wasn't but that she had been, and the receptionist was more than happy to give Susan the name of the employment agency that they used for temporary secretaries. In turn the agency didn't need much persuading to tell her where Emma was currently working. One more phone call and old friends were reunited and a reunion arranged.

Finding Emma was a distraction from thinking about Kwok-wah. She was undecided on whether she should see him again. Certainly it was against the rules, against all standard best practice, but then she'd been breaking the rules for some time now and she was unhappy with the way she had treated him. Used him. She was also worried that Kwok-wah himself might be in danger. They might have thought that Kwok-wah and Susan were working together. Would it be safe for him back in Shanghai? Was it even safe for him in Hong Kong? Should she at least try and warn him or was contacting him only putting him in even more danger?

Perhaps she wasn't really cut out for this business, she thought. Not hard enough. Not cold enough.

First though she had to find him in this city of six million. She couldn't ask the Consulate for help – as far as they were concerned she was going to be out of their hair tomorrow. The only lead she had was Alice Chan. She called her at work:

'This is Susan Khoo. We met the other day ... about Kwok-wah ...'

'I remember.' Susan thought Alice seemed cold. Distant.

'You said that he was going to be back in Hong Kong. Is he back now? I was wondering if it would be possible to talk to Kwok-wah, to see him again, but I don't have his address or number.' Susan paused, hoping for a reply from Alice. When none came, she continued. 'I was thinking you might be able to help?' Another pause. 'I'm quite close to your office. I could easily come round.' Silence. Susan wondered if there was a problem with the phone.

'I don't know,' Alice finally spoke. 'Do you know how upset he is? How much you've hurt him? Is there anything you can say or do that will make up for that? Or are you going to raise his hopes just to dump him again?'

'Sorry, I don't know what to say. You don't know how much I'm going out on a limb by wanting to see him again.'

'Who are you anyway? I've seen the papers you gave Kwok-wah. Where did you get them from? And why have you been playing with Kwok-wah? What's he done to deserve all this? I just think it would be better if he didn't see you again.'

'Please. Will you just think about it?' Susan was running out of arguments. There was another long pause. 'Hello?'

'I'll think about it. Call me again on Monday.'

Susan was indeed close to Alice's work. In fact she was calling from a phone in a *dai po dong* on the other side of the road from where Alice worked. It was late in the afternoon so she decided to order some food to keep the owner happy, and then she'd wait and watch to see when Alice left. Not that she knew what she was going to do then. Perhaps follow Alice to see where she went. Where she lived. Perhaps to see if she would lead her to Kwok-wah. Anyway, it was something to do. She could just see what developed naturally.

Thirty minutes later and a man arrived at the entrance to the building, but rather than going in he simply stood outside. Tall for a Chinese man was Susan's first thought. Certainly not Cantonese, perhaps from somewhere in the north. She watched him for a while. He was alert to everything around him. It was something that civilians probably wouldn't notice, it certainly wasn't obvious, but Susan could see the way he was taking in his surroundings. Watching people. He probably wasn't even doing it consciously. No doubt it was second nature to him. There was something about him that only a fellow professional would recognise. The more she watched him, the more Susan admired his technique. But what was he doing there? Watching someone himself? Following someone? Waiting for someone?

Later Susan was cross with herself for not realising the truth straightaway. After all, she had been warned that Hong Kong activists were being watched, but it was only when Alice left the building that she put two and two together. Even then she was surprised when Alice put her arms round the man and they kissed. Once Susan had got over her initial shock, she found herself laughing. The irony. This guy was playing Alice in much the same way that she had been using Kwok-wah, the only difference being that in her case Kwok-wah was only a means to an end. Susan thought for a moment about following them before thinking better of it. She wasn't really supposed to be in Hong Kong and there'd be hell to pay if she was spotted by the other side.

***

Alice had been disturbed by Susan's call and genuinely didn't know what to do. She was confused as to whether to give her Kwok-wah's number or not. Was there a chance of some kind of reconciliation or would it just make things worse? What was it people talked about … closure? Or would a clean break be better all round? Alice was completely undecided and hoped to take advantage of the evening to try and judge Kwok-wah's mood before Susan rang her again. Either way, she was pleased to see Liang-bao waiting for her when she left the office and threw her arms around him as they kissed.

'Tell me,' Alice asked Liang-bao, 'if I was to disappear tomorrow without warning, what would you think?'

'Do you think you're likely to?'

Alice explained the story of Kwok-wah and Susan.

'But, God, whatever you do don't let on tonight that I told you any of this. Okay? Promise? I shouldn't have told you really but … I don't know … I just don't know what's for the best.'

'I think I'd prefer the clean break. What's the saying in English? More fish …?'

'… in the sea. Yes, you probably would, wouldn't you?' Alice poked Liang-bao in the ribs. 'Just move on to your next conquest? But seriously, I don't know what to do. I just hope I'll know what to say when she rings on Monday. Perhaps I'll get a better idea after tonight.' Alice had been insistent that Kwok-wah should join her birthday bash. ('Come and join us. It will stop you from moping. You know Queen's Building? Meet us in the lobby there at seven.') The plan was to join up with Emma and Sam at his office and then to go on from there. A few drinks, dinner and who knows where the evening might lead. Anything to get Kwok-wah out of his room. Even his parents were starting to worry and they were complicit in Alice's attempts to get him out of their apartment. In the end Kwok-wah had given in.

Alice looked at her watch. 'We've got plenty of time

to kill before we meet the others. Let's go get a beer.'

***

Kwok-wah had spent the day writing up some of the results from his research. He should really have still been in Shanghai – term hadn't finished – but after Susan had disappeared he'd asked permission to come back to Hong Kong a couple of weeks early. He had been surprised, and perhaps in a way a little disconcerted, at how quickly Professor Ye had agreed. Although the memory of being shouted at was still vivid, he had imagined that he was becoming invaluable and yet it was almost as if the professor was glad to be rid of him for a while.

He didn't want to go out with Alice and her friends, but it was her birthday so he hadn't been able to put up much of an argument. In his heart he would much prefer just to stay in and watch TV rather than spend time with people he had never met before. Two of them *gweilos* as well. Not that he had a problem with *gweilos,* he just didn't really connect with them. Not the way Alice did. He'd always thought that Alice would end up with a Western boyfriend and he was more than a little surprised that she was seeing a mainlander. Still, at least that meant he would have something to talk about and somebody who would understand some of his experiences.

He was in plenty of time when he got to Queen's Building. Too early to expect any of the others to be there. There were a number of chairs in the lobby so he took one and watched the comings and goings.

A security guard eyed him suspiciously. Wearing just jeans and a *Star Wars* T-shirt, he saw how well-dressed everyone else was and wished that perhaps he had made more of an effort. Was there still time to cry off? Perhaps say that he wasn't feeling well and just go home? McShane Adams had their own dedicated lift, which he kept an eye on in particular; not that he knew why as he had never met Alice's friends before and had no idea what they looked like.

He wondered where Susan was, and what she was doing. He imagined that she was back home in California. Back with her family and friends. Did she think about him at all or was he just somebody she had toyed with? And who was she anyway? How did she get those papers about Shu-ming? He still had no idea of whether he was going to tell Granny Sun when he got back to Shanghai. Assuming he went back. He felt that it wasn't really working out as he'd hoped, but then he didn't want to admit that to Alice, his parents and the rest of the world who had all told him to go to the States or somewhere like that. Anywhere but China. All those thoughts and more were chasing each other around his head while he sat and waited for the others when the lift door opened and two men appeared. One was quite old and indeed old-fashioned, with his heavily-dyed hair parted in the middle of his forehead. He reminded Kwok-wah a little of his history teacher at school. The other man was younger, middle-aged anyway in spite of thinning hair, smartly dressed in what even Kwok-wah could see was an expensive suit. For a moment

Kwok-wah was confused; the context was so different that at first he almost failed to recognise the younger man. But there really wasn't any doubt about it. Swap the designer suit for a military uniform and this was undoubtedly the professor's army contact.

Absorbed in watching the two men as they walked across the lobby and out into the street, Kwok-wah failed to see Alice and Liang-bao approaching from another direction and he almost jumped with shock when Alice tapped him on the shoulder.

'Sorry, hello? Earth to Kwok-wah? Didn't mean to startle you, but you had a faraway look on your face, you know, the way you sometimes do when you are working on your projects. Have you had an idea about something?'

'No, sorry … no, nothing like that, it's just …'

'What?'

'Did you see those two guys who just left the building?'

'I didn't really notice anybody, there are so many people. What about them?'

'Well, you'll think I'm crazy—'

'No more than usual I expect.'

'—but I've just seen a guy I recognise from Shanghai.'

'That's not a big deal, surely?' asked Liang-bao. 'These days there are more and more people from the mainland here, I mean, look at me, and especially from Shanghai.'

'Yes, but this is different. If he's the man I think he is, I've seen him in the labs with Professor Ye. Only back in Shanghai he was always in uniform.'

'In uniform?' asked Alice.

'Yes. Some type of military uniform.'

'Are you saying he's PLA?' Liang-bao laughed. 'Here in the lobby of Queen's Building? Next month perhaps, but not just yet.'

'Are you sure?' asked Alice.

'Well, I thought I was, but … I don't know now …'

'Look,' said Alice, 'here's Emma.'

By the end of the evening, during which Kwok-wah had enjoyed himself far more than he thought he would, an evening in which wine was drunk, copious amounts of food consumed and songs sung, the question of why a PLA officer was visiting the offices of a Hong Kong law firm was long forgotten.

***

The strength of the sunlight sneaking into Liang-bao's bedroom through the gap between the curtains showed that it had been morning for a while. Liang-bao turned over in bed and looked at Alice beside him. She was lying face down and he reached over and kissed her on the back of the neck.

'Mmm …' Alice's voice was muffled by the pillow.

He pulled the sheet away from her and ran his fingers down her back, lingering gently on her hips. He traced a circle around the small of her back and then allowed his fingertips to brush the backs of her thighs as softly and delicately as he could, barely touching her body. Alice responded by moving her legs apart, creating room for his hands to explore further as his fingers caressed her.

'Mmmm …'

'Wake up, sleepy head.'

'I am awake,' said Alice, moving her head so that she could speak more clearly. She turned towards Liang-bao and put her arms around his neck. 'I've been awake for a while.'

'Good morning, birthday girl,' he said.

'That was yesterday. Now I'm just a year older. Still, last night wasn't bad for an old woman was it?' Alice smiled at Liang-bao as she remembered the night just gone. 'Not bad at all.' She pulled Liang-bao towards her until he was on top.

'Alice … what are you doing?'

'You mean you don't know?' she giggled.

'I should be thinking about' – he kissed her on the mouth – 'getting' – he kissed her left breast, his tongue flicking her nipple – 'a move on' – and then her right breast.

'Really?' Alice felt between his legs. 'You don't seem in that much of a rush to get up.' She rolled Liang-bao onto his back and straddled him, then, leaning forward, her lips found his lips, her tongue met his tongue. Breaking off the kiss, Alice sat upright again and started to move against his erection until she was ready for him and then adjusted her position and took him inside her.

'Nobody ever told me that Hong Kong girls were so demanding …' he said.

'Shut up.'

***

'Is there any fruit?' Alice, hair still wet from the shower and decent only by virtue of a towel, was in the tiny kitchen looking for breakfast.

'There should be some papaya in the fridge,' Liang-bao answered, still in bed. The flat was so small that they could easily have a conversation from different rooms.

'Got it.' Alice found a bowl and filled it with the fruit. At the back of the fridge she also found some yoghurt that was only one day beyond its use-by date. Alice sniffed the yoghurt and then added that to the papaya. She returned to the bedroom and sat on the edge of the bed while she ate. The bedroom floor was strewn with clothes and the detritus of the night before.

'How's your throat?' he asked.

'My throat?'

'You were belting out the karaoke last night.'

'Sorry. Did I get carried away?'

'A bit perhaps.'

Alice finished the fruit. She put the bowl on the floor and got back into bed.

'You seemed to be enjoying yourself as well, but your Cantonese is terrible. You were much better with the English songs.' They'd ended up in a Causeway Bay karaoke bar at the end of the evening. 'Your "Love Me Tender" was great. Sing it now … go on …'

Liang-bao ignored the Elvis request. 'What are you

going to tell your parents about where you were last night?' he asked instead. Spending the night together hadn't been planned, but when Liang-bao had suggested coming back to his place in Aberdeen it had seemed to Alice the natural thing to do, and much more satisfying than their previous times, which had had to be grabbed when the chance arose. Alice was still downplaying the relationship to her family and before last night she had never been able to stay over without lying about where she was.

'No need, they're away visiting family in Vancouver.'

'You mean we could have gone to your place?'

'No way!' Alice was horrified at the thought. 'Concepcion would tell them.'

'Concepcion?'

'The maid. Anyway, you've got a great place here.'

'It's nothing special, just a one-bed. Four hundred and fifty square feet including my share of the lift.'

'But with a view.' The flat looked out over Aberdeen harbour, where the fishing boats were moored and tied together to form a community of their own, and over to Ap Lei Chau, where at night the lights gave the illusion of glamour – buildings that sparkled like diamonds after dark, but which were revealed by daylight to be drab public housing blocks. 'I've never understood how you can afford it. I'd kill for a flat like this. I've got a full-time job but I'm stuck with my parents. What's your secret?'

'Do you really want to know? I'm a gigolo.'

Alice raised herself up on one arm and looked at

Liang-bao. She pretended to be upset. 'That explains it. I knew you were up to something. When you're not with me you spend your time seducing rich *tai tais*. I should have guessed. How much do I owe you for last night?'

'The rather more boring truth is that I get an allowance from my father.'

'So I'm not just another notch on your bedpost?' Alice kissed him on the forehead. 'What time is it anyway?'

Liang-bao leant over to look at his watch on the bedside table. 'Just gone eleven.'

'I'd better get going. I'm meeting Emma for lunch and I need to go home and change. I can't turn up wearing last night's outfit.' Alice got out of bed and started gathering her clothes together. 'Perhaps I should start leaving a few things here.' She glanced at Liang-bao to check his reaction before adding: 'Don't worry, I'm not moving in, but it would be nice to have some clean underwear.'

'Emma seems happy with Sam?' he asked.

'Yes. She seems much more settled and content these days.' Alice tried not to be disappointed that Liang-bao had changed the subject. At least he hadn't said no. 'Much more settled than last year anyway.' Alice had found her underwear and was pulling up her knickers.

'In what way?'

'Didn't you notice? I guess you'd only just met her then, but she seemed very preoccupied for a time. Miles away whenever you tried talking to her. And then do

you remember the scene that time at the Fringe Club?'
Alice was fastening her bra. 'Perhaps it was just her
hearing. Whatever. She wants to talk about the group.
She says she has some ideas.' Alice pulled her dress on
over her head. 'Can you zip me up at the back …?
Thanks.' Alice rubbed at a mark on the dress. 'Damn.
I knew I'd spilt something on it.'

'Emma's getting quite involved with the group, isn't
she?'

'She is, yes. I'm a bit surprised to be honest. It took
me ages to persuade her to come along, I was on the
verge of giving up, but as you say she's really getting
into it now.' Alice had now located her handbag and
she took out a hairbrush and started to work on her
rapidly drying hair.

'How long are you in Beijing for?' Alice asked. She
examined her hair in a mirror and sighed.

'Just until Tuesday, I don't want to miss too many
classes. My father's birthday is on Monday.'

'Well, if he's paying for this place you'd better keep
in with him.' Alice looked around. 'Have you seen my
shoes? When's your flight?'

'Four thirty.'

'How do I look?' Alice had discovered her shoes
under the bed.

'Terrific.'

'Liar. I look like a shameless hussy who didn't sleep
in her own bed last night. The taxi driver will know.'

'You could take the bus?'

'God no, that would be even worse. There'll be some

old woman who will give me the eye, or young guys making lewd comments. Oh well.'

'Next time bring a change of clothes that you can keep here.'

Alice smiled and kissed Liang-bao on the forehead. When she'd left, Liang-bao started to pack for his flight. He opened the drawer in his bedside cabinet and with his fingers felt for the key that he kept taped to the underside of the top of the cabinet. He then went into the kitchen and pulled out a small metal box from behind a pile of plates in a cupboard. He unlocked the box with the key, took out the contents and placed them in a large Manila envelope that he then added to his packing.

CHAPTER 22

WHEN THE TELEPHONE RANG ALICE answered in a brusque business-like manner. She'd only just put the phone down after dealing with an irate customer and wasn't in the best of moods. Alice had forgotten that Susan was due to call her back.

'Good morning, this is Susan, Susan Khoo? Do you remember? We spoke on Friday about Kwok-wah. You were going to think about …'

'Oh yes, sorry … I thought you were a customer.'

There was a silence while they both waited for the other to continue. Finally it was Susan who gave in.

'Have you thought about it? Do you think it would be okay if I could see Kwok-wah?'

'He's very upset, you know? You've really hurt him.'

'I'm sorry. I know it's a cliché, but I never meant to hurt him. That wasn't supposed to happen.'

'Did you know that he was in love with you?'

That was what Susan had feared.

'No, and I really didn't mean for that to happen. Please believe me.'

'I don't suppose you love him? No, don't bother to answer. That was a silly question. Of course you don't, you've just been using him for some reason. God knows why. Well, you tell me, what did you think you were doing messing with Kwok-wah's head like that? Why? What were you after? Oh, and while I'm at it, how the hell did you get those papers about Shu-ming? Who are you, Susan Khoo?'

'I'm sorry, I ...'

'Can't tell me, yeah, I get it.'

'No, I don't love him, but I am fond of him.'

'Fond of him? He's not a pet lapdog, he's a human being.' Susan was not encouraged by the angry tone in Alice's voice. 'Sorry, I didn't mean to shout at you. But unless there's anything you can say to him that is going to make him feel better then I just don't see what good it would do. Is there? Is there anything you can say that will help?'

Susan had spent all weekend asking herself this question and she knew the answer.

'No. There isn't.'

'Then I think you have your answer.'

Again, a silence. Susan knew that there wasn't much point pressing Alice any further about Kwok-wah. That discussion was over. Instead she was thinking of something else.

'There's one other thing I wanted to ask you about,' said Susan.

'I thought we were done with this call.'

Susan threw the dice one last time. Who knew how they would fall?

'Last Friday, when you left work, you met a man outside your office? A Chinese man, looked like a main-lander I think, quite tall?'

'What?'

Susan could tell that the change in topic had thrown Alice. She pressed on. 'I was watching from across the road. That's where I was calling from.'

'You've been watching me? What are you? Police?'

'I didn't set out to watch you. Honestly. I just hap-pened to see you meet this guy. Can I ask you who he is?'

'No!' Alice was clearly angry now. 'What business is this of yours?'

'It's none of my business, I know. But did you know he's an agent?'

'An agent? Don't be stupid. An estate agent? Insur-ance agent? He's a student, for God's sake. I know him from the university.'

'Yeah, well, not everyone at a university is who they say they are. You should know that by now. He's some form of Chinese intelligence agent and, wait, I know you're itching to slam the phone down on me, he's your boyfriend, right? Well if he's interested in you then it can only be because of you and your friends in that human rights group, and yes, I know all about that. I know you're not going to believe me now, and why should you, but please remember what I've said and think about it later. Is there anything surprising about him? Anything that doesn't seem right for a student?'

Another silence. Susan thought that she had said enough. Probably too much.

'Just think about it,' said Susan before she put the phone down.

Alice remained sitting at her desk in the office, a mouthless Hello Kitty toy staring back at her.

Susan, sitting on the bed in her cheap hotel room, looked at her rebooked plane ticket. She had plenty of time left and she was wondering what to do with it when an idea struck her. It was a long shot but she had nothing to lose and she could get directions from the reception desk.

***

Istanbul has its Grand Bazaar. Marrakech, the Medina. Barcelona, La Boqueria. Hong Kong has the Shamshuipo Golden Arcade Computer Centre. A maze of small shops and stalls selling new models of phones, games consoles, computers, joysticks, modems, motherboards, disc drives, graphics cards. The latest software, video discs and, above all, games. Some of them were even genuine. Everything from the computer nerd's wildest wet dreams. The aisles between the vendors were so narrow that two people could barely pass each other without becoming intimately acquainted. Geeks' heaven, and where Kwok-wah was happiest.

Kwok-wah never needed much of an excuse to go

the Golden Arcade, but when Alice had said that she had lost the charger for her laptop, he had quickly volunteered to find her a replacement. In fact he knew loads of places closer to home where he could have easily bought one, but it was the perfect excuse to go to the Arcade. The place where he felt most at home, where he felt that he belonged. A place he understood. A place where people behaved normally and didn't just disappear into thin air. A place where people didn't let you down. That was, of course, the great thing about computers. They behaved rationally. You could understand them, predict what they will do.

He found the charger quickly enough, and once that was done he started to look for things for himself. His computer had been running slow so he wanted to buy some extra RAM, and he was tempted to get a new hard drive at the same time. He had built his first computer with parts bought from shops in the Golden Arcade, but he hadn't been there since he went to Shanghai. Although he had been away for months, he was so well known that in a number of his favourite shops the shopkeepers would call out to him: 'Hey, Kwok-wah! Good to see you, we've missed you … How's Shanghai?' Kwok-wah would reply with a non-committal neutral answer, and perhaps talk a little about his work before steering the conversation onto the things he was looking for and what did they have that was new and interesting.

In this way the morning passed before Kwok-wah

noticed how long he had been there. Thinking he should get something to eat, and with most of his purchases already done, he started towards one of the exits. And there she was. He would have spotted her anyway but there were never that many women in the arcade so she stood out doubly; taller than many of the men in the Arcade, her hair in a ponytail, she stood between him and the exit, watching him.

'Susan?'

'Hello, Kwok-wah.'

They stood not saying anything for a moment until they realised that they were getting in the way as people jostled past them and they moved to one side.

'How are you?' Susan asked, since Kwok-wah seemed to be lost for words.

'Um … fine …'

'Look, if you don't want to talk to me I'd completely understand. Just say the word and I'll go, but I wanted to see you one last time.'

'How did you know I'd be here?'

'I didn't for sure, but you told me in Shanghai that coming here would be one of the first things you'd do when you got back to Hong Kong, so I thought I'd give it a try.'

'But today is the first time I've been here in months.'

'Then I'm lucky today.' Susan looked to where the heavens would be if they weren't indoors. 'The Gods are obviously smiling on me. Can we talk? Are you okay with that?'

'Sure, I guess. Do you want to go somewhere

quieter?'

'No. Quite the opposite. It's good being in crowds. Show me around the place while we talk.' They worked their way between shops, Susan keeping close to Kwok-wah, trying not to lose him among the throngs of people hunting for the latest techie must-have. 'First of all, I wanted to say sorry. Sorry if I worried you by disappearing. Sorry if you think I was stringing you along.'

'And were you?' said Kwok-wah. 'Stringing me along?'

'No … Well, perhaps, but it's not that simple.'

'What happened to you in Shanghai? I saw you taken away in a police van. They said it was drugs but—'

'You saw me being taken? I didn't know. I'm sorry you saw that. You shouldn't have had to see that. It wasn't drugs no, but …'

'What was it then?'

'Sorry, that's something I can't tell you. Please don't ask me about that.' Susan moved to where there was an empty shop waiting for a new tenant. 'Let's stop here for a moment, it's easier to talk.'

'Where did you get those papers about Shu-ming from?'

'Ah, good, you got them safely,' said Susan, not answering the question. 'Will you tell Granny Sun what you know?'

'I don't know. I haven't decided yet.'

'Yes, that's difficult, but I think she'd like to know.

I expect deep down she knows already.'

'I don't even know if I'm going back to Shanghai.'

'Really?'

'It hasn't exactly worked out for me.'

'I suppose that's my fault. Perhaps in a few months you'll feel differently? Don't burn your bridges. But … if you do go back, be careful.' Susan went to put her hand on Kwok-wah's arm but stopped short.

'Careful?'

'Don't talk about me. Don't ask what happened to me. Act as though you never knew me. And be especially careful around Zhao Zhanyuan. Don't trust him. Also, you know Alice's boyfriend I suppose?'

'Liang-bao? Slightly. I've met him a couple of times.'

'Well, be very, very careful around him. I've warned your cousin but I don't think she believes me. Can't say I blame her, I don't think she likes me one bit, but if you have any faith in me at all keep an eye out for Alice.'

Kwok-wah was trying to take everything in. He had come to the arcade to get away from thoughts of Susan and Shanghai, but instead of losing himself in the pleasures of technology, here she was talking like someone out of a movie.

'I thought I knew who you were, now I've no idea. Why should I believe anything you say? Is Susan even your name?'

'It is actually, yes. I am from Oakland and I follow the Warriors.'

'But building science isn't your thing, is it?'

'Oh my God, no. It was so boring!' Susan laughed

and Kwok-wah caught a glimpse of the woman he'd got to know in Shanghai. He remembered what Granny Sun had said about Susan just before he'd left. If she liked Susan, then perhaps whoever she was he should give her the benefit of the doubt.

'Do you remember back in Shanghai that I told you about a military guy who kept visiting the labs?'

'Yes, I do.'

'I've seen him here … in Hong Kong, that is.'

'Really? When was that?' It seemed to Kwok-wah that Susan was suddenly very alert.

'Last Friday. I was meeting Alice and some of her friends when I saw him come out of the offices of one of those big law firms in Central.'

'Which one?'

'Oh, I can't remember the name, but it's in Queen's Building. Alice and Liang-bao said I must have been mistaken but the more I've thought about it since then the more I'm sure I was right. You seem to know everything, what do you think?'

'I don't know, it seems unlikely. Did you get a good look?'

'I thought I did, but I don't know … Will I see you again?'

'No. I'm flying back to the States soon. You'll never see me again after today. I know it's probably not much consolation, but I did have real feelings for you … You're so kind-hearted, you deserve a proper girlfriend. Not a fake counterfeit. I'd better go now. Don't follow me, and it might be best if you stayed in the arcade for a while before you leave. Just in case.'

Before Kwok-wah had time to say anything, Susan had turned away and started to work her way through the crowds towards the exit. He didn't follow her.

***

Making her way back to the hotel, Susan smiled to herself. Even after everything that had happened, Kwok-wah still hadn't twigged just why she had been spending so much time with him. She'd felt a pang of anguish at how downcast he'd looked when she told him that they wouldn't meet again. Perhaps Alice had been right, perhaps it hadn't been a good idea to see him. But it had been worth it beyond her expectations, and perhaps staying on in Hong Kong to find Kwok-wah hadn't been just an indulgence on her part after all. Her mind was connecting up the dots and a very interesting picture was coming into focus.

The only thing that bothered Susan was how she was going to tell her superiors that a senior PLA officer they had been watching in Shanghai was visiting a major Hong Kong law firm when she wasn't even supposed to still be here. More than that, she knew exactly which firm it was that had an office in Queen's Building: McShane Adams. Where Emma Janssen's boyfriend worked. Susan never knew whether to believe in coincidences or not. But possibly, just possibly, she was starting to see the glimmer of a chance of redeeming herself after Shanghai.

CHAPTER 23

AT THE CLOSE OF BUSINESS on Friday, 27th June 1997, the last working day before a weekend like no other, the Hang Seng Index had risen by nearly seventy points, and the last two digits of the index rounded up to ninety-seven. People who believed in such things, and there were many, thought that it must be an omen. Those who were more cynical, and again they were not in short supply, thought that it must have been a fix, even though they had no idea how it had been done.

'A slight extension to the Colony,' Lord Salisbury, the prime minister back in 1898, had said, justifying the ninety-nine-year lease acquiring the 365 square miles that became known as the New Territories. Ninety-nine years? Even at the time there were voices saying that was too short; others said that no doubt it could be extended later. But then what was so special about the New Territories? Most of the land was mountainous scrub and rock. There was very little arable land, and what there was was low quality. Would they have thought differently if they had known what Hong Kong would become? Did any of those Victorian colonial officials ever imagine that a hundred years later Hong Kong would be a city of over 6 million people? A major trading port, a financial and legal centre? Would they have been so cavalier as to think that ninety-nine years was long enough, when in the eyes of the Middle Kingdom it was a mere instant?

In his more reflective moments Sam tried to imagine what anyone from those early days of Hong Kong would think if they could suddenly have been transported across the years. Even in more recent decades, in living memory, the changes had been rapid. Sam had come across older expats who had been in Hong Kong most of their lives and who could still remember when cricket was played in Central in front of the Hong Kong Club. A time when the tallest building was the old Bank of China, just a few storeys high. When there was water rationing with the taps only running on certain days. A time when the rickshaws at the Star Ferry pier were a genuine form of transport and not just a tourist gimmick.

However much people tried to ignore it and pretend that it wasn't so, it was the land and people across the border that shaped and changed Hong Kong. For better or worse it always was and always would be. In the 1950s and '60s it was the refugees that flooded across the checkpoints – legally and illegally – doubling the size of the population. Without homes for the incoming thousands, they were forced to live in ramshackle, and deeply unsafe, shanty towns. A series of fires, culminating on Christmas Day 1953 with the fire at Shek Kip Mei when over 50,000 people were left homeless, led to the massive public housing estates that still dominated large parts of urban Hong Kong. From the 1980s it was the money that started to come across the border. Pretty much every deal Sam had been involved in since he first arrived in Hong Kong had something to do with China or Chinese money. His clients were so often European or Americans using Hong Kong as a way into China, or they were Hong Kong companies opening factories in Shenzhen, and now increasingly it was Chinese money looking for a safe haven outside of the People's Republic. It was inescapable. The reality was that the return of Hong Kong to China started long before 1997 and that 30th June 1997 was just one waypoint on a longer journey.

But that wasn't to downplay the importance of the date. It was the day that the ninety-nine-year lease expired and, given that the parts of Hong Kong not limited by the lease were not viable on their own, the day that at midnight Hong Kong would officially return to China.

And yet even on 30th June itself life also went on its normal way, which was why Emma and Sam found themselves in IKEA in Causeway Bay looking at Billy bookcases and considering a new dining table. But the normality of shopping for flat-pack furniture seemed abnormal to them. Earlier in the morning they had been on the harbourfront in Central and a person would have had to have zero empathy not to sense an electricity in the air, to recognise that it was not in fact a normal day after all. But then there were not usually warships moored in the harbour and *Her Majesty's Yacht Britannia* (smaller than they expected) was not a common sight either.

***

The rain had started the night before with a violent thunderstorm, and although that had eased by the afternoon the clouds had started to gather again. When the flag was lowered for the last time at Government House the rain was only light. The flag was folded and presented to the governor with Government House staff watching on, some taking photographs, others mopping at damp eyes. By the time the schedule had moved on to the late-afternoon leaving ceremony in the open air at Tamar – once, long ago, before it was reclaimed, the British naval base – the rain had come on again in earnest. But the bands played on; the Hong Kong Philharmonic under shelter playing on cheap disposable violins, nobody prepared to risk valuable instruments to the heat and humidity of Hong Kong in June; military bands and pipers were not to be discouraged by such a minor inconvenience as a torrential rainstorm. When the Governor spoke movingly, declining the offer of an umbrella, the rain hid his tears.

In the evening Sam and Emma were part of a McShane Adams party in a Causeway Bay restaurant. It was barely a mile or so from the Convention Centre where the handover ceremony would be taking place, but a different world separated from the dignitaries by lines of police and security. It might have been any other restaurant on any other day, except that while they ate lobster and drank Meursault, an advance guard of PLA soldiers were already crossing the border, standing erect in the back of military trucks. Showing strict even-handedness, it rained on them as well. While Sam tapped his feet to a surprisingly good Filipina jazz singer and wished he'd brought his sax, in the streets outside the police played Beethoven's Fifth Symphony over loudspeakers to silence protestors. Whether the police had chosen the music deliberately or not, the irony of the choice was apparently lost on them.

For Sam the music distracted him from the clock and the TV screens that were set up to show the official handover ceremony. As for his own feelings, he was confused. For weeks he had regarded the handover with detachment. He didn't see that it would make much difference to him, and he was fed up with clients and friends in the UK asking him about it: 'What do you think will happen?', 'I suppose everything will be in Chinese?', 'Will it be safe for you there?' Repeatedly having to try and explain the concept of 'one country, two systems' – the fact that Hong Kong would continue to have its own legal system and its own currency – had become very trying long ago. He had become blasé about it, bored of it before it had even happened, and yet now that it was almost upon them he couldn't deny that he felt a little less confident. A little less sure that in the morning everything that mattered to him would be just the same.

Superficially it might have been any other dinner with friends, but it wasn't. Conversation was strained, even Kate was not her usual ebullient self. The banter was more than a little artificial at times as everyone tried to pretend that nothing special was happening, and Sam could tell that Emma was distracted by something. He assumed that she was also more worried about the change of sovereignty than she had let on, but when he asked her she simply put it down to her tinnitus and the noise in the restaurant. He was surprised at how slowly time passed. He'd thought that like when he was approaching something he dreaded, an exam or a trip to a dentist, the time would fly by, but it was quite the opposite. Whenever he checked the time it was only a couple of minutes later than when he last looked. He started to wonder if the watch was running slow. But then, as midnight approached, he found that time was suddenly accelerating again and Sam wished that he could stop all the clocks in Hong Kong, to hold back the inevitable for just that little bit longer.

But of course he couldn't and suddenly it was midnight. They watched the ceremony taking place in the Convention Centre; Jiang Zemin and Prince Charles standing like mannequins on a dais as soldiers in crisp dress uniforms lowered the Union Jack and the colonial Hong Kong flag before raising the new Hong Kong bauhinia and the Chinese flag. Golden stars on a red background fluttering indoors in an artificial breeze. In the restaurant champagne corks popped, toasts were made and whistles blown as if it was New Year again, but Sam felt a mixture of emotions. Pride and sadness. Hope for the future and the promise of autonomy for Hong Kong, and deep down an anxiety that somehow it wouldn't work out that way. Outside, in the streets, taxi drivers blew their horns at midnight and in cities across China firecrackers sparked.

So it was over. What had started when Captain Belcher of *HMS Sulphur* raised the flag on 26th January 1841 at a spot on a barren rock that later became Possession Street, ended with the lowering of a flag in smart new convention centre built on reclaimed land jutting out into the harbour of one of the greatest cities of the world.

CHAPTER 24

'*MY BROTHER LOVED GOING TO the races when he worked in Hong Kong, but of course he would never have been able to come here.*'

Those were the words that had brought down the façade of equanimity that Emma had carefully maintained during dinner at the Jockey Club. It wasn't just the words, but the way the speaker had looked at her. Ostensibly he was addressing the whole table, but they both knew that the words were carefully chosen and directed at her alone. That night, again unable to sleep, she replayed the dinner and remembered how she'd been taunted. Played with like a matador with a bull; the words the red cape to which she was supposed to react. Did he want her to rise to the bait and create a scene? Perhaps it was sufficient that he saw her flinch when she realised the significance of what he was saying. Perhaps he got enough pleasure from telling her that he knew; enough satisfaction from seeing the pain that he had inflicted on her.

***

'I don't know why you're so worried.'

Those had been Sam's words throughout the day. Emma knew that he meant well, but the more he tried to reassure her, the more worried she became. But how could he understand? Here she was, for the first time, about to be his plus-one at dinner with his boss and a major client. No, far more than a plus-one, she was his other half. His significant other, or whatever the current terminology was. And all that was without even thinking about who the client was, and things about the client that Sam didn't know. To make things worse, her hearing was playing up badly. Stress never helped and she hadn't been this anxious in months.

'You look fabulous, as usual,' Sam said when they were ready to go out. Here Emma felt on safer ground. She knew that she looked good. After much searching she had found the perfect dress; a Vera Wang copy at a fraction of the price of the real thing. Knee-length, it was long enough to be respectful while still showing her figure; and the red chinoiserie pattern seemed suited to what was after all meant to be a celebration, at least in the eyes of their host.

It was an old joke that the most important people in Hong Kong were the governor, the chairman of the Hong Kong and Shanghai Bank, and the head of the Jockey Club. Not necessarily in that order. Nobody thought that the handover made any difference, and entering the dining room of the Jockey Club's Happy Valley clubhouse did nothing to change that impression. There was the money, of course. That went almost without saying. From the marbled entrance to the plush carpets of the rooms, there was no shortage of evidence of wealth. But there was also an aura of something more than just money. Something more important than mere riches: control and influence. This was where the real deals were done, both in politics and business. In the restaurant all the tables were full; whether everybody was celebrating the handover or not she couldn't have said, but there were Chinese and new Hong Kong flags on all the tables. Chinese and expatriates united by the common bond of money and power. Emma had never before felt so much out of her depth.

They were six for dinner, including Sam and herself. Emma remembered Paul Ridgeway but hadn't especially cared for him; she recalled how his eyes would follow her around the office. His wife, Elizabeth, was the only other woman at the table and Emma had hoped that she would be somebody she could talk to. Instead Emma found her to be cold and haughty. Dressed in Chanel, she reminded her of the expatriate wives who would hang around the tennis club all day complaining about their maids. Emma also sensed that she didn't think much of her dress. Mr Leung, on the other hand, Emma did like. She remembered him from when she was working for Sam. He was very gentlemanly and courteous in an old-fashioned way.

The final dinner guest was a colleague of Mr Leung. He was quite different, younger and more contemporary in appearance in spite of thinning hair. Emma wondered what had brought them together.

'Paul, Sam,' said Mr Leung, 'you know Mr Gao, of course, but perhaps I might make the introductions. Mr Gao, may I introduce you to Elizabeth Ridgeway and Emma ... sorry, Johnson?'

'Janssen.' Emma tried to keep calm. Mr Gao? Surely not? Surely it couldn't be him? Mr Gao offered his hand, and in spite of her fears Emma took it and they shook hands. 'A pleasure to meet you,' she lied, 'Mr ... Gao?'

'Gao Shu-ming.' He smiled and continued to hold her hand for a fraction longer than would be normal. 'The pleasure is all mine.'

Emma relaxed a little when his given name turned out to be something quite different. And after all, she told herself, it was hardly an unusual family name. It could be nothing. Could be just chance.

Dinner progressed smoothly and Emma even started to enjoy herself a bit. There was the inevitable discussion of the handover itself and how they had spent the evening. Paul and Elizabeth at the Cricket Club, Mr Leung at home with his family.

'And how about you, Mr Gao?' asked Sam.

'I was at the official banquet in the Convention Centre.'

'That must have been quite an experience.'

'Oh, I was on a table right at the back, a long, long way from anybody important.'

'And were you at the ceremony itself?' asked Paul.

'Yes, but again right at the back. It's a huge place,

you know, I could hardly see anything. You probably had a better view watching on TV.'

'Even so … to be at such an event … with history being made and all that,' said Sam.

While Sam made polite conversation, Emma was starting to worry again. She didn't dare ask the question that was foremost in her mind. *Who are you, Gao Shu-ming, that you get invited to such an event?* The Convention Centre may be large, but it wasn't that large. Once you allowed for the people who had to be there, the politicians from all sides, the military, diplomats, overseas guests, there couldn't have been that many places left over. Emma couldn't believe that Mr Gao would have been invited unless he had connections in pretty high places.

'True, and forgive me, Sam, Paul, Elizabeth, Emma.' He looked at each of them in turn, his eyes finally resting on Emma. 'I appreciate that you may feel differently – but being Chinese, I did feel a lot of pride. We've waited for this so long and now Hong Kong is back as part of the motherland. All Chinese people feel the same about that, no matter what their politics. Foreigners shouldn't worry, Hong Kong is always going to be a great place to do business, but now, with Hong Kong people running Hong Kong, and support from Beijing, it's only going to get better.'

To Emma it was like listening to an editorial from the *People's Daily*, but she wasn't going to respond. It was the sort of thing that was being said all over town. You just had to smile and nod.

'Anyway, as long as the horses keep running, eh?' said Mr Leung.

'Of course! What would Hong Kong be without the racing and places like this.' Mr Gao gestured to the restaurant, and this was when the words came. 'My brother loved going to the races when he worked in Hong Kong, but of course he would never have been able to come here.' Gao Shu-ming looked directly at Emma as he said this. Nobody else seemed to notice this, but Emma knew that he was speaking to her.

'I didn't know you had a brother,' said Paul. 'That's not so common these days, is it?'

Emma was glad that Paul had diverted Mr Gao with a question while she gathered her thoughts and composed herself. She knew with sickening certainty who Mr Gao's brother was.

'Not these days, no. We were both born just before the one-child policy came in, but as it happens I was adopted. Our parents thought they couldn't have children so they took me in, and then to everyone's surprise my brother turned up. He's younger than me but, poor guy, he looks older because of his greying hair. It's a thing in our family – all the men go grey when they're young. Except me, of course …' Mr Gao ran a hand over his head. 'I should be so lucky.'

He was no longer looking directly at Emma, but from time to time his eyes came back to her, as if he was waiting for a reaction.

'What did he do in Hong Kong?' asked Paul.

'He worked at Xinhua for a couple of years. When was that now …? I think it was back in 1993 that he moved back to China. Anyway, working so close to the racecourse he used to go most Wednesdays, just in the public stands. Once in a while a business contact would invite him to a box, but for the most part back then business steered clear of anyone at Xinhua. Mind you, I mustn't make it sound like he was hard done by. It was quite a – how do you say in English? – a good posting. He used to have a car and driver pick him up from the racecourse rather than fight the crowds on public transport. I was the jealous older brother.'

Mr Gao's eyes were once more back on Emma, watching her, looking for any reaction. But after the first shock Emma no longer took in what he was saying. Indeed, she could barely make out the words at all such was the screaming in her ears: a vicious raw mix of frequencies that drowned out everything else. Nausea started to overwhelm her and she quickly excused herself, making it to the toilets just in time to throw up in the sink in front of a shocked attendant. When she was finished the attendant passed her a damp facecloth and Emma wiped her face, determined to return as if nothing had happened. Determined not to let Mr Gao win, not to let him see her suffer, and above all not to let Sam down.

***

Later that night, when she had finally grown tired and returned to bed, Emma dreamt of Peter. They were walking by a stream in woodland. The path was slippery and overgrown with ferns, but with Peter by her side her usual fear of the water had gone. It was summer and the trees were in full leaf, but sunlight filtered through the branches lighting the path in front of them. In the dream they are small children, but with the parallel logic of visions they talk as adults.

'You need to let this go, you know?' says Peter.

'I can't, Peter.'

'I know. You always were a stubborn so-and-so.'

A kingfisher suddenly flies across their path and lands on a branch of a nearby tree. The bird sits there and they stand and watch it. Since it was a dream neither of them are especially surprised when the kingfisher speaks.

'You shouldn't trust that Liang-bao,' it says. 'He's a bad'un.'

'He's right, of course,' says Peter. 'Liang-bao is definitely not to be trusted.'

'What do the pair of you take me for? Do you think I'm an idiot or something? I know that. I don't trust him one iota. Just who he is, though, I don't know.'

The bird flies away and Peter picks up a handful of small stones from the path and lobs them one by one into the water. He watches the ripples spread out for a moment before turning to his sister.

'Do you remember that time you visited me at uni and my room-mate refused to admit that he had a thing for you?'

'I was only sixteen, he was, what … twenty? Twenty-one?'

'Quite. And do you remember how you tricked him into admitting it on tape?'

'That was funny. He was so embarrassed afterwards, but … oh, I see what you mean.'

'Come on, sis, race you back to Mummy and Daddy.'

***

The frustration was that when Emma wanted to talk to Liang-bao in private, he was nowhere to be found. She only really knew him through Alice. She didn't have an address or telephone number for him, and she couldn't think of a good enough excuse to ask Alice. A couple of weeks ago it was like he was following her around wherever she went. Now he was nowhere to be seen.

She was glad of the distraction that Susan represented. Her call had come out of the blue. They'd first met in Chiang Mai when Emma was travelling with her then fiancé, Mike, and the three of them had shared a guesthouse for a few days. They took a day trip into the Doi Suthep-Pui National Park and got along so well that they talked about travelling together, perhaps going further north to explore the hill tribes close to the Burmese border. Then one evening, when they were in a bar experimenting by mixing Chang beer with potent local spirits, Emma came back from the toilet to find Mike flirting with Susan, his hand on her thigh. The argument that followed was only the final one of many.

But instead of being angry with Susan, if anything Emma was grateful that she had been the catalyst that finally brought an end a relationship that clearly wasn't going anywhere. Still, Emma hadn't wanted to travel on her own, so over the next few weeks she and Susan joined forces. They got to know each other well and one night in Laos, when they were in Vang Vieng heading for Luang Prabang, when the heat and humidity made it impossible for either of them to get to sleep, Emma told Susan about Peter. Some weeks later they'd parted to go their separate ways. They'd promised to keep in touch but Susan always seemed to be on the move. Meeting up again it was like old times and it didn't take many glasses of wine before Emma seized on the chance to unburden her worries in a way that she couldn't with Sam. Emma was reminded of what a good listener Susan was; she was always interested in other people.

Still waiting and hoping that she would bump into Liang-bao somewhere, Emma finally gave in and realised that she would have to do something to get his attention. Lacking any better idea, she telephoned Xinhua and asked to speak to either of the Gao brothers or Liang-bao himself. As she expected, she was told that there was nobody there with any of those names, but she made a lot of noise and fuss and made sure that they knew her name. That they knew who was asking. Then she waited. Emma didn't have to wait for long, and two days later she wasn't particularly surprised when mid-afternoon she bumped into Liang-bao in the street. They exchanged fake pleasantries before Liang-bao suggested that they find somewhere to talk. A nearby café suited Emma and they took a quiet table at the back.

'Give me a moment,' Emma said, 'I just need to put this in so I can hear you better.' Emma took out an earpiece from her handbag and put it in her right ear. 'There we are.'

'So how was the Jockey Club?' asked Liang-bao.

'Not really my sort of place, but it was certainly an interesting evening.' Emma didn't bother asking herself how Liang-bao knew about the dinner. She hadn't even told Alice.

'I gather Mr Leung took a shine to you.'

'He's a gentleman. I'm not sure why he's involved with someone like Mr Gao.'

'Ah …'

'Or does he have no choice about it?'

They paused while a waitress brought them the drinks they had ordered.

'Oh, he has a choice,' said Liang-bao, 'everybody does. We all have choices that we can make, but he knows what's best for him in the new Hong Kong. Do you, Emma? Do you know where your best interests lie?'

They were dancing round each other like boxers in the ring. Each keeping their guard up while throwing the occasional parry and feint. Emma was tired of this continued pretence.

'Who are you, Liang-bao? Who are you really?'

Liang-bao took a sip of his tea before answering.

'You may not believe this, Emma, but I'm a friend. Honestly, I really am. I know this is going to sound like a cliché, but you're playing with things you don't understand. You're going to get hurt if you're not careful. And so is Sam. I don't want to see that happen – I really don't. I'm sorry about what happened to your brother – yes I know about that – but that's all in the past and the driver was jailed for it.'

'Except that the right man wasn't, so please don't patronise me and treat me like a fool.' Emma kept her voice level and collected. She was surprised and pleased with herself for managing to be calm. 'The man who was actually driving the car, Gao Zhihua, got away scot-free and some poor sucker – God only knows how – was talked into taking the blame. Was he bribed? Threatened with something worse? Why on earth did he admit to something that he didn't do?'

'You can't prove that Gao Zhihua was driving, and even if he was, well … it was still an accident. Nobody meant for it to happen and nothing you can do can change anything. He had a career ahead of him, family in Shanghai. Do you know what would have happened to him, or to his wife and child back in China, if he'd been jailed in Hong Kong?'

'Excuse me?' Emma was aghast at the way Liang-bao was trying to spin things. 'Am I supposed to feel sorry for him? Fuck that. He was a senior mainland official who used his position to get away with killing my brother. It may have been an accident but he should have had the guts and decency to admit that it was his fault.' Emma stopped when her voice started to falter.

'Whatever … Like I said, you can't prove anything and it's history anyway. Do you think anybody is likely to be interested in revisiting such an old case?'

'Given that Gao Zhihua is involved with a company buying into a Hong Kong telecoms business, then yes, I think they might.'

'So Sam knows all about this?'

'No, he doesn't. Leave him out of it.'

There was a silence while they both took a breather after their initial skirmish. Emma wondered if she'd got enough of an admission from Liang-bao that Gao Zhihua had been driving. She wasn't sure that she had. This was going to be her one and only chance. She knew she mustn't let it slip by.

'Just out of curiosity, do you know why Chan Wah Man took the blame? What was he offered?'

'No, I don't as it happens. Not for certain anyway. I did hear a story that he'd been drinking and that's why Gao Zhihua was driving that night, so perhaps that was something to do with it.' Emma decided that was good enough. If she pressed the point any further Liang-bao might get suspicious.

'You didn't really answer my first question,' she said. 'Who are you? Who do you work for?'

'Oh Emma, I'm sure you've worked that out, in general terms anyway. I'm certainly not going to tell you the specifics.'

'And what if I tell Alice? My God ...' A thought had just struck Emma. 'She's not ... as well, is she?'

'Alice?!' Liang-bao laughed suddenly. A waitress stopped what she was doing and looked over to them. 'No, certainly not. She's a sweet little thing but not always that bright. You can tell her if you like but there's no way she'll believe you.'

'Alice was your way into the group? To keep a watch on them?'

'That was the plan, yes, but to be honest it turned out that the group was so small and ineffectual that they weren't really worth the effort until you turned up. If it hadn't been for you I would probably have quietly split with Alice and left the group to its own devices, but I stayed to keep an eye on you.'

'You knew who I was even then? You've been watching me all this time?'

'Of course. Just watching, nothing more than that. We've known that you were in Hong Kong ever since you first arrived, but until you started poking your nose into things you were quite harmless. But I think now it's probably time I did leave Alice. She's served her purpose and there are better things I can do with my time.'

'Served her purpose? You bastard, Liang-bao ...'

'Oh come now, Emma, bad language doesn't suit you. It's not your style. Alice has had some good times with me. If you tell her the truth, apart from the fact she won't believe you, she'll hate you, you'll lose a friend and it will just ruin her memories. Trust me on this if nothing else. I'm not a bad person. I'll let her down gently. I'll tell her that I have to go back to China or something. I expect I'll be called back anyway. I'm pretty much finished with my work here.'

'But your relationship was just a fake.'

'This is Hong Kong, what do you expect? Most relationships here are fake. People get together for all sorts of reasons that are nothing to do with love. Sometimes it's for money. Sometimes because their families want them to, or they do it to get away from their families, or to be able to buy a home. Or to get a visa or residency somewhere. *Gweilo* men with Filipina women, all sorts of reasons. Hongkongers are pragmatic people, you know that, they certainly don't marry for love.' Liang-bao gestured at the waitress to get the bill. 'Emma, like I said, I'm a friend, so will you take my advice?'

'Which is?'

'Don't be so cynical. The world isn't black and white. I'm not evil and neither is Gao Zhihua. Not really, he made a big mistake, of course – a tragic one for you – but don't think he didn't get punished in our own way. Do you think that it went down well with his superiors that he made such a mess here that needed tidying up? Let it be.'

'Or I could tell the authorities everything I know about Bright Talk, and Gao Zhihua's involvement with it, and about my brother.'

'None of which you can prove. Even if you could prove it, they wouldn't care. What do you know about

Bright Talk anyway? That there's mainland money involved? So what? Emma, this is China now. Yes, I know,
one country, two systems, and all that crap, fifty years
of autonomy and so on, but we've been waiting for this
for a hundred years. Leave with grace, leave with dig-
nity. That's what your politicians and army did. Chris
Patten was very proper in the end, did things the right
way, and your army were consummate professionals.
They left with their heads held high. A credit to your
country. You should do the same.' The waitress brought
the bill and Liang-bao handed her a few notes.

'I wasn't planning on leaving.'

'But you will be, Emma. You'll need a work visa next
year and I can tell you now that you won't get one.
Don't even bother to apply, it will just be refused. But
Sam, that's a different story. He's got a future here. Mr
Leung likes him, I like him. You know what happened
with Sam in London, of course? He thinks nobody
here knows, but we do. He will be very useful to us
so he'll get a visa with no problems, so long as you do
the sensible thing.'

'Which is?'

'Don't make a fuss, don't tell Sam or anybody else
about Gao Zhihua, and quietly leave Hong Kong
sometime in the next few months. You've got no choice
in this. You'll have to leave whatever you do or don't do,
but do you want to wreck Sam's chances as well? And
for what? Nobody will believe you or care. You may get
a sense of personal satisfaction for a short while but it
won't achieve anything except to make matters worse.'

'You can't make me leave, not if I marry Sam.'

'Is a wedding on the cards? I didn't realise. Many congratulations, but if you think that's the answer you're mistaken. Get married and Sam won't get a visa either.'

'And in the meantime I should be careful when crossing the road in Wan Chai,' said Emma bitterly.

'Don't be so melodramatic. Nothing's going to happen to you unless you're really stupid.' Liang-bao looked at his watch. 'I should be going, I'm meeting Alice from work and you know what she's like if you're late.' Liang-bao smiled and stood. 'Think about what I've said, Emma.'

When Liang-bao had left the café Emma took out her earpiece and turned it off.

'I'll think about what you said alright,' she said to herself with a smile.

CHAPTER 25

'WELL THAT'S PRETTY INCRIMINATING,' SAID Susan. Emma had finished playing the tape of her conversation with Liang-bao. 'And he didn't suspect anything?'

'Nothing at all. He just thought it was my hearing aid. Thanks to you for telling me about the Golden Arcade. I'd never been before. It's amazing the things you can get there.'

It was late afternoon and Emma had asked Susan to come round.

'So when will Sam be home?'

'I'm not sure – I know he's busy at the moment.'

'Have you told him what you know about Peter's death?'

'No, well some of the early stuff, that it wasn't the guy who was jailed. But I haven't told him about the connection to his client. I just don't know how to or even if I should.'

'So what are you going to do?' Susan asked. The air-conditioned cool of the Hong Kong apartment was a different world from that night in Vang Vieng when Emma had first told her about her brother. 'I hate to say it, but Liang-bao is probably right. Nobody is going to be interested in reopening a hit-and-run. Bright Talk is more interesting, though. Are you really not going to tell Sam?'

'I don't know, I really don't know. It could really screw up his career. I don't know how I can do that to him.'

Susan wondered how far she could push Emma. It was frustrating to be so close to finding out what the PLA was doing in Hong Kong. She could almost smell it. What she wouldn't give to get hold of a copy of Sam's Bright Talk papers. Would she be willing to give up a friendship, albeit an old one that had sort of died anyway?

'Do you think Sam would get you a copy of the Bright Talk file?'

'A copy of the file? I don't know … What would I do with that? Liang-bao made it very clear what would happen if I went to the authorities with what I know. You heard what he said on the tape.'

'Emma, I've not been completely honest with you, and given everything you've been through I think you deserve better than that.' Susan had decided that the prize was worth taking a chance on. Not that she had any intention of being completely honest. 'When I first got in touch with you it was simply to meet up again and chat about old times. Nothing more than that. I didn't even know you were in Hong Kong, and finding you here was a really nice bonus—'

'How *did* you know I was here?' Emma interrupted. Susan had been surprised that Emma hadn't asked that question when they'd got together a few days before.

'I was wondering when you would ask that. Let's just say your name cropped up in a different context. But I didn't even know if it was the same Emma Janssen.'

'But ...'

'Please, Emma, don't ask me more. Anyway, like I said, I just wanted to see you again for old time's sake. But then when we met up, and you told me what you'd discovered about Peter's death, about the Gao brothers and that they were your boyfriend's client, I couldn't believe my luck.'

'Your luck? What are you talking about, Susan?'

'Emma, please don't ask how I know this, just trust me, but Gao Shu-ling is an officer in the People's Liberation Army. I don't know about Gao Zhihua but it wouldn't surprise me if he was as well. You know yourself that they are both interested in telecoms. What you don't know is that they are working with a university in Shanghai to develop software that can be preloaded on mobile phones that they'll be able to use to eavesdrop on people. That's what Bright Talk is all about.' Susan paused to let Emma digest this before continuing. She tried to read Emma's face to see how this was being received but couldn't be sure. Having gone this far Susan didn't have much of an option but to go on. 'The people I work for would love to have evidence of what Bright Talk is doing, how it's structured, who is involved with it. All the stuff that will be in Sam's file.' Susan stopped again and waited while Emma took this in.

'The people you work for?' asked Emma. 'You work for a telecoms company?'

'I should just say yes. That would be the easiest answer, but it would be a lie and I don't want to lie to you. Emma, please don't ask me questions I can't answer.' Susan thought that she seemed to be spending all her time telling people not to ask her things. 'I just need you to trust me.' Susan played her last card. 'With that information, I can use it against the Gao brothers. Maybe Liang-bao as well. At the very least I can cause major embarrassment, at best we might even be able to stop Bright Talk completely.'

Susan watched while Emma was silent in response for a while. When Emma finally spoke Susan was taken aback by the bitter tone of voice.

'You're no better than Liang-bao, are you? Just using me the same way he's been using Alice.' Emma moved away from Susan and stood, staring out of the window.

Yes and no, thought Susan. She couldn't deny that she needed Emma's help, and Sam's, but she was on the side of the angels, wasn't she? Didn't that make a difference?

'Emma, all I can say is that I'm one of the good guys, and I can help you at the same time. It's not a one-way thing.'

There was another long pause filled by the erratic hum of the air-con unit and traffic on the main road. From somewhere beyond the apartment there was the sound of a mother scolding a child and a door slamming. Susan knew that Emma was on the edge and could go either way. She was scared to say anything in case it pushed Emma in the wrong direction. Finally, after what to Susan seemed an age, Emma spoke.

'If I get what you want, do you think you can keep Sam out of it? I mean, will anybody be able to work out that the information came from Sam?'

'I don't know. I certainly don't need to tell anyone.' Susan winced inwardly. Sometimes she was shocked at how easily she could lie to her friends. She'd have to tell her superiors where it came from if they were to believe in the information she gave them. 'But one day when the Chinese realise that we have this information – and they will eventually – they'll know that there are only a limited number of people it could have come from and Sam would be one of those. Not the only one, I mean it could be anyone at Sam's firm, or even someone within Bright Talk, but given that he knows you, and since ... well, you know what I mean. He probably would be their first guess.' Susan didn't mention the outside chance that she might have been followed to Sam and Emma's place. She didn't think she had been, she'd taken care, but she couldn't see what good would have been done by raising the possibility.

'Perhaps you'd better leave before Sam gets back. I don't see how the three of us can have a simple dinner together after what you've said. I don't think I can anyway. I'll make an excuse for you, Sam won't mind.'

'Fair enough.' Susan started to leave, feeling somewhat deflated. She didn't know what more she could have done.

'How long will be you be in Hong Kong for?' asked Emma.

'Two days. I've almost run out of money so I really have to go back to the States.'

'Can I get in touch with you?'

'I've got a better idea. Let me borrow a pen and paper and I'll give you my parents' address in Oakland. If you decide to help, you can write to me there, or even just send anything by post.'

***

That night Emma again found herself sitting on the sofa watching the ships moored in the harbour. She was starting to make a habit of spending the nights there. She wondered if perhaps she should keep a spare pillow and duvet to hand. Sam had come home a little later than expected. It had obviously been a long hard day and he wasn't remotely bothered that Emma's old friend hadn't stayed for dinner. They'd listened to a little jazz, shared a glass or two of wine and generally spent the evening in quiet intimacy. Emma had no idea whether she could ask him to risk his career and future to help her. She didn't even know how much she could trust Susan. She was wary of everybody now.

She also hadn't forgotten what Liang-bao had said. She remembered his comments about Sam. What had Sam been involved with in London? She didn't dare ask but it was obviously something they were prepared to hold over him if he got out of line. Liang-bao had said there was no chance that she would get a visa. Perhaps it was an idle threat. Did he or the people that he reported to really have that power? She could stay and try, see what happened, but she feared that Liang-bao was probably right. She'd stirred up too many things. Annoyed too many people. She remembered what Brian Lo had told her in Sydney. All of which meant that Sam would have to choose between her and his career no matter what she did about Susan. Would he choose her over partnership? She hoped so – surely he would? – but she wasn't certain. But more than that, it was still early days between them and who knew where their relationship would go. She didn't want to pressure him into leaving for her sake. If she did, and Sam left Hong Kong for her, then if it didn't work out he'd hate her for it later. No. If Sam was to leave Hong Kong to be with her, then it had to be his own free choice.

It was starting to get light when Emma returned to bed and Sam woke sleepily.

'Where've you been?' he asked.

'Just sitting watching the harbour.'

'Come here.'

Emma responded to his gentle embraces. He kissed her bad ear as if to make it better. They made love slowly and tenderly as the sun rose.

***

It was a week later that Emma stole the Bright Talk

papers. It had been a week of indecision and uncertainty. A week spent hiking on her own in the New Territories, trying to find some space to think things through. She turned down an invite to have lunch with Alice. Emma had no idea what she could say to her or even if it was safe to talk to her. Taking the papers herself wasn't what she had planned to do, but was something that she did almost without thinking when the opportunity arose.

In the end it was so ludicrously simple that when she thought about it later she concluded that the gods must have wanted her to have the file. It was lunchtime and she was in Sam's office. They were supposed to be getting something to eat and she was waiting for him to get ready to leave. Everything conspired to make it easy for her: she had a larger bag with her than usual because she was planning on going shopping in the afternoon, and Sam's secretary had already gone out for lunch. When Sam went to the toilet she simply took the file from the filing cabinet. After lunch she went to a photocopy shop and then returned to Sam's office on the pretence of having mislaid her keys. It was a trivial matter to leave the file on top of a pile when no one was watching. There was an outside chance, of course, that somebody might have wanted to see it in the few hours that it was missing, but she had worked in enough offices over the years to know how often files went walkabout for no obvious reason.

What she was going to do with the file she still

didn't know.

***

Although she didn't recognise it to begin with, in time Emma realised that she was saying goodbye to Hong Kong and the life she had made there. Without doing it consciously she was revisiting all the places that meant something to her. They all played a part in the story of her time in Hong Kong.

There was the casual restaurant on the beach at Deep Water Bay. A friend had taken her there on one of her first weekends in Hong Kong. There were seven of them that night sharing chilli squid and prawns. The sound of the waves lapping on the shore was only disturbed when two policemen came running through the restaurant chasing a burglar who had been trying his luck on one of the nearby apartment blocks. *'Probably an II'* one of the diners said. Only later did Emma discover that – fairly or unfairly – illegal immigrants were blamed for most things that needed a scapegoat.

One day she took the ferry to Cheung Chau and lay sunbathing on Tung Wan beach. It was mid-week so the beach was quiet and she had it mostly to herself. She enjoyed the warmth of the sun even if she went nowhere near the water. Her floppy sunhat covering her face, sand getting between her toes, her memory wandered back to family holidays in Cornwall when she would play with Peter building the most elaborate sandcastles with moats and turrets. After spending a couple of hours on the beach, she sat at a simple café with an iced tea from where she could see Hong Kong Island and Pokfulam. If she looked closely Emma could just about make out Sam's apartment building. She no longer thought of it as theirs, something they shared. It was his again. He'd be at work anyway but she wondered what he was doing. Was he working for Bright Talk today? Was he meeting one of the Gao brothers?

She dug out her hiking boots and went back to some of her favourite trails. She climbed the path up to the top of Pat Sin Leng. She remembered when she'd dragged Sam along with her. She'd known then that they would get together. She had smiled to herself when she'd seen him struggle up the hills. It was obvious how little hill-walking he did and how much he was doing it only to be with her. She had felt his eyes on her body even when she was striding ahead. She remembered how he had looked at her when they sat soaking wet in the restaurant; how a warmth had filled her when he looked away embarrassed. She wished she could go back to those simple days.

She walked the streets of Western District. She wandered along Queen's Road West close to where she had lived. There were shops that she found continually fascinating: the one that sold nothing but bamboo steamers, the bakery that made pastries in the shape of fish, the Chinese medicine shops with roots in glass jars and wooden drawers full of powders. Sometimes Emma was never quite sure whether you were supposed to drink the medicines they prepared or use them as an ointment. There was the shop that sold simple rice bowls, next to a shop that stocked every type of bucket and brush you could imagine. Her favourite shops of all were those selling paper funeral totems. Everything from sports cars and paper money to air-conditioners, all made of paper ready to be burnt to accompany the departed into the afterlife. She sat in the McDonald's below her first apartment. That was the first proper home that she had all to herself. Her place and her place alone. There was an old Chinese man who lived on the floor below her. She never knew his name or understood a word he said, but he always smiled when they passed on the stairs.

She went up to the Peak and escaped from the tourists who were hanging around the observation point. Instead she walked to where she knew there was a much better view. From there she could see the ferries going to and from Macau. Easter in Macau and the first time that she and Sam had slept together. His shyness, his gentleness. Looking in another direction she could see the extension to the Convention Centre where the handover ceremony had taken place. Somewhere nearby in Causeway Bay, somewhere in the warren of streets, was the restaurant where they had gone that evening.

And also somewhere down there was where Peter had been killed. And, of course, she also went to the junction, where only a few months ago she had laid flowers on the anniversary of his death. So much had changed since that day. The flowers were long gone, but to her surprise there was a little piece of ribbon still tied to the drainpipe, torn and faded but still recognisable as the one she had used. She untied the fragment and put it safely in her pocket. This was when Liang-bao's words came back to her: *'We all have choices.'* Of course he was right, though it was ironic that he of all people would be the one helping her to understand what she had to do.

The trigger had been Sam's partnership. He had been so excited, so thrilled. Emma was pleased for him – of course she was – but now it felt impossible to tell him. She had put on a mask for him, hidden her feelings and shared in his happiness when they celebrated the news. They'd opened a bottle of champagne and gone out to dinner. But inside, beneath the surface smiles and gaiety, Emma had made her decision, and she knew there was nothing to be gained by delaying. She had been on borrowed time ever since she heard that Chan Wah Man had been released from prison. As Peter would say, she needed to end it now. She needed to let it go. The next day she mailed the copy of the Bright Talk file, along with the recording of Liang-bao, to an address in Oakland. She felt a sense of physical release as the thick envelope slipped from her hand into the mailbox with its anachronistic crown and E II R lettering.

Emma had made her choice. Committed now to her course of action, she called into the travel agent that she normally used.

'I'd like to buy a ticket to London, please.'

'Return, I assume?'

'No. One-way.'

There was another letter that she had to write. A letter to Sam that she would post to him when she got back to the UK. She sat down at their dining table one morning when he was at work. She expected it to be a difficult letter to write, but once she had started telling him everything, telling him all that she had discovered, why she was doing what she was going to do, seeking his forgiveness and understanding, she found that the words came easily. She didn't want to type the letter, though – it needed to be handwritten – and by the end her wrist was aching. She hoped that it would speak to him not only through the meaning of the words but through the curls and lines. She hoped that her heart and love would cry out to him from the paper.

Emma had made her choice and now she would have to wait for Sam to make his.

EPILOGUE

CORNWALL, EASTER 1974

PETER WAS FIRST TO REACT to the scream.

They were walking in the woods near the holiday cottage that they had rented for the week. It was April in Cornwall, the Easter holidays, spring had come and bluebells transformed dark shaded groves into imperial splendour. His parents were somewhere behind him, lost in serious adult conversation that he either didn't understand or found incredibly boring. Instead of staying with them he'd taken a turning off the main path to explore a fallen tree that was softened with fungi, moss and lichen. In the tradition of small boys down the ages, he pulled at a broken branch that came away in his hands, disturbing a cityscape of beetles. He watched the insects as they tried to come to terms with the uprooting of their world.

He knew at once that the scream had come from his younger sister. More than once he had been the reason for her tears, but pulling her hair or dropping a worm down the back of her dress had never brought forth a sound with the intensity he'd just heard. Worse still, worse than the scream itself, was the ominous silence that followed. No crying, no tears, no sobbing. He knew that something was wrong. He dropped the branch and ran in the direction he thought the sound had come from, oblivious to the undergrowth that was in the way, the thorns that cut his arms and the nettles that stung. He tripped and fell more than once, but simply picked himself up and continued. He knew only that Emma needed him and nothing else mattered.

The undergrowth gave way to a clearing and he finally stopped running, gathering his breath not knowing what to do now or where to go. He heard his parents calling out to both their children. 'I'm here,' he shouted back, not knowing where here actually was. He called after Emma: 'Sis! Where are you, sis?' There was no reply. Only the sound of his parents continuing to call out her name, the clamour of his heart beating and the blood rushing in his ears. But as he looked around he realised that there was another sound: that of running water, a beck cascading over rocks. He started towards the water and soon he saw the stream, and by the water's edge, on a bank, he saw his sister's rucksack – red, decorated with smiling ponies, princesses and flowers. He'd often laughed at the bag and hidden it from her. It was an exotic orchid out of place in this ancient English wood.

Then he saw her in the water, one arm twisted unnaturally, her head resting on a rock as if she was sleeping. He could see that she had lost one of her shoes. He shouted to his parents: 'She's here, by the stream! Quick!' He climbed down into the water. The stones were slippery and the water was flowing faster than he expected. He almost fell, but steadied himself by holding on to an overhanging branch and worked his way to where she was lying. Her head was only just out of the water so he lifted it clear and was shocked to find blood on his hands.

***

They sat waiting for news in the hospital. Peter had washed his hands when they'd arrived, but there was still some of his sister's blood beneath his fingernails. Everybody had praised him: his parents, the ambulance men, the kind young nurse who brought him a Fanta. But he could only think that he might have done more. Could he have got there faster? How long had it been before he spotted her in the river? More to the point, why did he let her go off on her own in the first place when they did everything together? Why did he have to go look at that fallen tree? If he hadn't, it might never have happened. He was certain that it was his fault no matter what people said. He promised to anyone who would listen that he would always look after her if only she would be okay.

His mother had no more tears left to give. His father was trying to get an answer from any passing nurse or doctor. Peter tried to distract himself with the comings and goings of the hospital: emergencies being brought in from ambulances, doctors consulting charts on clipboards, telephones ringing, a man helping his wife walk on crutches. A mother comforting a child.

Later, at home, with her arm in plaster and a bandage around her head, Emma was a precious object to be handled with care. She got to stay in bed and didn't have to go to school for two weeks. Her favourite food was brought to her and she was always allowed seconds. Even of jelly and ice cream. He might have been jealous but he wasn't. Out of his own pocket money, and with a little help from his mother, he bought a new rucksack to replace the one that had been left in the woods in the panic. In time her bandage was removed, and his mother held her hand while the stitches were taken out. The nurse said that she would have a scar but that it would fade. Peter was impressed that she didn't cry at all.

Back at school she was the centre of attention. It wasn't until several weeks later that her teacher started to notice problems. Sometimes, the teacher said, she seemed to mishear things. Sometimes she wouldn't hear her teacher at all. Sometimes she would complain about the strange noises in her head. The doctors said it was probably the accident, but that there wasn't anything they could do about it. It might get better in time, or if it got worse then perhaps a hearing aid might help, but otherwise it was just something that she would have to live with.

Once more, he was impressed that she didn't cry.

ABOUT THE AUTHOR

In 2014 Graeme Hall abandoned the world of intellectual property law to become a novelist and short story writer. He has won the short story competitions of the Macau Literary Festival and the Ilkley Literature Festival. His first short story collection The Goddess of Macau was published in 2020 by Fly on the Wall Press, and his writing has been published in anthologies by Black Pear Press and the Macau Literary Festivalas well as online.

Graeme lived in Hong Kong from1993 to 2010 and still keeps a close connection to the city, and most of his writing comes from his love of that part of the world.He is an active member of the Leeds Writers Circle whose members have been a constant source of advice, support and encouragement.

Graeme lives in Calderdale, West Yorkshire with his wife and a wooden dog.

Twitter: @hongkonggraeme
www.graemehall.net